THE GREAT ADVENTURES OF

SHERLOCK HOLMES

Jaico Sherlock Holmes Series

THE GREAT ADVENTURES OF SHERLOCK HOLMES

Jaico Sherlock Holmes Series

DONALD THOMAS

JAICO PUBLISHING HOUSE

Ahmedabad Bangalore Chennai
Delhi Hyderabad Kolkata Mumbai

Published by Jaico Publishing House
A-2 Jash Chambers, 7-A Sir Phirozshah Mehta Road
Fort, Mumbai - 400 001
jaicopub@jaicobooks.com
www.jaicobooks.com

Published in arrangement with
Pegasus Books LLC
80 Broad Street, 5th Floor
New York, NY 10004

THE GREAT ADVENTURES OF SHERLOCK HOLMES
ISBN 978-81-8495-501-9

First Jaico Impression: 2014
Second Jaico Impression: 2015

Printed by
Repro India Limited, Mumbai

For Robert, Deirdre, Jane, and Christopher

I am most grateful for information on Byron's handwriting from Dr. Linda Shakespeare and for Charles Schlessiger's fellow enthusiasm for the Great Detective.

contents

1

The Case of the Tell-tale Hands

1

It was on a fine May morning in 1901 that Holmes and I first made the acquaintance of Raymond Ashley Savile, 3rd Earl of Blagdon. The Earl was in his mid-forties at the time of our meeting.

His grandfather, the 1st Earl of Blagdon, had gained a fortune and a title as the founder of Savile's Commercial Bank in the City of London in 1839. In the heyday of Victoria's England, Savile's Bank had been a name to conjure with. Plain old John Savile, before he acquired his earldom, made his first million in the railway boom of the 1840s. He then sold his shares in the Great North Eastern Railway and its rivals shortly before the bubble burst. Whatever his profit, he doubled it—and doubled it again—through his stake in Ocean Coal, as well as in several of the new "department" stores which graced London's West End in the later decades of the nineteenth century.

The old man died in 1897 and was succeeded by his eldest son, who outlived him only for a few months. It was old John Savile's grandson who then became the 3rd Earl of Blagdon. By that time, as Sherlock Holmes remarked acidly, the aristocratic title had passed through three generations and had been washed clean of the whiff and taint of "trade." In the House of Lords and elsewhere, Raymond Ashley Savile stood equal with the descendants of Plantagenet knights and Elizabethan statesmen.

The name most closely associated with the Savile family and its title as Earls of Blagdon was that of their country house, Priorsfield. It had been built no more than forty years before Holmes and I first saw it. Infinite pains had been taken to suggest that a 16th-century château of the Loire had been whisked up and set down in a valley of the River Thames, half way between Oxford and London.

Priorsfield was soon brought to our attention, and I must say a word about it. It was best seen from a distance, as passengers on the Oxford train glimpsed it across the Berkshire meadows beyond Windsor. Despite the best efforts of the architect and the builders, its French Renaissance design had too much of the "new" in its appearance to be anything but the plaything of commercial success. The dome between its round towers with their conical roofs might as easily have graced the Winter Gardens Pavilion or the Grand Hotel of a popular seaside resort.

Other stately homes might be known for suits of armour or the banners of chivalry. Priorsfield's fame came from glass cases of Sèvres porcelain, from gold lustre centrepieces with fresh flowers down the length of polished dining tables and overblown garden scenes painted in oils. The Earls of Blagdon walked on flower-decorated carpets ordered by Louis XIV for the halls of Versailles.

Raymond Ashley Savile came to see Sherlock Holmes by appointment. He was a tall, rather gaunt man, perhaps in his prime but already with a pronounced stoop. It was not only this stoop which made the fair-complexioned and clean-shaven aristocrat appear to bear the weight of the world on his shoulders. He glanced at me, uneasily as I thought, swept his long morning-coat about him and sat down. He turned to my friend.

"Mr. Holmes, what I have to tell you must remain between ourselves."

"Of course, my lord," said Holmes courteously. "However, you may speak as freely before Dr. Watson as to myself. Indeed, it is advisable that you should do so. The resolution of most difficulties benefits from a second opinion. It is far better that my friend and colleague should hear of the matter from your own lips. Indeed, I would consider it essential."

In this polite but inflexible manner, Sherlock Holmes had laid down the law to the aristocracy on many occasions. Lord Blagdon paused, as if he might even now stand up and take his leave. Then he sighed and began his explanation.

"Mr. Holmes, you are probably aware that my father's youngest brother was Lord Frederick Savile who together with his young wife was killed in the Clapham train crash of 1879."

"Indeed, my lord," said Holmes quietly.

"He left a five-year-old son, Lord Arthur Savile, who was brought up by my father as if he had been my younger brother rather than my cousin. We were not close, of course, because there was a gap of almost twenty years between us. However, I have always behaved towards him as though he were more than a young cousin. He will only carry the courtesy title of Lord Arthur Savile and therefore cannot inherit. However, I have seen to it that he need not want for money. He left Oxford without a degree but, curiously, he had the makings of a budding pianist. Were he not otherwise provided for—and had he the persistence—I daresay he might have made a career in that way."

"I take some interest in concert music," said Holmes casually, "and have heard of Lord Arthur's remarkable talent. I am sorry he has not cultivated it. His private impromptu performance at Priorsfield of Chopin's C-sharp-minor study, several years ago, was described to me by the great Vladimir de Pachmann himself as a tour de force. It might not have done for him to play in public, but he was a most accomplished performer."

The Earl inclined his head in acknowledgement.

"It is a matter of character, Mr. Holmes. Unfortunately, it is not his accomplishments which are the subject of my present visit. To speak frankly, he is better known in certain outlandish and Bohemian areas of London society than I should care to be. As for his music, he plays less and less, except occasionally in the company of his family. Let me be plain. I am attached to Lord Arthur and I have helped him, from time to time, as I have been able. But his conduct is become a matter of concern."

Holmes raised one eyebrow.

"I cannot presume, my lord, to take your cousin's conduct under my care."

The Earl of Blagdon reassured him with a lift of the hand.

"I do not suggest that he is vicious or wild. There is nothing of drink, or gambling, or womanising. Rather, he is not merely eccentric but he seems to collect eccentricities for their own sake, if you follow me."

"I believe I do, my lord."

"I certainly could not say that he is insane. A man may believe that character can be determined through phrenology by reading the bumps of the skull, as he has done in extremes, and yet he is not insane. He may enlist in the ranks of those Rosicrucians known as 'The Magicians of the Golden Dawn,' yet no alienist would lock him up in Bedlam. He may swear to the appearance of apparitions of the dead at the command of a spiritualist medium, yet that is his freedom of belief. It is when he becomes—shall I say a collector of such oddities?—that I am concerned for him."

"Unless there be fraud or coercion of some kind," said

Holmes gently, "I doubt whether I am the right person to approach. Dr. Watson, on the other hand. . . ."

"What if it should touch upon crime?"

"That, of course, is a quite different matter."

"What if he should burgle, by night, the houses of his own family? What if he should do it to no purpose? It is not only his eccentricities, though they are bad enough, but a growing oddity and perhaps criminality of conduct which brings me here."

Holmes straightened in his chair.

"I think, my lord, that you had better explain that a little."

Lord Blagdon seemed to bow increasingly under the weight of his concern.

"Last Friday, Mr. Holmes, a week ago precisely and in the middle of the night, Lord Arthur came secretly to the grounds of Priorsfield. He opened a sash-window of the library on the ground floor, pushing back the catch with a blade of some kind. He must then have climbed over the sill, which is easy enough, and walked through the lower level of the house to the north drawing-room. The chief feature of this room is a full-size Louis Phillippe display-case, containing the finest items of porcelain in the Priorsfield collection. One of the housekeepers had heard the window being opened and had gone to investigate. She was in time to see Lord Arthur entering the drawing-room. He did not see her. Because he is sometimes a visitor to Priorsfield, she did not challenge him at once but alerted my valet, who in turn woke me."

"I take it that your brother was a regular guest at Priorsfield but not on this occasion? If he wished to visit the house, he had only to ask?"

"Of course. He could treat it as his home, for, in a sense, it was. That is why such incidents have made his conduct so disturbing for some time. I came downstairs quietly in order to observe him without attracting his notice. I watched him open the cabinet. It took him a moment or two, and I cannot tell you whether he picked the lock or merely turned a key which he had had made. He may have taken an impression on one of his visits and had a key cut."

"We shall be able to determine that," I said quickly but Holmes frowned me into silence.

"He did not need to turn on the electric light," Lord Blagdon continued, "having chosen a night of full moon through open curtains. I could not see precisely what he was doing, for his back was towards me. However, he was facing the display of Sèvres vases, jardinières, dishes, and boxes, with the door of the cabinet partly open. These items are glazed in royal blue or pink, picked out in gold, inset with garden scenes of fêtes galantes or Classical mythology. He struck a match very briefly as he stood there, and seemed to find what he wanted at once. His movements were quick, though quiet. Indeed, I heard nothing all the time he was there and I cannot tell you whether he moved or opened any of the pieces, though I believe he must have done."

"What did he take?" I asked.

Lord Blagdon swung round to me.

"Nothing, Dr. Watson! Nothing! If the housekeeper had not heard the library window being opened, we should never have suspected that he had been there."

"Whereupon," Holmes interposed, "he closed and locked the display cabinet, passed from the drawing-room to the library, left by way of the window, closed it after him, but could not lock it?"

"Quite correct, Mr. Holmes. I was dismayed when I first saw him because I feared he had got himself into money trouble and was robbing his own family to pay off his debts. What if he was in such trouble and was robbing us at the command of criminals? You see?"

"Indeed I do. But has the window been found unlocked since then?"

"Never. It has been examined every morning."

"Excellent. And where did he go when he left the house on the night in question?"

"I can only assume that he walked across the garden, along the road to the village, and waited for the first morning train from Priorsfield Halt."

"That is good to know. It suggests that he had no accomplices and was probably not working on the orders of anyone else. Of course, he might have been examining the objects in order to facilitate a robbery by some other person. However, I think not. He could have done that more easily while he was a guest in the house. In any case, he has not returned in the past week."

"Had I known that he wanted to, he would have been welcome to come to the house and examine the porcelain to his heart's content. That is what makes it so disturbing. As it is, he did no harm that I could see. I thought it best to observe but say nothing."

"You did quite right, my lord," said Holmes reassuringly.

"The curious thing is that he did not wear gloves that night."

"Surely he had no need to," I said. "Chief Inspector Henry at Scotland Yard can read finger-prints like a book. But who would look for prints without evidence of a crime? Had the housekeeper not seen him, there would have been neither evidence nor suspicion."

Lord Blagdon shook his head.

"You misunderstand. For the past six months, Lord Arthur has worn gloves, invariably out of doors and frequently at other times. He says nothing of this, will not discuss it, but we infer that he suffers from a rash or some such ailment."

There was a note of scepticism in Holmes's reply.

"Does he wear gloves when he plays the piano?"

Lord Blagdon bridled a little at this.

"Of course not, but he has largely given up his music."

"Or at the dinner table?"

"Once or twice. Of late, when he has been our guest, he has taken meals in his room. That is the least of his eccentricities."

"And when did you last hear him play the piano—without gloves, as you say?"

"About four weeks ago. It was in the afternoon, with only a few family members present—and they were not paying much attention during their game of whist. He played one of the Schumann Carnaval pieces, just the first one. Then he stopped, closed the lid of the piano keyboard, folded his hands together, and left to go to his room."

"An accomplished musician indeed," said Holmes graciously. "Since you were present, did you see any obvious marks or disfigurement of the hands?"

"No," said Lord Blagdon. "I was, however, sitting at a little distance and naturally saw only the backs of his hands. I did not see a rash of any kind."

"Let us conclude, then, that whatever causes Lord Arthur to wear gloves, it did not do so while he was playing Schumann. And has the instrument been played since?"

"No, the lid is closed and locked when it is not in use."

"Has the keyboard been dusted?"

"I think not. It was locked as usual and I do not recall Mrs. Rowley, the housekeeper, asking for the key since then."

"Excellent!" said Holmes. "In that case, I believe we may take a first step towards the resolution of your difficulty."

When we were alone together, Holmes jotted two or three words on the back of his shirt-cuff as an aide-mémoire and then looked up.

"I confess, Watson, that this promises to be one of the most intriguing cases to come our way for a little while. First of all, however, by his lordship's leave, I think we must examine the locus in quo, as the lawyers call it—the scene of this little mystery."

2

So it was that three days later, on Monday morning, we stepped down from our train at the quiet wooden platform of Priorsfield Halt to find a pony and trap waiting for us. It was that time of year when the riverside elms were in full leaf. The broad stretch of the Thames sparkled in sunlight, carrying an occasional pleasure steamer rippling upstream to Oxford from Windsor.

Priorsfield House was huge and empty after a weekend party. The gardens were deserted, and the patter of water spilling from a triton's conche in the grand basin was audible across the main lawn. The housekeeper received us, in the temporary absence of her employer, and we were conducted at once to the north drawing-room. The windows had been orientated to avoid strong sunlight damaging the fabrics of furniture. With a small key she unlocked the display case.

"The piano too, if you please," said Holmes courteously.

She puffed herself up, cock-robin style, and clasped her hands. One look at her had been enough to assure me that she would never let drop tittle-tattle about Lord Arthur Savile's unorthodox visit to the house.

"Lord Blagdon left no instructions as to the piano."

Sherlock Holmes sighed.

"I fear we shall have wasted his lordship's time, as well as our own, if we are denied an opportunity to examine the keyboard. In that case, I must decline to proceed further with the investigation."

There was only a brief pause before this contest of wills was decided. Our chatelaine walked across and unlocked the lid of the fine black-lacquered Bösendorfer grand piano, folding it back on its polished brass hinges and laying bare an immaculate keyboard.

"It seems," said Holmes to me from the corner of his mouth, "that the housemaids here have been as careless as in most establishments when it comes to the matter of dusting. I daresay I should be so myself, in their situation. A good deal too much fuss is made about dust—which settles again almost as soon as it is brushed off."

The housekeeper had walked silently from the room, though we could feel that her eyes were still upon us from some vantage point just beyond the door. Holmes turned to the piano. He had come equipped with a black Gladstone bag that might more properly have belonged to a doctor. From this he took an instrument case, laid it on the table, and opened it. He chose two camel-hair brushes, such as a painter might have used for fine work. To these he added two small bottles. The first contained a dark powder, which was graphite of much the kind used for lubricating locks. The second was his own preparation, two parts of finely powdered chalk and one part of metallic mercury. These little bottles were accompanied by two insufflators to allow each powder to be blown gently onto any surface. In his waistcoat pocket, as usual, a folded magnifying-lens was readily available.

For the next twenty minutes, Sherlock Holmes worked

patiently and intently, his features drawn in a slight frown of concentration. He began with the light-coloured powder of chalk and mercury, puffing it gently but accurately onto the black keys of the piano. Then he removed a little surplus with a camel-hair brush. When this was done, he took the graphite and the second insufflator, applying the darker powder to the white ivory of the piano keys. It settled like a thin drift of snow—and like snow it revealed the contours over which it lay, in this case those slight ridges imprinted by the exudations of the human skin.

He took a little mirror from his pocket and angled it to catch the light from the windows. Then there began his long examination of each piano key in turn. I knew better than to interrupt him. It was half an hour before his back straightened and he stood up, the sharp profile animated and eyes glittering. He put down the little mirror into which he had been staring, seeking the best angle. The powders had now left on the polished ivory of the keys what I can only describe as a slight and brittle encrustation which a sweep of the hand would remove.

"Of one thing we may be sure, Watson. The last person to touch this keyboard played upon it the 'Préambule' from the set of pieces entitled Carnaval, by the late and sublime Robert Schumann. It has not been dusted nor touched since then."

He seemed a little too pleased with himself for my liking.

"How can you possibly say that?"

"Very easily, my dear fellow. To begin with, we are only concerned with the last person to touch the instrument. I can assure you that all these prints belong to the same pair of hands. Only one person has played upon it since it was last dusted."

"Lord Arthur?"

He raised a finger.

"Look at the two topmost octaves of the keyboard in the right hand. No prints appear on the four highest keys. That is to say,

G, A, and the raised notes of F and G. They are very often not required. We can safely forget them. But four other notes are also free of prints. Those are significant."

"Of what?"

He sighed tolerantly.

"Significant in your case, my dear Watson, of hours wasted in concert halls, fighting back sleep when the air was shimmering with the genius of Rubinstein or Paderewski. Before our little outings to the Wigmore Hall, I like to read the scores of the pieces to be played. Consequently I may tell you that in the right hand of Robert Schumann's 'Préambule' there are only five other keys—black or white—which are not touched. All are in the same two topmost octaves. They include the lower B natural, upper D flat and, in both octaves, the keys of E natural. Now you may study the keyboard of this splendid instrument and tell me for yourself which of those five keys have produced no finger-prints."

He was right, of course. I tried to salvage as much dignity as I was able.

"Hardly conclusive proof of anything but Lord Arthur playing Schumann. Not much to go on."

"My dear fellow, I am nowhere near my conclusion yet. I promise you I have a good deal more to go on. Look at the lower half of the keyboard, by the way. Tell me what you see."

"There are no prints on the lowest eleven keys, black or white. All the rest seem to have been touched."

"Exactly. It will not surprise you to learn that those are the very notes not required in playing Schumann's exquisite sketch."

"But Holmes, there is no dispute that Lord Arthur played that piece on this piano."

"There would have been a great deal of dispute if we had asked Lord Blagdon, or indeed Lord Arthur himself, for a set of our subject's finger-prints as though he were a common criminal. He is a young man of excellent family and as yet unblemished reputation. Therefore he is likely to resist being treated as a suspect. None the less, we now have what we want: a set of his finger-prints is essential if our investigation is to be successfully carried out."

There was little point in arguing. In any case I must either concede that Holmes was right or, at least, suspend my judgment. He left the lid of the keyboard open and turned instead to the display case with its magnificent collection of Sèvres porcelain. It was the most remarkable example of eighteenth-century craftsmanship. Its vases, cups, tableware, and bonbon dishes were fit for a royal drawing-room.

He carefully opened the unlocked glass doors.

"I think we shall find very few finger-prints of any kind here, Watson. The servants in great houses are taught to dust such treasures, on the rare occasions when they do so, by holding them in a cloth without allowing their fingers to touch the polished surface. It would not do for a housemaid's or even a butler's greasy thumbprint to blemish the display."

"Lord Arthur used no duster."

"No. Curious, is it not, that a man who wore gloves on most occasions—except when playing the piano, which he could hardly do with gloves on—should have left them off while practising the art of burglary. That may be the answer to everything."

"He cannot have expected to be caught."

"He cannot have expected to be seen, rather," said Holmes with quiet emphasis.

"Then why play the piano without gloves in front of others?"

"We shall have an answer to that without leaving these rooms. For the moment, I should value your assistance in taking the pieces of porcelain as I hand them to you and putting them gently on the table behind you. Please avoid marking them with your own fingers and preserve the prints already there. We shall not need to look far. We have it on Lord Blagdon's authority that whatever interested his cousin was comfortably within his reach as he stood at the opening of the cabinet doors, where we are now. I doubt whether we need examine more than a dozen items."

As it proved, we required eight. Four of these were a fine set of Sèvres vases with gilt handles and ornament, each bearing a garden scene set in royal blue lustre, taken from a painting by Fragonard. Holmes tested all four with dark powder. They had been dusted some time ago but not marked since. A satin-pink gilt-edged dessert plate bore the signs of the zodiac but no finger-prints. Two Meissen vases decorated in blue on white with a pattern of Indian flowers required both light and dark powder but yielded no prints. Holmes was evidently correct that all these had been dusted, polished and then put away without the fingers of the servants touching their surfaces once the cleaning had been completed.

Then my friend took a dainty Sèvres bonbonnière. It was in richly enamelled porcelain, a rectangular chocolate-box, some six inches across. Edged by a motif of golden fleurs-de-lys, its centrepiece was a golden knob by which the lid was lifted. On each of its sides, the face of one of the winds was painted in natural tones, Boreas for the North, Auster for the South, Eurus for the East, and Zephyr for the West. Holmes handled it so that none of his finger-tips touched the polished surface.

"A little out of place among the vases, I should say," he remarked as he set it safely on the table. "An afterthought to the display, and therefore most interesting. On such light surfaces as these, I believe our graphite powder will suffice."

He positioned it on the window-table where the sunlight would fall as he required it. With his insufflator he puffed a light drift of the darker powder onto the outer surfaces. Judiciously, he blew off a small amount of the powder and applied his enlarging glass to the golden knob at the centre of the lid, as well as to the left-hand side of the box itself. Presently he straightened up, offering me the glass.

"We must make a more detailed inspection presently, Watson. However, it seems the only prints to be seen are exactly where I had anticipated. There are two complete and two partial prints on the golden knob at the centre of the lid, as well as four finger-prints on the left-hand surface and a separate thumb-print on this side. Let us suppose they are the prints of someone who has steadied the box with the left hand while lifting its lid with the fingers of the right. I believe you will find that these prints are exact replicas of those on the piano keyboard."

I am no expert in the matter of finger-prints, but the similarities in the papillary ridges in every case, as Holmes now demonstrated, were certainly striking. In the case of the left index-finger, the manner in which three of the ridges forked prematurely in an upward direction and two in a downward direction were identical on the porcelain and the piano keys. There were also two short independent ridges which seemed to me a carbon copy. I also noticed an identical small feature known as an island or a lake. Conclusive, in my opinion, was the slight disfigurement of a minor cut or abrasion, such as we all suffer from time to time. It had long ceased to trouble the man whose finger sustained it, yet it had not quite vanished on either surface.

Taking the lid of the exquisite bonbonnière by its edges, Holmes lifted it gently and put it on one side.

"I think we may say that the box was dusted and put away behind glass some time ago, untouched by the servant's fingers. Since then, one person has touched it and removed the lid. Even if we had not the prints on the piano keyboard, the evidence points to Lord Arthur Savile."

He peered into the interior of white glazed china.

"As one might expect, Watson. Out of sight, out of mind! The servant who dusted the exterior of the box did not think it worth the trouble to open it and clean the interior!"

He showed it to me. The glazed white china which formed the little floor of the interior was marked by two caramel-stained deposits, each about the size of a postage-stamp.

"This box has merely been used for its original purpose of holding chocolates," I said. "Heat of some kind, perhaps a fire in the background or the sun through the window, has warmed the interior sufficiently to melt the chocolate or even the contents of one of the bonbons."

"Two of them, I think," said Holmes quickly, "and quite recently."

He touched his forefinger to one of the marks and then to his tongue. He mimed a disappointed face and shrugged. Then he repeated the process with the second caramel deposit. This time he stood still, his features immobile for several seconds. Very suddenly, as if he were about to vomit, he drew his handkerchief, stuffed it to his lips and spat into it with all his strength. In a few strides, he crossed to a small table on which stood a syphon of soda water. Like a singer lubricating his tonsils, he squirted the water into his mouth, crossed to the window, flung it up, and spat again, unceremoniously, into the flower-bed.

I stooped over the box and sniffed its interior. There was a mustiness of stale sugar and condiments of some kind, but nothing more. Very carefully, I touched my finger to the same deposit.

"Before you go further, Watson, the word 'aconite' may give you second thoughts. Unless I am very much mistaken, the terms Indian aconite, or Aconitum ferox, or the so-called Bish poison would be a more accurate description here—to judge by the speed with which it affects the tongue. I believe there has been poison in this box, and it would hardly have been introduced without murder in mind. I tasted the minutest quantity but my lips and the tip of my tongue are still tingling and a little numb. Concealed in a bonbon, of course, it would have done its worst before there was any suspicion."

"And Lord Blagdon?"

"For the moment, we shall say nothing. However, in case we should require to verify his lordship's account of Lord Alfred's visit, I should like to take one more finger-print sample from the sill of the library window. I do not think our client has misled us, but this case now takes on a graver complexion."

3

We took the print from the library sill. By the time we returned to the north drawing-room, it was occupied by the tall and stooping figure of Lord Blagdon, who turned from the oriel window to greet us.

"Well, Mr. Holmes," he said uneasily, "I see that you have been at work. To what conclusion have you come?"

"To little more than I had already come," said Holmes crisply. "In playing Schumann on the grand piano, your cousin left a perfect set of his finger-prints. Those prints also appear on the window sill of the library, corroborating your version of events."

"When I came to you, I was not aware that my version would require corroboration," said Lord Blagdon reproachfully.

"But you have it none the less, my lord," Holmes replied, yielding no ground. "The same finger-prints appear on the Sèvres bonbonnière near the front of the cabinet. So far as we can establish at the moment, that was the object of Lord Arthur's visit."

Lord Blagdon seemed genuinely taken aback.

"What possible interest could he have in it? He certainly did not attempt to steal it. Indeed, I should have made him a present of it, if his heart was set upon the thing. It is not of great value, compared with the other pieces."

"I do not think he ever wanted to steal it. Perhaps, however, you would not mind giving me an account of its recent history."

Holmes had gained the initiative, and Lord Blagdon now looked a little perplexed.

"It has no recent history to speak of, Mr. Holmes. It is only as a matter of convenience that it appears in the display. During her lifetime, it was the possession of our father's cousin, Lady Clementina Beauchamp. Lady Clem, as we all called her. Like so many of our more distant family, she was never well off, but we all cared for her as best we could. She had inherited a few items like the bonbon dish from our grandfather, and she left them to us when she died."

"What did she leave to Lord Arthur?"

Lord Blagdon raised his eyebrows.

"To Lord Arthur? Why, nothing. She had no reason to. He had no expectations from her. It was my own side of the family from which she had received kindness. She was fond enough of my cousin, of course, as I have always believed he was of her. But then, Lady Clem was fond of everyone because it was in her nature. I do not think she and Lord Arthur were more closely acquainted."

"They were on visiting terms, however?"

"Oh, to be sure, we all were. To what extent, in his case, I cannot say."

"When did Lady Beauchamp die?"

The expression on Lord Blagdon's face suggested that this line of questioning had gone on long enough but that he would indulge his hired detective a little more.

"Almost exactly two months ago."

"And where was Lord Arthur then?"

"Lord Arthur had been in Venice for a week or two with my

wife's brother. He was unable to return in time for the funeral. Now if that is all for the present. . . ."

"I fear, my lord, that it is not nearly all."

The tone of this stung our host.

"Mr. Holmes! On the recommendation of a close friend, I have invited you to investigate a most sensitive family matter. You now inquire into things which I cannot see are in the least necessary. I am anxious to benefit from your advice, but I am bound to say that there is a point beyond which I shall feel compelled to do without it!"

Holmes did not even blink.

"I trust not, my lord, for if I am compelled to relinquish the case, the advice which you will receive is likely to be that of the Metropolitan Police. Most probably, as matters stand, it will come in the person of Chief Inspector Lestrade or Inspector Tobias Gregson, both of the Criminal Investigation Division of Scotland Yard. My lord, I cannot afford to be party to compounding a felony."

It is a cliché to say that a man looks stunned, but that was exactly how Lord Blagdon appeared. Holmes allowed him no retreat.

"I have to tell you, Lord Blagdon, that the bonbonnière before you contains two deposits of melted chocolate or something of the kind. One of these, in my opinion, contained a lethal dose of Aconitum ferox, the most deadly and still one of the most secret of all poisons."

"Stuff and nonsense! Balderdash!"

I had expected Lord Blagdon to be further stunned by this news, but he came out fighting, as the saying is. Even Holmes paused, and this gave me the chance to intervene between them.

"Since I am a medical man, Lord Blagdon, it may help us all if you can tell me quite simply how Lady Clementina died."

He almost laughed at me.

"Quite simply, she died of heart failure at an advanced age, sir! Though she put on a brave face and went out and about as much as she could, she had been ailing for years. It was not unusual at her time of life. The wonder is she lived as long as she did. I have served in India with the 17th Lancers, and I too know a little of vengeance by secret poison. I have some notion of what the symptoms are. She did not exhibit them."

He turned away to the window, as if to conceal from us his exasperation. Then he swung round again with a spin of the hem of his morning coat and a wagging finger.

"Suspect me, if you like! I was present when Lady Clem died, and I can tell you that she died of heart failure. Her final illness lasted for more than a week. During that time, the bonbon dish you refer to was never within her reach and, believe me, she had no use for it during her last days. The Duchess of Paisley visited her just before the end and took dinner in Lady Clementina's room. The poor old woman could manage nothing apart from broth and plain water. Her physician, Sir Matthew Reid, and a nurse were in constant attendance. A man of Sir Matthew's eminence may be allowed, I think, to know the difference between heart failure and acute poisoning. Your suggestions are quite preposterous!"

"Lord Arthur—" Holmes began, but he got no further.

"I have already told you, Mr. Holmes, that Lord Arthur was several hundred miles away. You or your friends at Scotland Yard may check for yourselves that he was staying at Danielli's Hotel in Venice. When he was not at the hotel, he was yachting on the Adriatic or with a shooting party in the Pinetum, accompanied by at least a dozen witnesses. As for having a motive to murder, that is the most absurd thing of all. He would not benefit by her death, and he knew it. Her intentions were never in doubt. I grant you, Lord Arthur benefited a little in the end—only because after her death, I asked that I should not have certain items she bequeathed to me. Lord Arthur did not know beforehand that this would happen. Despite your reputation, if this is the best you can do, Mr. Holmes. . . ."

"Perhaps it would help," I said, with some sense of desperation, "if you could tell me what happened to the contents of the bonbon dish."

"The dish was bequeathed to me as a keepsake. I lack a sweet tooth for such things and, in any case, there is something unappealing in eating the bonbons of the dead. I threw away such as remained in it and left the dish for the servants to clean. It was evidently dusted. I had assumed that the servant who did this would also have washed it out. If it should contain evidence of criminality of any kind, then of course I am glad that that did not happen."

This discussion of the dish had calmed the atmosphere somewhat.

"In that case, my lord," said Holmes, "there is little more that I can suggest. The curiosity of Lord Arthur's visit here in the middle of the night is a matter for your own consideration. Unless you wish to pursue it, the mystery may rest where it is. As to the death of Lady Clementina, however. . . ."

"Very well, Mr. Holmes; as to that, I am there before you. I am, after all, a magistrate and know something of the law. You mean to have your way. Yet you must understand that I could not bear the thought of that kind old lady being made the subject of public gossip and the sniggerings of the gutter press."

"It is the last thing I should wish. However. . . ."

"Fortunately, she lies in the family vault at Beauchamp Chalcote. I will go this far with you. I will communicate with Sir Matthew Reid, who attended her from first to last. I will take his opinion whether an autopsy might be the proper course to silence speculation. If Sir Matthew thinks so, I shall make no objection. He may deal with the coroner. I will suggest, perhaps, that terms in her will, favouring medical science, make an examination desirable. I hope that may suffice. Because it is our family vault in the church at Beauchamp Chalcote, no unseemly public exhumation from a churchyard or municipal cemetery is necessary. If it must be done, it must also be discreetly done."

Holmes gave a half bow and said, "Your lordship is too kind."

He made it sound as if Lord Blagdon might withdraw his offer of an autopsy if he chose. Yet both men knew that his lordship had been allowed no choice.

As all the world does not know, because the secret was kept within the family circle, an autopsy was carried out within the week. The body of Lady Clementina Beauchamp showed no trace of poison whatever, let alone the atrocious effects of Aconitum ferox.

"I fear we have put Lord Blagdon to unnecessary distress," I said to Holmes across the breakfast table, when the post communicated this news to us.

"I think not."

"We were misled by the evidence of a smear which in itself would have killed no one. On that evidence, we allowed for the possibility of a far greater quantity of aconite in the bonbons before the box was emptied. Suppose there was not. Then all we have is a medicinal trace which may have leaked from a pastille or a gelatine capsule used to make a tonic dose palatable. A homoeopath might well have prescribed it for a failing heart."

"No doubt," said Holmes in the tone of one who is listening with less than half his attention.

"At the worst, it was a quack remedy, bought and neglected. It lay in the box until heat and moisture caused chocolate and gelatine to melt. That is the rational explanation."

"You really think so?"

"I cannot see why not."

"I entirely accept that you cannot see why not. That is where your problem lies."

"Mark my words, Holmes, you will find that we have seen the last of Lord Blagdon."

"I think not."

After this exchange of words, it seemed that our case had come to an end—and a most unsatisfactory end at that. The bonbonnière was thereafter washed, polished, and returned to its shelf. The presence of aconite had been a red herring, if ever there was one. As I had remarked to Holmes, in medicinal doses even such poison has its place in every pharmacy cupboard, as a homoeopathic remedy for the onset of acute conditions, from the common cold to a congestion of the vital organs.

It was hard to see that the case could go any further. Certainly no murder had taken place. Such a minute trace of aconitum was not even sufficient evidence of attempted murder. What was left? A minor figure of the English aristocracy had behaved oddly, but that was hardly a novelty. He had arrived and departed, unannounced, at his cousin's house in the middle of the night. While there, he had inspected several items of porcelain but had taken nothing. This, at any rate, was how the matter rested as the London season ended and the beau monde looked forward to country estates and shooting-parties.

4

August is the month which the newspapers characterise as "The Holiday Season." A lack of serious information caused the columns of the press to be filled with stories that one was afterwards ashamed to have wasted time in reading. Something of the sort also affects the life of the consulting detective, as Holmes was apt to complain. Humbler folk, not part of the London season, take their families to the beaches of Brighton or the sands of Margate. The criminal classes are hardly to be seen from Putney Bridge in the West of London to Bow Church in the city's East End. We were at the mercy of every eccentric or lunatic who chose to pester us with his story. I suggested to my friend that we might refresh our minds and bodies among university dons or the legal and medical professions, where the Atlantic Ocean rolls sonorously in at Ilfracombe or Tenby.

He would have none of it. Better to be pestered by clients of doubtful sanity or questionable morals than to travel without purpose and linger one's life away—or, as his old Calvinist nursemaid had cautioned him, to sleep oneself silly.

When the Archdeacon of Chichester, the Venerable Doctor

Josephus Percy, visited us, he was the first client to cross the threshold for almost a fortnight. Dr. Percy, despite his archdiaconate and his attachment to scholarship, had made little impression upon the world of theology or church politics. He was known principally for a certain eccentricity of conduct and his devotion to the worlds of books and clocks.

Several years ago, he had attracted a certain notoriety and a rebuke from the coroner on the death of his housekeeper. This amiable churchman had been at home with her when the unfortunate lady succumbed to a heart attack. It had despatched her within half a minute. It was a Thursday afternoon, just before two o'clock. At two o'clock every Thursday, the Archdeacon was a visitor to Goodley's Fine Prints and Rare Editions in the market square of his cathedral city. On this occasion, having propped the deceased housekeeper in the corner of the sofa, he was seen upon his errand as usual, bicycling through the streets of Chichester. An hour or so later, with a brown paper parcel in the basket of his machine, he had pedalled home. Only then did he summon assistance.

In appearance, the Archdeacon looked not so much an old man as a younger man made up for the stage to look antique. The bulb of his vinous nose suggested a gutta-percha beak surmounting a smaller and less inflamed protuberance. The hump of his back belonged surely to the properties department of Quasimodo. The dark locks of a younger man were assuredly bunched up beneath the white wig. His mutton-chop whiskers suggested an aura of spirit gum. But it was not so. The youth of Josephus Percy, if he ever had one, had long since passed away.

"Mr. Holmes!" The voice was firm and precise. "What can you tell me of exploding clocks?"

Sherlock Holmes touched his finger-tips together as he confronted the Archdeacon across the unlit fireplace.

"Very little, I fear, Archdeacon. A clock, like almost any other mechanism, can be designed to explode. However, it is not usual. Indeed, a clock is more often the means of regulating the time of an explosion. Perhaps that is what you mean?"

The Archdeacon shuffled his gaiters—there is no other term for it—and impatiently tapped the carpet twice with the ferule of his stick.

"What I mean, sir, is this. Four days ago I received through the post a black marble clock in the shape of a classical Athenian facade—with figures. If you know anything of me, you will know that I am a collector of clocks and a past president of the Horological Society of Great Britain, as well as a Fellow of the Society of Antiquaries."

"I was indeed aware of that," said Holmes graciously.

"Well, then! The clock of which I speak came from a dealer in Greek Street, Soho. I had not heard of this dealer before and there was no explanation as to why it had been sent. I assumed it must be a gift or presentation of some kind and that a letter explaining this would follow. No such letter has arrived."

"Perhaps you would do me the kindness of describing the clock in detail."

"It was a most unusual one, Mr. Holmes. It appeared to emanate from the French Revolutionary period and even to sing the praises of that unfortunate event. At the quarter, it sounded the first two notes of the Marseillaise. At the half, it sounded four, at the three-quarters six, and at the hour the first ten, completing the opening line of that distasteful anthem."

At this point the Archdeacon broke briefly into song.

"All-ons, en-fants de la pa-trie—uh—uh! After that it struck the hour."

"How singular," said Holmes as if the tedium were well-nigh unbearable. "Pray, do continue your most interesting account."

"On the top of the pediment stood a figure of Marianne, wearing a Cap of Liberty, as though at the head of a mob. To either side, in niches, were two figures, whom pennants stamped in gold identify as Danton and Marat. My manservant, Parker, unpacked it and after breakfast we stood it upon the mantelpiece in the library. It was soon wound up and ticking. At midday on Friday, I was reading in a chair just beside the mantelpiece. The clock played its ten notes and then struck the hour. At once, there was a whirring sound from the mechanism, a sharp crack and a puff of smoke from Marianne's pedestal. It was such a mouthful of smoke as might be exhaled during the consumption of a cigar. The figure in its Cap of Liberty fell off the pediment."

Sherlock Holmes shifted his long legs to ease them.

"I fear, sir, you have been the victim of an elaborate practical joke. I am bound to say that your views upon revolutionary outrages are quite well known."

"You fear that, do you?" said the Archdeacon testily. "Wait until you have heard the rest. I thought, as you do, that the device was sent merely to try my patience. I summoned Parker and ordered that the object should be removed at once and placed in the potting-shed. That seemed the most appropriate place for it. I replaced it with a testimonial clock from a grateful congregation at the Tabernacle Church, Ebbw Vale, which had been there to begin with."

"This story has scarcely brought you all the way to Baker Street," I said helpfully.

Once again, the Archdeacon's forefinger pointed in the direction of heaven and his eyes grew wider.

"Wait! That night the household, such as it is, had gone to bed soon after eleven o'clock. At what must have been midnight, I was woken from a doze by a blast which sounded as though a gas-main had exploded. I got up at once and looked from the window. The potting-shed was just in my view—or rather it was not. It had gone. There was a smell of burning fabric in the air and the moonlight was reflected on several shards of broken glass. Anyone in the vicinity at the time of the explosion would have been killed."

"And it was in the light of such danger that you sought our advice?" I asked sceptically.

"No, sir. I do not keep a dog and bark myself. I summoned the police but unfortunately they were very little help. They pointed out that the evidence I offered had been destroyed most efficiently by the explosion. They promised to look into the matter but, meantime, advised me to be patient. They said that explosions in potting-sheds are invariably caused by paraffin oil heaters! Such things are always happening, they told me. Their inspector thought it a great joke. 'I wonder you don't go and consult Mr. Sherlock Holmes in Baker Street!' he said, and his constables all laughed. Hence, you see me here."

Holmes frowned.

"One thing you may be sure of. The name of the clockmaker on the parcel was false."

"But I have not told you what the name is, Mr. Holmes."

"That is no matter. It is my business to know the streets of London better than other people. I can assure you that there is no clockmaker of any name in Greek Street. It has had its share of bomb-makers, but they have not been active of late."

"You confirm my suspicions, then. Now, what do you make of this?"

The Archdeacon handed my friend a small tube-like bottle with a cork in it.

"Where did it come from?" Holmes inquired, tipping a little of the powder into the palm of his hand. He sniffed it carefully.

"When the clock emitted its puff of smoke from the library mantelpiece, a very small amount of this fell onto the tiles of the fireplace."

"Did it indeed?" said Holmes. "Well, wherever it came from or wherever it fell, this is gunpowder. However, it is certainly not gunpowder of the best quality. Were it so, the explosion which occurred in your garden shed might have taken place twelve hours earlier on your library mantelpiece. I daresay that most of the percussion caps failed to ignite the bulk of it on the first occasion."

"And what do you suggest?"

"That you should go home and stay there. Take every sensible precaution. Leave the rest to me. I do not think you will be troubled again."

The Archdeacon's face was a study in indignation and dismay. "You will not come to Chichester? I surely need to be guarded?"

"The threat to you is not from Chichester but from London. If a man with a gun appeared in the doorway of this room and offered to shoot, you would not want me to stand beside you over here but to disarm him over there."

"Very clever, Mr. Holmes. But you do not know who the assassin is!"

"On the contrary, Archdeacon, I have a very good idea who he is, and I do not think he will trouble you again."

"Then give me his name!"

"It would not help you. Indeed, I think it would mean nothing to you. It would merely distract you from doing the best and safest thing, which is to live quietly and sensibly at home until this case is concluded. It will not be for long, a week at the most, probably much less. Of one thing you may be quite sure: your persecutor will not come near you again."

"But you have told me nothing!"

"On the contrary, I have given you precise instructions and specific assurances. For the rest, if you wish me to take your case, you must trust me."

"It seems I have very little choice, so long as the police will not listen to me!"

With that, our visitor left. However disgruntled he might be and however often he might hint at refusing to pay a fee for this sort of advice, the Archdeacon knew that he would get no further with Sherlock Holmes that morning.

5

Such was the visit of the Venerable Josephus Percy to our consulting rooms. I cannot say that I was much encouraged by Holmes's performance but, at least, he was correct in telling the Archdeacon to go home and stay there. Hardly had this clergyman left us when there was a sharp sound of hooves in the street and the grating of wheels against the stone kerb, followed by a sudden pull at the door bell.

"This, I think," said Holmes, without getting up from his chair or going near the window, "will be the Earl of Blagdon. I have been expecting him for several days."

"Really? Why?"

"I imagine he will tell us in his own good time that it is a matter of his cousin's hands."

At that point our visitor was announced by Mrs. Hudson. A great change had come over Lord Blagdon. He was a worried and a contrite man. Placing his hat on the stand, he sat down in the chair indicated to him.

"Mr. Holmes, I have come to ask you not to abandon the case of Lord Arthur."

"That does not surprise me, my lord."

Our visitor looked puzzled but not startled.

"Perhaps you had better listen to what I have to say. I wish you, and your colleague Dr. Watson, to keep watch on him for the next few days. By then I hope arrangements can be made with those who will have him in their care. Since we last spoke, I have made enquiries among the family and the servants. I am told by her former maid that for the past two months Lord Arthur had brought bonbons from Florestan's of St. James's Street to Lady Clementina. I cannot dismiss from my mind the suspicion that she did not die from aconite poisoning—only because she died of heart failure first!"

Holmes gave this a little thought. Then he turned to our client.

"I believe, my lord, that your cousin may be deranged but not ostensibly so. More specifically, I believe that he is a victim of cheiromancy, the so-called science of palm-reading."

"But that is what I have come to tell you!"

"Then you betray no secrets. I had concluded as much from his curious habit of wearing gloves at all times except when playing the piano, which as you say he did less and less. We know that he does not suffer from any infection or disfigurement. If that were so, the hands would show it on their backs. It matters only to him that the world should not see his palms. Why? Because that is where secrets are read by all who can do so. He believes that catastrophe lies in wait for him as surely as a beast in the jungle."

"But is not the whole thing absurd?"

"To you or me it is, my lord. To one who, as you say, has been a devotee of astrology, phrenology, the Magicians of the Golden Dawn, the materialisation of the dead as ectoplasm, then the appeal of palmistry may be strong. Such arts of divination, however specious, are too familiar to the criminal investigator. Palmistry is deep-rooted. It goes back through many centuries to a superstition of examining the cracks and lines of a shoulder-blade. It was brought back to England from the medieval Tartars and anciently known as 'reading the speal-bone.'"

Holmes stood up and crossed to the bookcase. He took down a tattered volume bound only in sheepskin, its yellowed pages printed in the "blackletter" of five hundred years earlier, a rarity even in his collection.

"Johann Hartlieb, Die Kunst Ciromantia, published in Augsburg in 1493." Holmes handed it to Lord Blagdon. "There you will find the arts which are still practised as cheiromancy. Their exponents claim that they can read predictions of evil and disaster in the lines of the palm. The Line of Life, for example, runs in an arc from the side of the left wrist to the edge of the hand midway between the base of the thumb and the index finger. Pale and broad, it may indicate evil instincts. Thick and red, it may betray violence and brutality. All this may be read easily in the course of an evening at the dinner table by a fellow guest who is an initiate. That, I believe, was the sort of discovery that Lord Arthur feared."

Lord Blagdon sat for a moment as if trying to compose the words in his mind. At last he said, "I am told by the Duchess of Paisley that my cousin attended an evening party a few months ago. It was the first reception of the spring at Lancaster House. Clever people, but not sound. There was smart talk and someone, who professed the ability, read a number of palms. Lord Arthur naturally offered himself as a subject. The man who had started the game, Podgers was his name, I believe, took Lord Arthur's right hand. Then he dropped it suddenly and seized the left hand. When he looked up, the Duchess tells me, his face was white but he had forced a smile."

"A believer in his art, therefore," said Holmes coldly. "To me, however, it reeks of rehearsal and fraud."

"Podgers had examined the palm long and closely, but he

would only say, 'It is the hand of a charming young man.' That was all. Lord Arthur pressed him to reveal what he had seen. The rascal then went so far as to admit that he had glimpsed the death of a distant relative. There was plainly more to it than that. The Duchess assures me that Septimus Podgers is a professional palm-reader with rooms in West Moon Street."

"Nothing more was said by either man at the party?"

"Lord Arthur and the palmist were seen together later on, very briefly. Lord Arthur was heard to say, 'Tell me the truth, I am not a child,' before Podgers rushed out. When he spoke these words, my cousin had his cheque-book in his hand. Whatever the secret was, he must have purchased the truth of it."

There was a moment of silence. Then Holmes asked, "Can you be sure of this account?"

Lord Blagdon nodded.

"Positive. Now I am told that one of his friends called at Lord Arthur's rooms the next day. There is a small Sheraton table in the window of his drawing-room at which he writes his letters. The visitor noticed on the blotting-paper an imperfect imprint in mirror-writing. The servant had not yet had time to change it for a new sheet. This friend read the name 'Podgers' and the sum of £105. One hundred guineas, Mr. Holmes! Unhappily, he did not hear the Duchess's account of the party until her return from a French tour a few days ago. Now we have both halves of the story."

"A great deal to pay for such information," said Holmes thoughtfully. "Something of which you may be sure is that it was not a prediction that he would poison Lady Clementina with aconite, since this did not happen."

"Then who else was in danger—if it was to be murder?"

"I have reason to suppose that Lord Arthur may have been the person who despatched an exploding clock to the Archdeacon of Chichester. It failed in its purposes."

Lord Blagdon looked blank.

"I do not know the Archdeacon of Chichester from Adam! Nor, I am sure, does Lord Arthur. What possible purpose could there be, unless this scoundrel Podgers put a spell upon him or exercised black magic of some kind?"

Sherlock Holmes's fine profile was a study in distaste.

"I am not a believer in spells, my lord, nor in black magic. Scoundrels are another matter. I believe that I can best discharge my duty to you—and indeed to Archdeacon Percy of Chichester, who has been good enough to consult me—by keeping the closest possible watch upon your cousin for the immediate future."

"You will find that his manservant, Crayshaw, shares my concern about his master. Crayshaw will keep watch on his movements indoors. It is for us to do the rest. I shall occupy his time as best I can without alarming him. For the immediate future, I may tell you that he has no engagements this afternoon but that he will attend the House of Commons this evening."

"In what connection?" I asked.

"Mr. Joseph Keighley, the Member for Manchester South, is a modern rationalist. He has put down an amendment to the Sale of Goods Act. It would make fortune-tellers legally liable for any loss or distress suffered in consequence of their mischief. It stems from the Hevingham judgment in the High Court last winter. Mr. Justice Strode urged the legislature to take some such course in dealing with what he called 'pious fraud.' You may recall that one of these charlatans terrified an elderly lady with predictions of death and disaster in order to buy her house for a song because it had a 'curse' upon it."

"Indeed," said Holmes, almost stifling a yawn.

"Lord Arthur, as you may know, is Member of Parliament for Chalcote. Though he bears the courtesy title of 'Lord,' as the grandson of an earl, he is not a peer of the realm. Therefore he is entitled to sit in the House of Commons. He will be sure to attend in order to vote against the proposed amendment."

"He will not take part in the debate?" Holmes inquired.

"He has never spoken in the five years he has sat in the house, except to say, 'Hear, hear,' on two or three occasions. He does not often attend. His seat is safe enough. Chalcote has been our land for a century past and our tenants are loyal. My cousin has been returned unopposed at two elections."

So it was that Sherlock Holmes and I attended the Strangers Gallery of the House of Commons for the first time. We did so on the nomination of Lord Blagdon, who was by title a member of the House of Lords—and therefore a Member of Parliament in his own right.

6

We should never have been able to track Lord Arthur that evening without permission to enter the precincts of Parliament. Once there, it seemed impossible to lose him. The policeman at the gate of Palace Yard saluted our passes and gave us directions. It was already growing dark, though a full moon lit the river and the gothic pinnacles of Westminster. Downstream, along the Victoria Embankment, gas-lamps on their wrought-iron pillars stretched like an even row of pearls. This was the hour when members, having dined, attended the house to discuss the matters on the order paper as long into the night as might be necessary.

A Gothic door whose architraves were filled by plain glass admitted us to a world which mingled Plantagenet architecture with the comforts of a gentleman's club. Pale stone arches formed sprays of fan vaulting above the tracery of Norman windows. Long murals in Pre-Raphaelite pastel showed the deposed King James II throwing the Great Seal of the realm into the Thames in 1688 and the new King William finding it again in 1689. King Charles I bowed before the headsman's axe on a cold January morning in Whitehall.

As we made our way towards the Strangers Gallery of the Commons, the floor tiles were diamonds of blue and yellow and brown, patterned with clubs, spades, and hearts. The officials in their red livery and buckled shoes might have been kings and knaves in a pack of cards. The brass-furnished oak door of each room bore a title which powerfully suggested the nonsense logic of Alice in Wonderland. One was the home of "Motions" and another of "Questions." On our right was "The Court Postmaster" and to our left "The Table Office." I half expected to turn the corner of a corridor and meet a white rabbit in Tudor jacket and tights.

We made our way up the steps and into the Strangers Gallery, where every seat was taken for the contentious debate on the legal liabilities of fortune-tellers. Lord Blagdon looked round and inclined his head as we took our places.

The House of Commons was much smaller than I had expected, not unlike the nave of a medieval parish church with rows of benches in green leather facing one another on either side. At the far end, upon his dais, Mr. Speaker faced us in his wig and gown. Behind him rose the Press Gallery and above that the Ladies Gallery, whose occupants were concealed by a lattice screen, as though this were a Turkish harem. In front of him was the table with its clerks and the two despatch-boxes at which members addressed the House.

The debate had already begun. Joseph Keighley, the Member for Manchester South, had brought forward the motion standing in his name and was addressing the House from the despatch-box on our left. Tall and spare, his black swallow-tail coat falling open, his grey hair sparse and windswept, his spectacles glinting, he looked every inch a rationalist in argument and agnostic in matters of belief. We heard the story of the widow whom only the Chancery Division and the High Court had saved from being cheated out of her property by a fraudulent fortune-teller.

Mr. Keighley glowed with indignation and demanded protection by parliament and new legislation against robbery in the guise of superstition.

He was answered on the other side by a Junior Minister from the Home Office. This functionary was as placid and mellifluous as Mr. Keighley had been indignant and hectoring. Was it really suggested that the inoffensive fortune-telling tent at every village fair or church fete should be made subject in all particulars to the criminal law? As for black magic, said to have been worked on the poor old lady in this case, the art and its practitioners had always been punishable at common law without the need for new legislation. On the advice of the learned Solicitor-General, they remained so to the present day.

There was much more of this sort of thing and, before long, I confess that my eyelids were heavy. I had not realised before, when reading the report of an interesting parliamentary debate, how much of the proceedings are omitted by the press. In their entirety I found them insupportable. I heard the junior minister refer jocularly to the reading of palms as "the harmless pastime of the tea-party and the fairground tent." Then I knew no more until Holmes dug me sharply in the ribs.

A younger member was on his feet, demanding to know on what grounds the minister was entitled to judge whether such arts were a harmless pastime or not. I screwed my eyes up and peered forward. I needed no one to tell me that the young man, who had risen among the benches and was wearing the black silk hat which entitled him to speak, was a blood relation of Lord Blagdon. The points of resemblance in the face, the dark curls, and the patrician stoop were plain. This, then, was Lord Arthur Savile. After a career of parliamentary silence, something had goaded him into eloquence.

I listened to his words and wondered if I was still dreaming. He demanded angrily how it could be said by the government's

Junior Minister that there was no harm in the "fun" of fortune-telling? Examples of its harm might be seen on every side. He began to list examples. I stared at the young man and thought that surely he was now speaking on the wrong side—in support of criminalising fortune-telling rather than permitting it! What had changed his mind so suddenly and so dramatically?

The Junior Minister made a jovial riposte to this outburst, brushing aside the "intemperate remarks of the noble member for Chalcote." The government would not intervene to criminalise the practice of fortune-telling. This ministerial spokesman rambled on but I was no longer listening. Like the Earl of Blagdon, I assumed that Lord Arthur would attend the debate to vote against any change in the law which might persecute fortune-tellers. Now he had changed sides and was supporting the amendment. I glanced at Holmes but if he was surprised by this volte-face, there was no sign of it on his face.

Only then did I notice a man sitting in the row ahead of me and to one side. He was fat, to put it plainly, with a face that might have been yellowed by jaundice and was deeply lined. His lightweight summer suit, of thin brown cotton, fitted his corpulent form no better than a bag. When Lord Arthur stood up and put his question, this man had emitted a sharp exhalation of breath. Having heard the question answered and dismissed by the Junior Minister, he now turned round to us all with a beam of mingled triumph and relief on his sickly features. It was as if he was inviting us to share his amusement at Lord Arthur's failure.

At last a division was called—and a vote was taken, though the House was by no means full. About a quarter of its members now divided. The "Ayes" who supported the new law against fortune-tellers filed into the lobby on the left and the "Noes" into the lobby on the right. To judge from the numbers crowding into the right-hand lobby, those who thought fortune-telling a harmless occupation were going to win hands-down. But Lord Arthur Savile was not among them. I switched my gaze to the left and saw only two or three dozen members voting in support of a law against such practices. At the tail of the queue was Lord Arthur.

The members returned to their seats and the tellers brought their totals to Mr. Speaker. The result was as I expected.

"They have voted. The Ayes to the left, thirty-one. The Noes to the right, ninety-five. There were no abstentions. I therefore declare that the motion is defeated by sixty-four votes. The House will proceed to the third reading of the Stockbreeders and Poulterers (Hygiene) Bill."

"How very singular," said Sherlock Holmes.

7

Lord Arthur had returned to his seat on the government benches for the very good reason that he was to act as teller for the Ayes at the end of the stockbreeders debate which now began. We knew where he would be until that debate ended or was adjourned. Lord Blagdon led us to his room beyond the House of Lords with its fine view of the Houses of Parliament terrace running above the Thames. He stood at his desk, pouring whisky from a decanter into three glasses. Then he straightened up and handed us each a glass.

"Why did he ask his foolish question? Why did he vote in support of the very law which he had condemned in my hearing as an abuse of freedom and a mere expression of prejudice against the enlightened?"

"Blackmail," said Holmes simply.

"Blackmail! How could he be blackmailed?"

"With great respect, my lord, has it not occurred to you that the so-called cheiromancer or palmist foretold something which, if true, would have made Lord Arthur liable to the criminal law or exposed him to public disgrace?"

"But what?"

"Nothing less than murder, I think."

"But my cousin has murdered no one!"

"Possibly not. Not yet."

Lord Blagdon had left instructions that the door-keeper should warn him as soon as a vote was called in the present House of Commons debate. Lord Arthur, as teller, could not leave until the result was announced. We should be alerted in good time to pick up his trail as he left the Houses of Parliament. Or so we thought.

I realised too late that something had gone wrong with Lord Blagdon's arrangement. We had received no message of Lord Arthur preparing to leave the building when I heard a familiar call echoing through the corridors outside. It is the cry that ends every day's business in the Palace of Westminster, calling like a watchman through the streets of a city.

"Who goes home? Who goes home?"

We looked at one another. Where was he? Holmes and I could scarcely go and search for him. Much of the building was forbidden territory to us and we should hardly know where to begin.

"Wait here, if you please," said Lord Blagdon peremptorily. "I will go and find him. If the door-keeper sees him preparing to leave, he will get word to you. Lord Arthur must still be somewhere in the building."

As it proved, Lord Arthur Savile was in the precincts of Parliament, but he was no longer in the building. Left to ourselves, Holmes and I stood at the latticed window. It looked down across the terrace and the river which ran at the base of its wall. By the lights of the far bank we could see cabs moving along the Albert Embankment. A tugboat pulling a string of three lighters was proceeding down the river towards the wharves of Battersea or Lambeth.

"I do not understand it," I said, not for the first time.

"Possibly not," said Holmes patiently, "Have the goodness, however, to keep quite still and watch the river. I would rather not be noticed."

I was surveying the river terrace which extends from New Palace Yard almost the entire length of parliament. There was a man walking by the wall, his back to the river. He was pacing up and down as if in expectation, wearing a black silk hat and smoking a cigar.

"That is the fellow who was sitting in the Strangers Gallery," I said at once, for there was no mistaking his bulk and the material of his bag-like summer suit, "the man who turned round and smiled at us after Lord Arthur had made his faux pas by interrupting the Junior Minister."

"Just so," said Holmes quietly. "If it will help your understanding a little further, I was able to read the card which he was holding and which admitted him. He is the correspondent of the Psychical Research Quarterly. Had it been a more exalted publication, he might no doubt have claimed a seat in the Press Gallery."

"What is he doing out there?"

"Wait! Give your attention to the facts and the events. Nothing else. From his presence in the gallery and the title of the publication, we may deduce that this is Mr. Septimus Podgers and that his reading of palms at the Lancaster House spring party is probably responsible for Lord Arthur Savile's curious change of mind this evening. His sudden antipathy to fortune-telling."

"And the wearing of gloves to conceal his hands?"

"To conceal his palms, Watson. He cared nothing about the backs of his hands when he played the piano. I think you will find that it was the Line of Life on his left palm which promised murder, according to Mr. Podgers."

"You cannot believe that, Holmes!"

"It is enough that simple-minded Lord Arthur believed it. You follow his reasoning? If he was doomed to murder, as his belief persuaded him, let it be someone whose life was of little account and with whom he would not be connected. Imagine Lady Clementina Beauchamp—despatched by aconite in a chocolate taken from the bonbon box and eaten with her coffee after dinner. Who would look for a sinister event in the death of one so frail? Who would suspect Lord Arthur, so many miles away in Venice and with no motive for murder? Only when he heard of her death by natural causes did he take fright. He must, at all costs, inspect the interior of the bonbonnière and remove whatever chocolates chanced still to be there. But there were none. With luck, he must have thought, the smear of chocolate on the porcelain base was no more than a smear of chocolate."

"And Archdeacon Percy?"

"I confess that gave me a little more trouble. The reason that there is no clock-maker at 199 Greek Street is that there is no such address at all. The numbers stop before 199. The clock's explosive mechanism was put together most inefficiently by an amateur elsewhere in London. The first percussion cap evidently detonated only a small part of the gunpowder at noon. I suspect that it merely ignited a brief trail of it, which had leaked in the post and now burnt without any significant explosive force. It was only when the hands met again at twelve midnight that the remaining percussion caps were struck and the main detonation took place."

"Lord Arthur was the bomb-maker?"

Holmes shook his head.

"I think not. It was a botched job, but even that would have been beyond him. Let us say he commissioned it. As for the timepiece, clocks of this model were made after 1871 in France to celebrate the advent of the Third Republic. They are a rarity in England, merely a curiosity. We have no taste for these revolutions. Through the agency of Inspector Lestrade and the records of Customs and Excise, I have established that no more than half a dozen have been imported into England in the past twelve months. One of these was addressed to Mr. Elivas Ruhtra in the care of the Serbian News Agency in Lisle Street."

"Who on earth is Elivas Ruhtra? What possible interest could a Serbian anarchist have in Archdeacon Percy?"

"It is a fact, Watson, that one who adopts an alias or memorises a combination of numbers for a lock is almost always more fearful of forgetting or muddling the pseudonym or the numbers than of a thief discovering them. For this reason, the most common combination of numbers chosen is 1,2,3,4 or the numerical date of a birthday. Lord Arthur Savile is only an amateur assassin, scatterbrained enough to muddle a pseudonym, devoid of much rationality. If he were not the grandson of an earl, he would probably be in the workhouse or selling matches on the street. Yet even he would hardly forget his own name."

"He is Elivas Ruhtra?"

"Arthur Savile is Elivas Ruhtra spelt backwards. Even his uncertain mental grasp could hardly let that slip from his memory. The Archdeacon, with whom he had no connection, beyond choosing him from the octogenarians in Crockford's Clerical Directory, gave him a second opportunity of homicide without motive or association. The evidence of the clock, such as it was, would be destroyed in the explosion, along with the Archdeacon. His predicted murder would be committed, the dreadful prophecy would be realised. Lord Arthur would be a free man."

I pointed at the window.

"And Septimus Podgers? What part had he in all this?"

"Blackmail. Podgers had kept him in view. He had only to tell the world, perhaps in the shape of Scotland Yard, that Lord Arthur believed himself doomed to murder. His acquisition of aconite or gunpowder would be easily traced. The deaths of

Lady Clementina or the Archdeacon would take on a very different appearance. The cheque for a hundred guineas, whose impress Lord Blagdon read on his lordship's blotter, was the final piece of evidence which convinced me. It is absurdly high for a palmist's consultation but scarcely excessive when the object is to conceal murder."

"That is your proof?"

"Not quite. I believe the rest will follow very shortly."

As he spoke I saw another figure, moving towards Podgers through the doorway which opened from the library staircase to the terrace. There was lamplight enough to make out the youthful aristocratic stoop of Lord Arthur Savile. If Holmes was right, this was a private rendezvous between a blackmailer and his victim. It was a place where no one else was likely to be found at this time of night, as members hurried homewards.

I prepared myself for a confrontation between the two, a loud argument perhaps, ending in the submission of Lord Arthur, the exchange of a further cheque or bank notes. However slippery and odious, Podgers had the whip-hand over the young man. Lord Arthur came on, stooping, his hands clasped under the tails of his evening coat.

He came closer and for some reason Podgers uttered a cry that was no louder than a distant bird-call by the time that it reached the height of our window. The cheiromantist was making sudden motions with his hands, as if he were trying to push his adversary away. But he was trapped in a corner of the stone wall which rose to the height of his waist. Lord Arthur moved his hand quickly and I swore that the lamplight caught the blade of a knife. I looked at Holmes but he made no movement.

Septimus Podgers did what any man might have done in the circumstances. He put his hands on the wall, jumped up backwards and was soon sitting on it, his feet flailing at the man who stood before him, as if to ward him off. I cannot say whether Lord Arthur welcomed this or, indeed, whether he had engineered it. In another second he had dropped the knife, if that was what it was. He snatched Septimus Podgers by the ankles, tipped him back, and let him go. There was a second cry, softer than the first, and, I could swear, the bump of a body against stone, followed by a splash.

Lord Arthur stood at the wall, watching the river tide. There was little that he could have done, even had he wished to. The terrace of Parliament drops sheer and implacable to the Thames, the ebb running fast downstream. The tugboat and its barges were in midstream, the currents flowing powerfully toward them from both the Westminster and Lambeth banks of the great waterway. I could not see whether Podgers was alive or dead, nor even where he was. He had disappeared from the eyes of mortals. I thought I could make out a black silk hat floating directly in front of the powerful tugboat as it threshed downstream.

Holmes made no movement and said only, "Even if Lord Arthur were to raise the alarm, the miscreant is beyond all hope. It is far too dark and the tide is running far too fast for any help that might be offered. It is better so. Justice moves in mysterious ways. I cannot deny that it has dealt with Septimus Podgers as he deserved. The man was the architect of his own murder. He planned it to the last detail."

"Planned his own murder?"

Holmes began to button his coat and draw on his gloves.

"To be sure."

"How?"

He looked at me, his head on one side in a gesture of despair.

"My dear Watson, if a palmist were to tell me that I was preordained to commit murder—and if I believed him—I should rid myself of the burden at once by murdering him. What else? It is only because Lord Arthur is so soft-headed or soft-hearted that he chose victims who were likely to die before long in any case."

"Then we are to do nothing?"

"There is nothing that requires doing, my old friend."

"Ought we not at least to search the lodgings of this man Podgers in West Moon Street and remove any compromising documents or evidence relating to the case?"

He chuckled.

"It is only to their victims that blackmailers pretend to have an archive of incriminating evidence. They know too well that such documents are like a knife which is more likely to injure its owner than his victims. It is the invariable practice of these scoundrels to carry the important or crucial items in their heads—or, in the case of Mr. Septimus Podgers, what remains of his head now that the tugboat and its barges have passed. We will, if you please, take our leave of Lord Blagdon and return to Baker Street. I daresay it will be as well to keep an eye upon the columns of the press for a week or two."

With a sense of foreboding I followed his advice. The next week brought a letter from Lord Blagdon informing us that Lord Arthur Savile had suffered a nervous collapse and was now in the care of a keeper at a clinic for such disorders in Bexhill-on-Sea. He was well cared for in every way and, so far as he could ever be, he was happy. It was not thought that he would be released at an early date, therefore the services of Holmes and myself would no longer be required for his protection. Lord Blagdon added his thanks and enclosed fifty guineas in settlement of his account.

There the matter stood for a further week. Then, as the breakfast-table was cleared on a fine September morning with a hint of autumn in the air, I opened the pages of the Morning Post and knew that our anxieties for Lord Arthur Savile were at an end.

> On Sunday morning at seven o'clock, the body of Mr. Septimus R. Podgers, the eminent cheiromantist, was

> washed on shore in Greenwich, just in front of the Ship Hotel. The unfortunate gentleman, whose mortal remains appear to have been in collision with a steamer of the river traffic, was identified by the contents of his pockets and the prints of his fingers. He had been missing for almost a fortnight, and considerable anxiety for his safety had been felt in London's cheiromantic circles. It is supposed that Mr. Podgers committed suicide under the influence of a temporary mental derangement, caused by overwork. A verdict to that effect was returned this afternoon by a coroner's jury. Mr. Podgers had just completed an elaborate treatise on the subject of the Human Hand, that will shortly be published, when it will no doubt attract much attention. The deceased was sixty-five years of age and does not seem to have left any relations.

Holmes read this. He put the paper down and gazed at the mellow sunlight beyond the window.

"I was a little short with you, old fellow, in the matter of a week or two at Ilfracombe or Tenby. September is not too far advanced and the sunny days are not yet too misty. I have for some time been meditating a monograph on criminal aberrations of the benevolent impulse, what the poet Browning calls 'the honest thief' and 'the tender murderer.' Warm autumn days on an Atlantic coast would do as well as anywhere for the composition I have in mind."

Before he had a chance to change his mind, I had consulted Bradshaw's railway guide, wired to a comfortable hotel reserving our rooms and also to the Great Western Railway, securing a first-class carriage from Paddington to Barnstaple, via Exeter.

11

The Case of the King's Evil

1

Of the letters addressed to our detective agency at 221B Baker Street, almost all bore the name of Sherlock Holmes and very few came directly to me. I had remained in medical practice for some time after our first meeting, and my patients necessarily had first call upon my services. When I encountered men and women in the critical moments of their lives, it was more often in my own consulting rooms. I was therefore all the more surprised, on an autumn morning in October 1884, when my services as a criminal investigator were requested by telegram.

Whatever distress had overtaken Miss Alice Chastelnau, mistress of the Openshaw Academy for Young Ladies at Mablethorpe on the Lincolnshire coast, was plainly a matter of urgency. At the time, Holmes and I were not otherwise occupied. I replied to Miss Chastelnau at once by wire. Noting the distance she must travel to reach us, I proposed a consultation at Baker Street on the following day at 4 P.M.

Within the hour I received a confirmation of this. Her second message added that her two brothers had been missing since Sunday evening, two days previously, in very disturbing circumstances. If that were so, I thought it a little curious that she had not consulted Sherlock Holmes in the first place.

As I explained all this to my friend, pipe smoke continued to rise from behind the copy of the Morning Post which he was reading. At length he chuckled, though without lowering the newspaper.

"The disappearance of her brothers, indeed! That at least adds a little piquancy to an otherwise unpromising case. Have no fear, Watson, I shall vacate our sitting-room tomorrow afternoon upon your client's arrival."

"She might prefer you to remain," I said hastily. "Unless, of course, the lady's own medical condition is at issue. If that were so, I should be obliged to see her privately."

He chuckled again but offered no further reply. As the hours passed, I felt increasingly that I would have preferred Miss Chastelnau to ask the advice of Holmes in the first place, thereby allowing me to play a supporting role in any inquiry. I could scarcely introduce him as my subordinate. In that case, I feared I could not introduce him at all. Holmes knew this as well as I did. Indeed, he was enjoying my predicament of being "senior man," as he called it, relishing this far more obviously than was decent.

Miss Chastelnau was in good time to take afternoon tea with us on the following afternoon. Her manner was earnest, as befitted the occasion. In appearance, she was neat and dainty without being self-consciously elegant. There was a spinsterly attractiveness in the demure oval of her face, and in the old-fashioned style in which her light brown hair was pulled back tightly to frame it. She put me in mind of those portraits of Charlotte Brontë and the "bonnets" of the 1840s. I judged her to be more than forty years old but not yet forty-five.

Sherlock Holmes was at once courteous and courtly, bowing

her to an armchair by the fireplace. As I had foreseen, he had no intention of vacating the sitting-room beyond saying, "If you would prefer to speak to Dr. Watson alone, you need only say so."

Miss Chastelnau did not say anything of the kind. She produced an envelope from her bag and came at once to the point of her visit.

"I have brought a letter, addressed to an unnamed doctor by my half-brother, Abraham Chastelnau. I doubt if he knew any doctor well enough to put a name to it. I hope you will overlook my custom of referring to both my half-brothers as 'brothers,' for it stops speculation and gossip which might be painful to me."

I thought that this certainly indicated a delicate and fastidious nature, such as became a mistress of Miss Openshaw's academy. Our visitor continued.

"The letter in its envelope was found by me after both Abraham and Roland disappeared on Sunday night. I have shown it to no one. In the first place, I should like it to be read by a medical man. Even at Mablethorpe, I had heard something of Dr. Watson who works in partnership with Mr. Sherlock Holmes of Baker Street. The letter, combined with the disappearance of my brothers, persuaded me that I should come to you."

She seemed an admirable young woman, polite but determined. If she appeared more composed than might have been expected at such an anxious time, I put that down to the inner strength of a quiet personality. I have seen such a balance of characteristics often enough in medical practice.

"First tell me a little about your brothers, Miss Chastelnau."

"They are the two keepers of the Old Light on the river estuary at Sutton Cross. It lies on the coast of the Wash about forty miles south of Mablethorpe and just above King's Lynn. It is not a proper lighthouse, but a beacon standing on nine wooden stilts. There is a barrack-room and a lantern-room above. It is on the mud-flats near the river estuary and is cut off from the land for an hour or two each side of high tide."

"And the letter?"

"It was before dawn on Monday morning that the mechanism stopped and the flashing beam from the lantern failed. The absence of my brothers was discovered soon afterwards, and I was summoned from Mablethorpe later that day. I found the letter at the back of the barrack-room table drawer. I have naturally read the contents, Dr. Watson, and I beg you to do the same."

With that, she handed me the envelope. I was at once struck by the disparity between the quiet but self-possessed manner of the schoolmistress and the deliberation of the ill-educated hand in her brother's writing. I should hardly have thought them brother and sister unless I had been assured of it.

I read the single sheet of paper carefully. It certainly seemed like a letter, for the address of the sender was at the top: "The Old Light, Sutton Bridge, Boston Deeps." It is common knowledge that the Boston Deeps remain the one navigable channel through the shallow and silted waters of the Wash. The sea has receded for centuries on that part of the Lincolnshire coast. The channel is little used now, I believe, except as a temporary anchorage for the coastal trade. I had supposed the land to be so flat, like the rest of East Anglia, as to make a lighthouse something of a rarity. Presumably, this light at Sutton Cross was a warning to ships of the point at which the Boston Deeps give way to treacherous sand-banks.

I glanced at the foot of the page and saw printed in uneven capitals the name of Abraham Chastelnau. It is an unusual surname for an Englishman. Yet it reminded me that East Anglia had become the home of Protestant Huguenot craftsmen, fleeing from France at a time of religious persecution two hundred years earlier. They were industrious and law-abiding folk who had done well in their new home.

The writer's appeal was addressed to "Dear Doctor." Who that might be, I could not tell.

> I am a man that is afflicted with evil beyond endurance. I have lived with it many years and once or twice thought I had come out of it. But I was wrong. I have heard that in days gone by a holy man might have helped me. I once thought I had found his secret but now it is lost again. If I could take a wife I might be better for it. The truth is I bear the brand upon me and no woman could tolerate the company of such a man. I cannot hide what I am and none will come near me. I need a physician who can do miracles. If you are that man please write what the cost will be.
>
> Your respectful servant,
> Abraham Chastelnau.

I read this through and then laid the paper down.

"I hoped when I read it that perhaps he had heard of you and your friend," said Miss Chastelnau softly. "But I cannot tell who this was meant for. Surely it was someone like you, for he knew no doctor at Sutton Cross."

I looked at it again. It was a strange letter in more ways than one. The handwriting showed a semi-literate deliberation. Yet the composition of the sentences betrayed a certain education. Here was a man who wrote "physician" rather than "doctor" or "afflicted with" rather than "suffering from." No doubt Abraham Chastelnau lacked instruction. Yet he had heard of holy men in days gone by. From whom had he got this piece of history? Here was a man who could scarcely write and then, on the few occasions when he did so, apparently expressed himself in a way that suggested some familiarity with those who had received a schooling. Had the letter been dictated to him in part?

"There are many unanswered questions here, Miss Chastelnau. If the letter was at the back of a drawer, how long had it been there? When did your brother write it, for there is no date upon it, and did he truly intend to send it to anyone? Will you allow my colleague Mr. Sherlock Holmes to read these lines?"

Alice Chastelnau nodded. Holmes, in his turn, glanced down the page. He stretched his legs towards the fireplace while he read it again, more slowly. Before he could give an opinion, we were interrupted by Mrs. Hudson's knock and the arrival of the silver tray and table linen. After tea had been poured and the sandwiches handed round, our landlady closed the curtains against the gathering fog and retired. The gas was now lit and shone brightly on the white cloth, the glimmer of china and metal. Holmes turned to our visitor.

"I think you must help us a little more, Miss Chastelnau. There are two distinct matters here. Your brother, if I may also call him so, is troubled in spirit. Hence the letter which we have just read. Since writing that, he and your younger brother have disappeared. Do you believe that these two things are connected? Or is it only one of them that requires our advice?"

She looked at him, directly and expressionlessly.

"I cannot tell you, Mr. Holmes. That is why I am here. Because my brothers are my half-brothers, they are comparative strangers to me. My father, John Chastelnau, was an oil-cake manufacturer, supplying the dairy farmers with food for their cattle. He married a second time after my mother died. When Abraham, the elder half-brother, was born, I was sixteen. I had been unwell for more than a year. A touch of consumption was suspected, the very illness which took my mother from us. My step-mother found lodgings on the coast near King's Lynn and I recuperated there for several months. A little while later, Abraham was born, she returned home, and I left for instruction at Miss Openshaw's Academy in Mablethorpe. I remained there subsequently as her assistant teacher. After she died four years ago, I was employed by her trustees."

"You are to be congratulated," said Holmes gently. "Pray continue."

"My life has been very different to that of my brothers, and our ages are some years apart. They remained in the little coastal village of Sutton Cross. At first, they followed my father in the trade of making oil-cake for cattle. With the draining of the fens and the coming of dairy farming, his works at Sutton Cross had been profitable and he employed a dozen men. With such farming in decline and cheaper animal foods brought in by the new railway, my brothers found it a meagre inheritance."

It seemed evident that there was no close relationship between the sister and the two brothers. This allowed Sherlock Holmes to slip the leash.

"If you wish us to investigate this disappearance, Miss Chastelnau, we should be obliged for whatever else you can tell us about your brothers. In the first place, what manner of men are they? I do not wish to be peremptory with you. However, if a search is to be successful, it must be pursued with urgency. In these mysteries the scent soon grows cold."

She remained so composed under this warning that, had we not known of her distance from the two men, I should at length have thought Miss Chastelnau quite without feeling.

"I have had little to do with them, Mr. Holmes, but that is not a matter of indifference. Like many brothers and sisters, our lives have been lived apart, in different worlds. Yet I will be frank with you. I am aware that they have not been popular in the district. I believe there was once a quarrel and some violence. As to their dispositions, both my brothers are by nature reclusive. Abraham prefers his own company, and Roland resents any curiosity on the part of those around him."

"And how did they come to be keepers of the Old Light?"

"Their troubles began after my father's death, more than ten years ago. His oil-cake manufactory did not long survive him. The old building by the river bridge stood empty for a while and then became a warehouse. After that, my brothers were employed at the Old Light. For many years now, it has only been in use as a simple beacon. Abraham and Roland have acted as keepers, and in return they have had a roof over their heads. It is a strange life. They are hardly a mile from the village and yet surrounded only by mud-flats and quicksands, cut off by the sea for several hours out of every twelve."

"Perhaps," I suggested, "you could tell us something more of the Old Light."

"It is a foreshore light, on the silt at the mouth of the estuary. The wooden supports raise it some eighteen feet above the low-water mark. It stands a mile or so downstream from the bridge. There is an iron ladder from the beach to a door at the level of the barrack-room. The area around it is marsh and sand-banks, with quicksand here and there. They call that part of it 'the quivering sands.'"

"And what of the village?" I asked.

"Sutton Cross is built on the old Roman sea wall. It had the first road bridge across the river estuary, built fifty years ago. Before that, the river could only be crossed by fording it. Now there is also a new iron bridge, carrying the Midland and Great Northern Railway from Spalding in Lincolnshire into Norfolk. Everything downstream from the bridge is marsh and sand-bank, dangerous to boats and hunters alike. The village has grown a good deal since the river was bridged, though the inn and the old church were there centuries ago."

Holmes slipped his hand into his pocket and stared thoughtfully at the fire. He smiled.

"I was once a visitor at Sutton Cross for several days, Miss Chastelnau. It was one of Professor Jebb's undergraduate reading parties from Cambridge. Just before the final examinations for the Classical Tripos. I recall that there is a river-bank footpath on the Lincolnshire side of the bridge, just by the inn. It follows the stream as far as the mud-flats of the estuary. At that point, I recall, there used to be a light on either bank, both in Lincolnshire and in Norfolk."

Miss Chastelnau nodded. "Until fifty years ago, two lights were needed to guide vessels from the sea into the river as far as up as Wisbech. Now the silt and the receding sea have made such navigation impossible. With a bridge standing across the river a mile from its mouth, there is no scope for coastal trade and little demand. Only the Old Light on the Lincolnshire bank is kept in use. It has a single beam directed seaward to advise ships at anchor in the Boston Deeps to stand clear. Even in that anchorage there are few enough vessels of any size nowadays."

"And the church beacon?" Holmes inquired. "I recall from my visit a quite charming medieval parish church with a high turret forming one corner of the old tower. There was a spiral staircase in the turret and a lantern at the top of the tower which must have pre-dated any lighthouse. Is that still in use?"

"Not as a guide to shipping. It would not carry so far. Its purpose, in conjunction with the Old Light, is as a landmark for eel-catchers and wild-fowl hunters on the mud-banks. The sands are dangerous, particularly after dark or in fog."

"Very good. Now may we return to your brothers and my question, which I think you have not quite answered? What manner of men are they?"

"Roland is the younger," she said simply. "The young people in the village taunt him as a stilt-walker." She turned to me. "Perhaps you know what that means on the coast of the Wash, Dr. Watson?"

"I have no idea."

"Roland is called a stilt-walker because he is an enemy to

change, even when others welcome it. The sea on that coast has been receding for centuries. Land is reclaimed from time to time by warping, as they call it. Sections of the marsh and sands are enclosed and dried out. They become pasture in the possession of sheep-breeders or dairy farmers. They are lost to those who have always treated them as common land. The old fowlers, fishermen, goose-breeders. Centuries ago, these men roamed the treacherous flats and sands by going on stilts. For years now they have been a dying breed. Their territory is stolen from them, even by the railway companies who have built embankments across the marsh and caused large sections of it to dry out. In short, to be called a stilt-walker is to be despised by the younger men."

"And what of your elder brother, the author of the letter?"

Miss Chastelnau thought for a moment and then spoke carefully.

"I know he is lonely. I fear that John Bunyan's giant, Despair, is his companion. There is nothing of Roland in him. They both live by what they can get, by what they can make, hunt, and catch. Yet Abraham also lives in a world of dreams and legends, scraps of history and romance. Would that he could find comfort in such things, but they all seem to fail him."

"Yet it is admirable that he should dream," said Holmes abruptly, sitting upright. "Are they loving brothers?"

"No," she said quietly, "I think they are not. Force of circumstance obliges them to share a single life in the barrack-room of the Old Light. I have no close knowledge, but I think it is a life of indifference at the best."

She drew herself up in her chair as though she had come to the end of the matter. There was a pause.

"That will not quite do," said Holmes gently. "Unless I am much mistaken, there is something more to this mysterious disappearance. Something which you know and which, as yet, we have not heard. That will not do, Miss Chastelnau, if we are to be of service to you. Come now, pray let us have the rest of this most interesting account."

She blushed a little but looked straight at him.

"Mr. Holmes, you have already mentioned the old church at Sutton Cross, the turret tower with a winding staircase to the roof and the beacon. After dark, it still guides hunters and fishermen going to their nets or traps on the mud-flats or the marsh. If a man can see that lantern and the foreshore lighthouse, he can judge his position on the flats long after dark. He can find his way home even when the tide is racing at his heels or in the fog. Men depend upon those two lights. By this time of autumn, fog and mist are as much the enemy as the incoming sea and the quivering sands."

She paused and for the first time showed a moment's difficulty in continuing her story. Then she resumed.

"Last Sunday, after Evensong, the sexton and the rector went up the tower in the dusk to light the lantern. Twilight was coming on, but it was not quite dark. A mist was gathering with the incoming tide, coming down like a curtain across the shore. It had not quite reached the level of the marsh. As the two men began to climb the stone steps of the winding stairs, they heard a gunshot."

"A weapon of what kind?"

"A shotgun, Mr. Holmes, fired from somewhere on the marshes. It is not uncommon by daylight but unusual in the dusk, except as a signal. By the time the two men came out on to the lead of the flat roof, the incoming tide was running fast, as it does across the mud-banks. The narrowing of the estuary channels it in. Yet the worst of it, Mr. Holmes, is that the marsh and the mud-flats may look level but they seldom are. You may stand on a stretch of uncovered sand, where the sea is a hundred yards out, and you may think yourself safe. But the ripples have outflanked you. Your retreat is already cut off by the depth of water gathering at your back or by the softness of the flats where the tide has percolated below, undermining the firmness and turning it into quicksand. Then the sea comes rushing in on either side of you, sometimes as fast as a man can run. All this is a hundred times worse in the dusk. You see?"

"Entirely."

"Anyone on the marsh or the flats by that time last Sunday evening was in peril. The sexton lit the beacon at once. The Old Light was already flashing. Then Mr. Gilmore, the rector, and the sexton saw two men on the soft mud, below the mist that was coming with the tide. It was so far off that, with daylight fading, it was hard to tell who they were. But it seemed that they were fighting. One man appeared to seize the other, and they fell together. The second man got up and ran off, but the first caught him and threw him down again. Or so it seemed. The dusk thickened and the mist drew round them, but a struggle of some kind went on. The mud was so soft and so slippery and they fell so often that, if there was a fight, neither seemed able to win it. There was nothing that the rector and the sexton on the roof of the tower could do, even at the risk of their own lives. They were too far off."

"Did they think, perhaps, that these were two young fellows playing the fool?" I asked.

"No man who knew the sands would do so in such a place, Dr. Watson."

"Very well."

"They were too far away by that time for Mr. Gilmore or the sexton even to tell their ages. Yet, since then, neither of my brothers has been seen. It was the following morning, after the tide turned, that two policemen went to the Old Light. A Tynemouth collier, at anchor across the water, had seen the beam of the Old Light fail an hour or so before dawn. When I came from Mablethorpe, they helped me to climb the ladder and I was able to get into the barrack-room. There lay the letter in the table drawer."

Now that she had come to the true end of her story, there was a moment's silence, broken by Holmes.

"And there was nothing else that you noticed when you went into the barrack-room next day?"

"Abraham's jacket was hanging behind the door. I went through the pockets. There was a piece of a pebble in one pocket."

"What sort of pebble?"

"I should not have bothered with it—I should not even have noticed it—except that he had folded it carefully in a piece of paper. I thought at first that the paper might have a message on it. There was none, only a pebble."

"Where is it now?"

"I took it with me. It could not possibly be of use to the police."

"I fear you may be in error as to that, Miss Chastelnau. Do you have it with you now?"

She reached into the pocket of her dress and took out the folded paper which, as she had said, was quite blank. I got up and stood beside Holmes as he unwrapped the pebble. Before us lay what I can only describe as a small piece of clay-coated grit or possibly a rough pebble from the shoreline. It was the size of my thumb-nail, certainly no larger.

Holmes stared at it for a moment longer and then again spoke slowly to our client, as I may now call her.

"With your permission, Miss Chastelnau, I should like to retain this item for a few hours in order to examine it. You must return to Mablethorpe tonight, I believe. We shall see you safely to King's Cross station. You may depend upon Dr. Watson and me being in Sutton Cross by noon tomorrow. I will bring the pebble with me then. I fear that I cannot assure you what the outcome of this mystery will be. However, from what you have told us, I have every confidence that the riddle of your brothers' disappearance will be resolved within the next three days."

"Of what possible use to you can a muddy pebble be?"

"Had it not been wrapped with such care, I should probably have thought it of no use whatever. However, such careful treatment reminds me that this is hard stone, though it came apparently from a bed of soft clay to which it did not belong. I do not call that conclusive of anything—but in the light of all the other evidence, it is suggestive of something."

2

That evening, after we had seen Miss Chastelnau safely to her train, Holmes ate his dinner from a tray beside him on his work-table. The table's disreputable surface was stained by hydrochloric acid and the results of numerous chemical "experiments." Scattered upon it now were a lens and a pair of forceps, a stained penknife in a butter-dish, and a medical scalpel. A dismembered revolver had awaited his attention for two or three weeks. Close at hand were two skulls, whose owners had been hanged for murder at Tyburn a century ago and publicly dissected before a large lively audience at Surgeons Hall. These two macabre fetishes now acted as book-ends for a brief row of well-thumbed reference volumes, required for immediate purposes. My friend had exchanged his formal black coat for the familiar purple of his dressing-gown.

It was after ten o'clock and his long back was curved once again over the Chastelnau pebble, as I had better call it. He had been examining it for several minutes by the aid of a jeweller's lens screwed into his eye. Removing this eyepiece, he straightened in his chair.

"I believe we can do better, Watson. We are no common high street supplier of watches and bijouterie."

He had scarcely spoken a word since we had come home from escorting our visitor to King's Cross Station and he had certainly not invited conversation in the half hour since our return. Rising from his chair, he now went across to his "natural sciences" cupboard and drew out a piece of apparatus. This was a hydroscopic balance, cased in mahogany and stamped along its base in gold, "E. Dertling, London." He sat down and placed it in front of him.

The device resembled an open-sided box of polished wood about ten inches in height, twelve inches long, and six inches deep. Within it, the pivot of a brass balance was screwed to the centre of its floor. A minute weighing pan was suspended to either side of this. From the lower edge of the box protruded a small brass knob for the alignment of the scales. This had been calibrated to calculate weights to within one milligram.

"I believe we may allow for a room temperature of sixty degrees Fahrenheit, Watson. Would that be your guess?"

This was conversation at last.

"Certainly no lower than that, with the fire glowing as it is and the curtains closed."

Holmes took Miss Chastelnau's pebble. With a fine brush he worked over its surface to displace any loose substance that might still have adhered to it. Then, placing it in a loop of thin wire which was suspended from the pan on the right hand of the balance, he adjusted the mechanism and noted the weight of it in air. Next, taking the pebble with a pair of tweezers, he placed a small jar of water under the right-hand scale-pan, so that when he lowered the pan the pebble was immersed. Almost as an afterthought, he dipped the slender brush into the jar and went over the stone again, apparently to dislodge any bubbles of air which might give buoyancy to so small an object.

As I watched the intensity with which my friend worked, I could not help thinking that Sherlock Holmes seemed less like the great consulting detective of Baker Street than like a happy child on Christmas Morning. Perhaps there was a slighter difference between the two types than I had supposed. Now he took his brass propelling pencil and made several notes on the immaculate starch of his white shirt cuffs. At length he had his answer.

"If our estimate of the room temperature is correct, Watson—and I do not think we can be far out—the specific gravity of this mineral is registered as 3.993. I do not believe it can be andradite, for I have tried it judiciously with a penknife and that will not produce a scratch upon it. Nor, I think, can it be zircon of whatever type. I therefore deduce that what we are presented with appears to be a species of corundum. Only caborundum and the diamond are harder than this. Indeed, in the scale of hardness drawn up by the admirable Professor Friedrich Mohs in 1812, only the diamond exceeds it. This cannot possibly be a diamond, for its specific gravity is far too high. That, I believe, is as far as we can go for the present."

Holmes had given me the opportunity I had been looking for. I had not wished to annoy him or to suggest that a piece of grit picked up from the Lincolnshire fens was unlikely to be of any value or relevance to the case whatever. However, I had been thinking wistfully of sleep. A long journey lay ahead in the morning. I yawned, stretched, made my excuses and withdrew to bed.

I suppose it was about half-past eleven when my head touched the pillow. I was woken after several hours by a dreadful screaming. It might have been a banshee—or at least the sound which I had always assumed a banshee would make. I sat up with heart pounding and, at the same time, a sense of considerable irritation.

By the time I had lit a candle, the high-pitched sound came

again. It was a demented shrieking from somewhere below me. Now that I was fully awake, I recognised that, whatever its origins, they were mechanical and not animal. The time by my watch was ten minutes past three in the morning. It was plain that Sherlock Holmes had not yet gone to bed.

I had not the least doubt that this disturbance would be heard on every floor of the house, and more importantly throughout those of the houses on either side. Pulling on my dressing-gown, I tied its belt and made my way by candlelight to the stairs. I began to descend to our sitting-room. Half-way down, I was aware of a lone figure on the little chair outside the door of that room. The flickering candle showed me Mrs. Hudson. She was wrapped in a shawl round her nightdress, rocking to and fro a little. With her face buried in her hands she uttered a repeated protest that was almost a dry sob.

"Oh, that noise! Oh, that dreadful, dreadful noise! Why will he not stop?"

She looked up and saw me with a candlestick in my hand, standing at the top of the staircase like Banquo's ghost on the stage of the Lyceum Theatre.

"Oh, Dr. Watson! None of my gentlemen, in all these years, has ever been such a trial as Mr. Holmes! What am I to do? What am I to say tomorrow morning to Mrs. Armitage next door?"

"This is too bad," I said soothingly. "Go back to bed, Mrs. Hudson, and leave this to me. I promise you that the noise will stop."

I was becoming more impatient with every moment of delay. I tried the handle of the sitting-room door and found it locked. I hammered on the oak panel with all the majesty of the law. There was a pause in the din. I sensed Holmes coming towards me and a key rattled in the lock. He flung open the door and almost pulled me into the room, his eyes gleaming. I now saw that he had screwed his carborundum wheel to the edge of the work-table and that it was the friction of its hard grey stone cleaning a penknife blade that had caused the din. The wheel had apparently also been at work upon Miss Chastelnau's pebble. On one side of the dun-coated stone was now revealed what looked like a dull speck of royal blue glass.

"Corundum, Watson! The stuff of rubies and sapphires. A blue sapphire fit for the crown of England! Lost in the muddy dullness of time and neglect! After I heard the good lady's story, I suspected that something like this must be the truth, though I hardly dared to believe it. Once we had been given a specific gravity of 3.993, I was certain. The figure is sometimes a fraction higher, but the room temperature would account for that."

"Corundum?"

"Corundum yields the ruby or the sapphire, according to the form of its crystals. In white light, the ruby absorbs every shade but red and therefore it glows red. Sapphire reflects only blue, as in this case. Take the jeweller's glass and look. You will observe that the crystals are quite clearly tall and pointed, as in the sapphire, and not shorter and rectangular as in the ruby."

"It looks very little like a jewel to me."

"Nor should it, after so many centuries in the earth. That is something which skilled polishing will amend in due course."

"But not tonight, unless you want Mrs. Hudson to throw both of us out into the street."

He chuckled, as if in a fit of mischief.

"Not tonight, then. We know enough now to put us on the track. Tomorrow will be soon enough to prove that we are right."

"Meantime, we are to assume that the Chastelnau brothers have been made away with for such a miserable little object as this?"

"Oh no, my dear fellow. I believe you have entirely failed to understand the nature of the problem. More is at stake than this. Far, far more."

3

The next morning saw us on the train to Cambridge, Ely, King's Lynn, and finally across the new river bridge to Sutton Cross. The fog dispersed on the northern outskirts of London. A fine October day with a pale blue sky faded to a yellow edging at the horizon. One sees almost nothing of the Cambridge colleges from the railway and very little of the fine medieval cathedral towers of Ely. But Holmes was not concerned with the view. He had wired Inspector Lestrade at Scotland Yard, mentioning our interest in the case of the missing brothers and requesting him to smooth our path with the Lincolnshire constabulary as far as was possible. Lestrade's reply suggested that if we wished to waste our time over a commonplace case of "missing from home" or "found drowned," we were welcome to do so.

Holmes read a good deal on train journeys but always with a set purpose. I could never imagine him feeling that he should cultivate the charm of Jane Austen or the melodrama of Sir Walter Scott. On the other hand, he would immerse himself in certain works of Robert Browning or Thomas Hood. He admired their insight into macabre aberrations and the "morbid anatomy" in the personalities of men and women. If he read for pleasure, it would be with his pipe, a pouch of shag tobacco, and something like the Notable British Trials volume of Dr. William Palmer, "The Rugeley Poisoner."

He spent the journey to Sutton Cross dipping into several books which had been packed into his portmanteau. The subject-matter on such journeys was not designed to encourage conversation from our fellow passengers. In the past, we had had Maudsley on Insanity, Stevenson on Irritant Poisons, and, on the most trying occasion of all, Krafft-Ebing's Psychopathia Sexualis. Holmes had perused this volume unremittingly for two hours in a corner seat, opposite a rural dean returning to his Oxfordshire parish.

On this occasion, his choice was unexceptionable. From Liverpool Street to Cambridge, his attention was held by Shakespeare's King John. Thereafter, he was absorbed by Professor Plucknett's edition of Pipe Rolls of the Plantagenets. I knew only that these were official records of the reigns of Henry II or King John.

At King's Lynn, we changed from the London express. A local train ran unevenly along the last few miles of the Norfolk coast and across the wide estuary of the Wash into Lincolnshire. It paused at every little platform and country halt, under the vast open skies of the fens and among the numerous marshes and waterways that ran everywhere. Here and there were glimpses of creamy breakers and a brown tide drawing away across long gleaming expanses of sand. Such was the North Sea—or "The German Ocean," as some people still called it.

At length the carriages of this local train rattled over an iron bridge across a wide river with flat muddy banks, and drew into the wooden platform of Sutton Cross. Holmes had wired for rooms at the Bridge Hotel, not because it was the best but because it was the only accommodation which the village could boast. It rose white, foursquare, and a century old, beside the river, within a stone's throw of the railway halt. This hotel was to be what he called our "base of operations." We briefly made ourselves known there and deposited our possessions. I noticed that Holmes had brought his black leather Gladstone bag as well as his portmanteau. Its principal contents appeared to be the jeweller's lens, the hydroscopic balance, and the carborundum wheel with a clamp which held it to the table-edge.

Had it not been for the case upon which we were embarked, I should have found a week or so at Sutton Cross very agreeable. The fresh wind from the North Sea and the tranquil pastureland made a pleasing contrast to Baker Street. As it was, Holmes had already wired for an appointment in an hour's time with the Reverend Roderick Gilmore, rector of the parish. This good man was formerly a contemporary of Holmes's elder brother, Mycroft, at Trinity College, Cambridge. That seemed enough to be going on with.

We found Mr. Gilmore at home, a comfortable middle-aged man who owed his incumbency to the fact that the living of St. Clement's, Sutton Cross, was in the gift of Trinity College. He, like Brother Mycroft, had distinguished himself in the Mathematical Tripos but preferred a quiet living on the Suffolk coast to a college fellowship. He talked as if we were old acquaintances, showing off the fine nave of his church with its Norman bays and clerestory, its fourteenth-century south aisle. As we sat at tea in his study, the lattice windows looked out across the yew-hedged churchyard towards a bright afternoon sky above a calm sea. I thought that had life called upon me to be Rector of Sutton Cross, I should have been well content.

After we had complimented him upon his church and his grounds, he said meekly, "We are also rather proud of our little railway bridge. It was built by Robert Stevenson, you know."

We murmured our approval, and then Mr. Gilmore came quietly to the reason for our visit.

"It is a bad business altogether that we should have lost the two Chastelnau brothers in this manner. A very bad business. They were not greatly liked and, indeed, they refused to consider themselves my parishioners, but that makes the tragedy all the more poignant."

Holmes put down his teacup.

"We understand from Miss Alice Chastelnau that you and the sexton were on the roof of the tower last Sunday evening, when the beacon was lit. You saw two men fighting—or, at least, struggling?"

Mr. Gilmore looked mournfully at us.

"I heard a single gunshot just as we climbed the tower. It was a shotgun without doubt, such as most of the hunters carry here. The Chastelnau brothers at the Old Light were the nearest inhabitants to the marshes and the mud-banks. Like many others, they sometimes used a gunshot as a convenient signal to one another. Yet it was far too late for a hunter to be out on normal business. The dusk and the mist were setting in. All the fishermen had already been out to their nets to retrieve their catch. The fowlers and the eel-catchers had long come in."

"Which surely makes it strange that the brothers should still have been out there?" I said.

"Not exceptionally strange, Doctor. It is true that one man should have remained to guard the Old Light—or at least should be absent for as short a time as possible. Yet it is not human nature for one brother to ignore a possible distress signal fired by the other. After all, they were never out of sight of the Old Light and its beam was in no danger of extinction at that time. Besides which, the Old Light is hardly a landmark like the Eddystone or the Bell Rock. It serves little purpose but to mark the river estuary for such vessels as pass. They no longer enter the river nor even approach it since the bridge was built to carry the railway across. Its lantern will be done away with before long, mark my words. Who would want the job? Who would choose to be a keeper, living well beyond any other habitation, surrounded by the marshes and the mud-flats?"

Holmes interrupted this a little too brusquely.

"Tell me, Mr. Gilmore, what did you and your sexton see from the tower?"

"See?" Gilmore shook his head. "It was difficult to see very clearly, Mr. Holmes. They were some distance off, half a mile perhaps, and the light was almost gone. It was very hard, by then, even to tell the appearance of their clothing. The mist was coming in with the tide. If they were carrying lanterns, which surely must have been the case, they were not shining towards us. Though I could not swear to it, I believe there was a second gunshot—the second barrel perhaps. What I saw was not so much a prize-fight with fists, not a striking of blows. It was far more like a wrestling match, as if for the possession of some object."

"Who possessed it in the end?"

Mr. Gilmore shook his head.

"That I cannot tell you. I do not think we saw the end of the affair between them. It was not done with before the darkening twilight and the mist obscured them completely. It appeared to me as if the first man snatched at the second. That second man fell but struggled free and scrambled up again. Then the first man brought him down and this time pulled him up. There was too little light to see more. I explained all this to Inspector Wainwright, but I do not know how much I could swear to in court."

"We expect to meet Mr. Wainwright this afternoon, at the Old Light."

"Wainwright is a good man, Mr. Holmes. As to the nature of the struggle between the two brothers, the greater danger would be for them to get lost among the tide and the quicksands. But that could hardly happen with the beacon on the church tower lit and the Old Light clearly visible with its beam flashing out to sea in a constant direction. That was why I was most anxious to see our beacon lit upon the tower. Moreover, these brothers had known the sands and the mud-flats all their lives. All the same, neither has been seen again and so we must suppose that the two men in the dusk were they."

"And that was all?"

"There was one thing, Mr. Holmes, which I told Inspector Wainwright. In the hope that we could retain communication with them, the sexton went down from the tower and came up with a rook rifle. He fired a single shot into the air, in case they could reply and tell us where they were. I heard no more, but a muffled shot or breaking surf can be much the same at that distance."

I intervened in what was, after all, my case.

"Were they greatly disliked in the village?"

Mr. Gilmore paused, choosing his words with care.

"I should rather say they were mocked, Dr. Watson, and that a hatred of those who abused them was their response. Local people can be very cruel at a time of misfortune. After old John Chastelnau died, the oil-cake manufactory failed. You can still see the rough stone building, just opposite the Bridge Hotel. Those who had disliked the old man's miserliness—and some who scoffed at his second marriage to a younger woman—took no care to conceal their satisfaction at the failure of the enterprise. There was a fight outside the Bridge Hotel one evening. Roland Chastelnau broke a man's nose after insults were exchanged. Sir Walter Butt, the magistrate, discharged both men with a caution, for fear of making matters worse. After that, neither of the brothers entered the inn or the church again. Indeed, they were already strangers to the church."

"Did their animosity extend to each other?"

"I was once told that they fought like two ferrets in a sack. That was the exact phrase used to me. I cannot believe it was as bad as that. Of course, they subsisted by tending the Old Light. I understand that they were paid out of the county rate. Their accommodation was provided by the barrack-room under the lantern."

"And what else?" I inquired. "How did they feed themselves?"

Mr. Gilmore looked as if he thought I might have known without asking.

"Roland was the hunter and fisherman. Even for those who are not hunters by profession, the snaring or shooting of wildfowl, geese, or the eel-catching and fishing nets for small fry commonly become additional trades. Abraham was the brother who usually took the watch and kept the light flashing out to sea. He also cultivated a vegetable plot just above the river bridge on the far side. How they lived otherwise, I cannot say."

"They had no inheritance?"

"I do not think they had anything except debts from the oil-cake works when the business was sold. They belong to that class of our nation, Dr. Watson, who live like serfs on next to nothing but never quite fall to the level of the workhouse. They seldom attract the attention of their betters until some mean crime or scandal breaks open in the columns of the press. Let us hope this is not a case of that kind."

"And what of their sister, Miss Alice Chastelnau?"

Mr. Gilmore brightened up at her name. He gave a brief smile and his voice became more buoyant.

"I know little of Alice Chastelnau, though I met her when she attended her father's funeral, and also concerning the arrangements made for it. I met her again at the death of her stepmother several years later. Miss Chastelnau lived in the village before my time and left it when she was still a girl. Indeed, I cannot recall that I have ever met her apart from those two occasions. Her health was a little delicate. She seems by all accounts an admirable young woman and has fulfilled her promise in the little school at Mablethorpe."

"There has never been a young lady in the lives of either of the two brothers?" I asked carefully.

Mr. Gilmore inclined his head.

"Not that I am aware of. I believe I should know of it, for gossip of that kind spreads very quickly through a village."

There was a finality in these words which indicated that the rector of Sutton Cross had said all that he proposed to say on these matters. As we stood up and thanked him, however, Sherlock Holmes inquired, "May we see the tower and the beacon? I believe it would help us to get the lie of the land and I should not wish to trouble you a second time."

Mr. Gilmore did not quite slap us on the back. However, the expression on his face suggested that the opportunity to show off another of his treasures was entirely welcome.

I had been conscious during our discussion in the rectory study that Holmes had said nothing whatever about the pebble which Miss Chastelnau had left for our examination. As we now walked back towards the church, my friend inquired, "Were either of the brothers treasure hunters, Mr. Gilmore? I imagine you must get a great many such people here in the holiday season."

The rector stopped and laughed among the gravestones. He was far happier on such topics.

"You have been reading far too much romance, Mr. Holmes, or possibly the Bard of Avon's famous play. What dreadful news was brought to King John upon his deathbed in the year 1216! If you recall, his jewels and royal ornaments—the coronation regalia, as tradition has it,

Were in the Washes all unwarily
Devourèd by the unexpected flood.

Not two miles from here, on 12 October in that same year.

Perhaps it was the greatest loss of royal treasure in our entire island story."

"So I believe."

"It happened, you know, when the king was campaigning here during the Barons' War, a few days before his death. He and his party had gone on ahead, making for Swineshead Abbey that night. The baggage train, with all the royal treasure and the furnishings of his chapel, set out to cross the estuary here at low tide. Just before noon. Of course, the line of the coast was different seven centuries ago, but the river was where you see it now. In those days, however, the uncovered estuary was several miles across at low water. The quicksands were everywhere and the sea could come in at a terrifying speed in October with the neap tides, as it still does. A little before noon, the foolish baggage train tried to cross the mud-flats and the stream without a guide. A guide would have probed the mud with his pole to find a path where the ground was firm. 'Moses,' they called him, you know, after the crossing of the Red Sea."

"So I understand."

"Then you have read the old chroniclers, perhaps? The Abbot of Cogershall and Roger of Wendover? Matthew Paris in his Historia Anglorum a century after the tragedy? How the rushing tide caught the column in mid-stream? The quicksands were flooded at once and swallowed up men, pack-horses, baggage-wagons, jewels, crowns, ornaments and chapel furnishings. Much of it was booty seized by King John in his campaigns across the country. It was a time of long civil war between the Crown and the nobles. Such was the tragedy that happened in our estuary all those years ago. Even now, if you stand alone out there in the quietness of the ebb tide, it is said you may sometimes catch the cries of men or horses, the pandemonium of the lost ones. It is a story that every schoolboy knows!"

"What I wondered," Holmes insisted mildly, "was whether you get treasure hunters?"

The rector laughed again.

"They come, and they go away disappointed. The sea has withdrawn and the land has been reclaimed. All that remains of King John's treasure is probably deep down in the silt or the clay that has formed, a mile or two inland under the fields. Do not waste your time, Mr. Holmes."

"Nothing has ever been found?"

Roderick Gilmore frowned slightly.

"That is not quite correct. In the later Middle Ages, and almost up to the present day, discoveries have been made. These generally consist of a few items which were first discovered a century or so after the disaster. Then they were hidden away, forgotten and so lost once more. A handful of these trinkets have been found for a second time. The great collections, including the coronation regalia, seem to have been lost forever."

"Most interesting," said Holmes politely. "Most, most interesting!"

As the rector told his story among the tombstones, and as I thought of the blue pebble, I felt a prickling along my spine. Had the Chastelnau brothers been treasure hunters after all? Was there a secret along the windswept shore of the Old Light which mingled murder with such majesty?

We climbed the winding stone steps and came out from the darkness of the tower shaft into the sunlight of the square leaded roof with its medieval battlements and flagstaff. The lantern of the beacon was supported against this staff. I had begun to get my bearings in the brightness, taking a birdseye view of the flat green fenland stretching inland and the mud-banks at low water running down to the sparkling tranquil sea. On such a fine afternoon as this, it was hard to imagine that any danger could lie there. Then I heard Mr. Gilmore behind me and saw several figures stooping over an object on the foreshore.

"Dear me," said the rector apprehensively, "I believe they have found something after all. It is when the tide withdraws that such discoveries are usually made. About the third or fourth day, the sea gives up her dead, if she gives them up at all. I wonder which of the Chastelnau brothers it can be?"

4

Inspector Albert Wainwright's appearance, like his Christian name, recalled the late Prince Consort. His was a somewhat heavy face with large and mournful brown eyes. There was a doglike reproof in his habitually melancholy expression. Sometimes such features hide a wry but lively personality. In Mr. Wainwright's case, they concealed nothing. Indeed, his dark hair and his trim whiskers seemed like a deliberate attempt to copy those early daguerreotype photographs of her Prince Albert whose untimely death Queen Victoria still mourned.

"I have exchanged wires with Scotland Yard, as our superintendent requested," he said sadly, "for one never knows where these cases may lead. My instructions from Chief Inspector Lestrade are quite plain, gentlemen. I am to show you every courtesy but not to let you overreach yourselves. You are to have the run of the Old Light, now that you have been retained by Miss Chastelnau. I cannot say that such a thing is usual but, to speak frankly, I would rather allow you that privilege than have Mr. Lestrade coming down from Scotland Yard himself, which he was otherwise threatening to do. We shift for ourselves quite well as a rule."

Holmes smiled pleasantly.

"I am quite sure Mr. Lestrade did not mean to suggest that I am employed to remedy deficiencies in such an admirable body of men as the Lincolnshire police force."

Inspector Wainwright seemed unsure how to take this. He resolved the difficulty by breathing out heavily without actually saying anything, as if the heavy breath alone constituted a reply.

Holmes and I had left Mr. Gilmore and made our way along the village street to the river-bank and the Old Light. The white-painted wooden structure with its black under-surfaces and ironwork stood raised on nine substantial square "stilts." It was a round beacon standing almost forty feet high and capped by a windowed dome. Beyond it, across the sands, reeds, and mud-flats, I could see that the afternoon tide was on the turn from ebb to flood. The black iron ladder, which we had climbed to the door of the barrack-room, had the knobbly texture of metal that is regularly and inexpertly painted but never rubbed down beforehand. It smelt strongly of sand and algae.

Presently we stood with Inspector Wainwright in the cramped barrack-room, where the prevailing smell was of damp woollen clothing and oilskin. It was more than anything like the cabin of a yacht, every space taken by cupboards, shelves, a table, and two chairs with black seats of horsehair padding. There was a curved bunk built against the wall at one side and a door leading to a smaller space where the second keeper evidently slept. A wooden ladder fixed against the wall and a trapdoor in the plain ceiling indicated the way to the lantern-room above.

"What information we have is not much," said Wainwright, "but, such as it is, you shall have it before you go down to the sands. Dr. Rixon is there, but we may assume from the details that the body is Roland Chastelnau, the younger brother. They're bringing him up on a hurdle. A further search has been made of the sands and the dunes, as high as the tide might reach. We have found a broken lantern and a damaged shotgun, empty and soaked by sea-water, not far from where a body would be swept away. Whatever may have passed between the brothers, it looks very much as if both of them died at flood tide last Sunday night. A great tragedy."

The inspector frowned. Then he added, "You notice, gentlemen, I say 'died' and not 'drowned.' If Abraham Chastelnau went down in the quicksands, we shall never have a certain verdict."

"And in that case," I said, "you will never know if he died—or how."

"We are not likely to see him again, Doctor. If we do happen to find him alive, of course, I shall have some strong questions to put to him. He may be the murderer of his brother Roland. That would be something, as they say, in a place like ours."

By this time I could not help feeling grateful that we enjoyed the protection of Lestrade. In consequence, the Lincolnshire officer acted as if the case had been taken out of his hands and put into ours. Had Abraham Chastelnau survived, I believe Albert Wainwright would have been well-pleased to bring a charge of murder against him. As that seemed unlikely, he lost interest.

The inspector opened the barrack-room door and stepped out onto the small iron platform with its ladder to the sands. He paused, framed by the lintel of the door.

"As to the lantern-room, gentlemen, the mechanism is clockwork, as it is in all these beacons. Similar to an old-fashioned grandfather clock, but on a larger scale. A stout iron chain bearing a weight is cranked up to the top. Its gradual descent for eight hours is controlled by a governor, as is the case with a pendulum in a clock. And just as the weight in a clock turns the minute and the hour hands, so the descent of the weight here turns the banks of reflectors which direct the light of the lantern as a single beam across the sea. Until we have new keepers, a deputy keeper will come over from Freiston Shore to crank it up, to wind the clock and governor. He will also ensure that the reservoir tanks are full of paraffin oil to keep the lantern burning. They will send new keepers from Lynn in a day or two. Until full tide, my constable will be at hand to answer your questions and help you as you may require."

"One moment, if you please, Mr. Wainwright," said Holmes courteously. "What were the duties of the keepers while they were here?"

"One man is on watch at a time. He notes the speed of the wind, the pressure of the barometer, and so forth. One of them must polish the lenses of the reflectors every morning. He also cleans the panes of the lantern windows when necessary. Of course, ours is nothing but a local beacon. Not much shipping comes near us."

"As Mr. Gilmore says," remarked Holmes, "it is like the church tower, a beacon for those on the shore and the mud-flats after dark."

The inspector left us the run of the Old Light, with a uniformed constable at the foot of the iron ladder. Presently we climbed down and trudged over the marsh to a broad ribbon of sand where the discovery of Roland Chastelnau's body had been made. Dr. Rixon had finished his examination, and four men were bringing the corpse up the beach on a white sheep-hurdle.

Of the two men following the hurdle, one was Mr. Gilmore and the other was recognisable as Dr. Rixon himself, if only because he wore a tweed suit and cap and carried a black medical bag. I introduced myself. On such a coast, this could not have been the first time he had been called to the scene of a drowning. He appeared to regard the duty as an entirely impersonal matter and had no objection whatever to discussing it.

"It would seem that the poor fellow was drowned," I ventured.

"The inquest will find it so," he said readily. "Of course, we must see what an autopsy reveals."

"He was not marked about the face or head?"

"No. There was post-mortem staining, as one might expect, but he would scarcely be dashed against rocks on such a shore as this. Not with the flood tide as quiet as it usually is in these parts."

Sherlock Holmes joined us.

"Permit me to ask, Dr. Rixon, does there exist a photograph of either of the two brothers?"

Rixon put on a scowl of perplexity.

"I do not think so—Mr. Holmes, I presume? I should be most surprised if there were. They were alike in many features as most brothers are, but this is Roland and not Abraham. We have known them all their lives."

"And his pockets? Is there nothing there to prove his identity?"

My friend tapped the pockets of the faded and bedraggled jacket on the corpse. It seemed evident from his face that his fingers felt nothing.

"No," said Dr. Rixon, disinclined even to issue a reprimand as Holmes slid a hand into each of the side-pockets, "No, Mr. Holmes. I think under the circumstances, whatever Scotland Yard may consider. . . ."

"Only relics of the beach such as this?" Holmes asked innocently. He was holding between his finger and thumb a dun-coated pebble that might have been the twin of the one presented to us by Miss Chastelnau. "Or this?"

There were three or four of these objects altogether. Yet even before Dr. Rixon could reply, Holmes dismissed the matter for him.

"It is common enough," my friend added with a shrug. "The detritus of the beach and its shallows will easily find its way into the folds and wrinkles of clothing, after several days of washing to and fro by the tides."

I was sure he had thrown the pebbles away. They were no longer in his hand. On reflection, I had no doubt that they had been transferred subtly from the pocket of Roland Chastelnau to that of Sherlock Holmes.

5

In the absence of Albert Wainwright, I assumed that we might spend much of the coming night searching the drawers and cupboards of the Old Light before the inspector's return. I did not anticipate that in the meantime, we should come close to sharing the fate of the unfortunate Roland Chastelnau.

On our return to the foreshore lighthouse, with only a uniformed constable standing temporary guard on the wet sand below, we climbed the iron ladder again. The constable called up and informed us that he would be leaving shortly: in another hour or so, the sand on which he stood would be covered by the tide. Holmes thanked him and then moved across the room to the wooden ladder under the trapdoor of the lantern. His feet disappeared and I heard him moving about above me. Then his face reappeared in the opening of the trap.

"Come up, Watson! The pebbles can wait until later. See what a wonderland is here!"

I followed him up to the tall lantern-room. It was, in effect, two rooms in one, the upper level occupied by the machinery of the powerful reflectors. Within its glass dome, formed by the large window-panes, the air was still warm from the autumn sun, the heat reflected by silvered metal. The space was also filled with a strong mineral tang of paraffin oil from the iron reservoir tanks below the apparatus.

To do justice to the intricate design would test the reader's patience. At the lower level of the lantern-room, where we stood, there was a table with the keepers' log-book. On a central shaft, a heavy iron weight on its chain descended slowly through the eight hours of its cycle, turning the banks of reflectors overhead steadily. When cranked up, the chain was wound on a large drum above us. A tall case in plain wood with a white enamelled dial and two keyholes, like a long-case "grandfather" clock, controlled the mechanism. The hole on the left appeared to be for winding up a weight whose descent turned the clock hands of a dial, while on the right the same key wound a governor of some kind, which kept the mechanism of the reflectors at an even pace.

Above us was the white brilliance of the lantern. The light of each flame at its centre was intensified by being sealed in a glass funnel with a mirror behind it. This was surrounded in turn by square banks of parabolic reflectors in silvered glass like rows of shallow cups standing on their edges, turning slowly. A beam shone brilliantly out to sea, day and night, but was seldom visible during daylight, except in fog or adverse weather.

Black iron shutters in their runners were adjusted across many sections of the glass window panes. By this means, the revolving beam flashed out to sea intermittently, at one angle only. This corresponded with the markings of the Old Light on the charts of the Boston Deeps. After the silting up of the little ports and the building of the bridges at Sutton Cross, no shipping used this estuary. The corresponding light on the opposite bank of the estuary, which had once shown red and so measured the river mouth, was no longer in use.

Holmes finished his inspection of the gleaming apparatus.

"This, Watson, is the dioptric system of Augustin Fresnel: in other words, a stationary chandelier of white light surrounded by banks of Bodier Mercet's silvered reflectors. The device is no longer modern, of course, but it is sufficient. Our French colleagues were pioneers in such matters. I daresay this one will be replaced before long or may be taken out of service altogether."

Even if antiquated, it was a magnificent creation—a wonderland, as Holmes had called it. The effect was almost hypnotic as the rows of reflectors rotated slowly, endlessly, and almost silently in the warm air, except for an occasional creak of wood at their axle. In the lower level of the lantern-room, standing before the tall wooden case with its clock dial and governor, Holmes opened the pendulum door. The mechanism of its smaller descending weights also controlled the flow of paraffin oil to the lamps. I noticed that a measuring scale of some kind had been carved on the interior of the case to indicate the progress of the weights. The length of time before the device must be wound again was clearly indicated.

To prevent the reflectors from coming to a halt, a metal strike-bell was attached a little above the base of this scale. Like the incessant striking of a clock, this alarm system would summon those in the barrack-room or nearby before the weight was fully unwound. According to Inspector Wainwright, "our man from Freiston Shore" had attended to the winding early that morning and again while we were with Dr. Rixon.

I turned to the little wooden table and opened the log-book. It was divided into columns for the date and time of winding, another for the point on the scale which the weights had reached before the winding took place, and a fourth for any comments to be read by the next keeper on duty. Underneath was the name of the keeper on watch.

These columns indicated that Abraham Chastelnau had

wound up the weights for the night watch just before 8 P.M. on Sunday evening. The time must have been almost immediately before Roland's warning gunshot had lured him to their fatal confrontation on the flooded sands. An entry by the Freiston Shore relief on the following day confirmed that the Old Light had ceased flashing by 5:20 on Monday morning, according to the collier's signal.

Holmes glanced at the entries and closed the book.

"The log and the pebbles can wait their turn. We have all night for them. Before it is too late in the day, it would pay us to take a stroll along the beach and visit the scene of the brothers' last encounter."

I looked out of the window across the ribbon of sand darkening to grey, and a tide that had already turned to the flood.

"I should have thought, Holmes, that it was already rather late. The sun has almost gone and the twilight will be upon us very soon."

"All the better. It will be just as it was at the time of the quarrel. In our case, however, we are not going to quarrel and we shall have the strong beam of the Old Light to lead us back. Keep that in view and we shall not go far wrong."

I noticed, however, that he had brought his redoubtable walking-stick, that "Penang Lawyer" which settled all arguments. We lowered ourselves down the iron ladder and stood upon the wet sands. The filling estuary was immediately to our right and the incoming tide lay ahead. I feared I might have better reason for my caution than I guessed. The pale yellow sun of that October evening had disappeared half an hour ago behind a silhouette of black Scotch firs which marked the flat inland horizon of Sutton Cross. Darkness was gathering across the wide sands with their low dunes and deserted shore. This impression of twilight was intensified by a contrast between the beam of white brilliance flashing out to sea, followed by sudden darkness as the silvered reflectors of the Old Light turned away from us behind their black shutters. They then shone only upon the interior of the iron, which covered the panes of the lantern on the far sides.

Holmes, swinging the stick in his hand, set off across the dark mud towards the point where Roderick Gilmore and his sexton had seen two diminutive figures struggling on Sunday evening. We were about half a mile seaward from St. Clement's church tower. Now, as then, a descending night mist was rolling in with the tide, progressively veiling the spot from onlookers ashore.

We had turned our backs on the Old Light and were walking away from its intermittent beam, which shot across the waves. No ship's light marked the horizon anchorage of the Boston Deeps. By comparison with the brilliance of the Old Light, even the beacon on the church tower was a mere glimmer confirming our position on the treacherous sands.

As soon as we had completed our reconnaissance, we needed only walk back in a straight line until the Old Light shone straight in our faces. Then we should turn right at forty-five degrees and make our way steadily towards its iron ladder, along the raised path of the river bank. Or so it seemed. I could already feel the sand yielding more easily underfoot as the tide seeped beneath us. By the yellow oil-light of my lantern, I could also see that each of my footprints now flooded progressively deeper and more quickly as my boot was lifted from the mud.

Holmes was at his most dogmatic.

"I think we need another half mile to reach the scene of their encounter. I should like to determine a direct line from St. Clement's beacon to the incoming surf."

As he said this, I noticed that the blurred but luminous line of surf was now the only thing visible to our right between the darkness of sky and sea. We walked for about fifteen minutes more, scarcely exchanging a word. I felt the coldness of the

October night coming in with the mist. Even the lemon afterglow of sunset had vanished from the inland horizon beyond the village. The rest of the shoreline was obscure, and the descending mist which the rector had described now hung between us and St. Clement's beacon, condensing slowly into fog. I tried a cheerful note.

"The ground seems a little higher here, Holmes, a rib of firm sand. If we follow it back, when we turn, and keep Mr. Gilmore's beacon in view to the right, we should soon have the beam of the Old Light full in our faces."

"I daresay," he said impatiently but with no sign of turning back. "If I had been the survivor of that fight between the two brothers on Sunday night, I should have assumed much the same."

"I thought we had agreed that there was no survivor of the encounter."

"On the contrary: that is a matter which we are about to put to the proof."

By this time, I had very little wish to put it to the proof. Indeed, with the light gone, I began not to like the whole business. We were not more than eight feet apart, but it had become increasingly difficult to make out the gaunt purposeful stride of my companion or anything but the hazy flicker of his lamp.

As if reading my thoughts, he added, "We must keep together. It may be firm going here, but it would be well not to get separated where the sands are more perilous."

So we walked on until we were, at the very least, level with the beacon of the church tower. It seemed far away now, across the flooding sands.

"We must take care that the tide does not get behind us," I said a little breathlessly.

Holmes was not listening.

"Now stop a bit," he said. "Let us have our bearings. We are the

Chastelnau brothers. Here it is that either you or I kill the other. The killer may have carried out a long-prepared plan. Alternatively, it may have been provocation, a sudden heat and a terrifying accident. In either event, what would the survivor do next?"

"Get back to the Old Light! Where else should he go?"

"Very well, Watson. You have committed murder or, at the least, manslaughter. Now, pray lead on."

This was not what I had bargained for, but I was relieved to be turning back before the flood tide encroached any further. As a soldier, I was not unprepared for the challenge. There was no light along the western horizon nor a moon in the sky. The lamps of the village were scarcely pinpricks. I heard an insistent murmuring from the dark billowing sea which was a good deal louder now than when we had set out. For the first time, I noticed a sharp north-east wind gathering at our backs, a light spot or two of cold rain. It was a reminder that, despite the pleasant sunlight of that afternoon, this was the season of equinoctial storms.

When I had joined the Army Medical Department a decade earlier and sailed for Afghanistan with the Northumberland Fusiliers, even a surgeon's training for service overseas included a course of instruction in map-reading, compass-bearings, judging distances, and identifying terrain. In my mind I now constructed a square map. In the top right-hand corner was the beacon of the church tower; in the top left-hand corner, the Old Light. Along the bottom was the line of the incoming tide. Holmes and I were in the bottom right-hand corner, walking parallel with the foot of the map.

We were following what I had judged to be a rib of sand six inches or more above the level of the dark beach around us and therefore firmer. The temptation was to cut a diagonal across the square map towards the Old Light. Fortunately, I had surveyed the terrain from the windows of the barrack-room that afternoon and had seen that such a diagonal would take us into lower ground, probably already flooded by the tide and possibly containing quicksand. The prudent line of march was still to follow the bottom line of the map until we were face-to-face with the lighthouse beam. Then we should know that we had reached the bottom left-hand corner and need only take a right angle and walk straight into the beam to reach the safety of the iron ladder to the barrack-room.

The sand beneath our feet was softer, but there was no doubt that we were still on slightly higher ground. I thought of Holmes's question and my answer. Suppose I were my brother's murderer, making my escape. In the first place, it was impossible that I should go anywhere but the Old Light. I assumed that I would not have intended murder when I set out. Therefore, I would not have been prepared for immediate flight without returning to the barrack-room.

Holmes said nothing in all this time but appeared content to follow where I led. The light of St. Clement's beacon was dropping away behind us on our right. The beam from the Old Light was ahead but shining at an angle, slightly away from us. We seemed in danger of pulling inland behind it. That must be avoided at all costs, for it was where I had noticed earlier that the mudflats lay and the treacherous "shivering sands" might be. It was easy enough to set a course a little further to our left. This brought us slightly closer to the tide but also took us further round on an angle that should put us in the lighthouse beam. Once there, we were safe.

I had begun to feel that a man could make too much of such difficulties as this beach had presented. Then I put my right foot forward and, before I could pull back, felt the leg sink half way up the shin in freezing mud.

"Stop! Stop, Holmes!"

We were almost level with the lighthouse beam but were

somehow in the very terrain I had tried to avoid. To one side, among what was now fathomless mud rather than firm sand, I could see strands of grass, limp and wet. Fresh water could mean only the river, which we should not have encountered at all. Though we were still short of the lighthouse beam where it crossed our path, we had somehow come too far. How could that be? How could we be where we evidently were—and how had we got there? The doomed baggage-train of King John, all those centuries ago, had thought themselves secure. Had we made an error in common with them? I had dipped into the chronicles which Holmes had brought and now recalled with dismay a warning that the first step to destruction in shifting sands and estuaries is when the victims lose their way—as we had done now. The ground opened in the midst of the waters, wrote the medieval chronicler Roger of Wendover, and whirlpools sucked down men and horses. It was already too late. To those who might help us, our cries would be inaudible.

The true terror, in the darkness and the fast sinking mud, is to know that one has followed meticulously the path to safety but come only to the verge of a cold and cruel death. There was no explanation and, without that, we were done for. We must move instantly or the incoming tide would overwhelm us—but where was our path? There was nothing but the surf and the sinking sand around us, on every side.

By every calculation, we should be on a firm river-bank path. It must by any logic lead us directly and easily back to the Old Light and the village, both of them now lost in the mist. The intermittent beam which must be our salvation was drawing us ever deeper into the deadly chill of the river mud. This was surely impossible, which was only to say that we were utterly lost in the darkness and the sea fog. And now there was a quiet but sinister ripple of incoming water across the path behind us with nothing but the filling estuary about our legs in front.

Where, by all reason, there should have been firm ground, the softening mud offered no foothold but a fathomless trap.

I hope I should not have fallen into a panic, but the cliché of not knowing which way to turn was never more true. The square map firmly in my head was now submerged as surely as the drowning Roland Chastelnau.

"I think," said Sherlock Holmes, "you had better leave this to me after all."

I was never more glad to do so. In that familiar voice there was assurance and a confidence which I was far from feeling.

"Step back!" he said.

His hand gripped my upper arm, as I performed a grotesque about-turn with my left leg, relying on his support. The last of the firm ground, from which I had stepped a moment ago, was under my right foot once more. I saw by the reflected light of the beacon that he was probing the mud with his walking-stick. It was a painstaking business, but after a dozen carefully chosen steps the fearful sense of bottomless silt became something which yielded a little but then held firm. But now we were walking away from the beam of the Old Light—surely in the wrong direction?

"A little further still, I think, if my calculations are correct," Holmes remarked casually.

What those calculations were, I could not say. By mine, we were heading straight into the shivering sands. Yet the mud underfoot was still turning to firmer ground. Presently, at each step that I took, the slush did no worse than engulf the lower portion of my boots. And yet the Old Light seemed to fall further behind us. This was no time to argue the matter. I took one more step and felt what seemed like compact earth under my boot.

"Now a little more to the left, I think," said Holmes cheerfully.

Surely we were by-passing the Old Light and walking into the same quicksand that I had seen earlier? Yet it was still firm going, and gradually I could just make out the ghostly contours of the Old Light with its heavy wooden supports and the round body of its barrack-room. Yet if that was so, then the beam which should have been directed out to the Boston Deeps was shining a little more in the direction of King's Lynn. It was a discrepancy that might not be noticed at a distance where the beam was more widely reflected but was just enough to lead us a hundred yards out of our way across the mudflats. Was this not the sort of trick which, a century earlier, the wreckers had employed to decoy a ship onto the rocks and loot it?

Presently we found our way to the black-painted iron ladder and climbed it, the first ripples of the surf swishing about our feet. Holmes lit the oil-lamp in the barrack-room. There was no policeman on guard on the sands below, for the tide would soon have covered them. We should be undisturbed for several hours until the tide had turned and the Freiston relief arrived.

Holmes drew his silver flask from his pocket and the comforting spirituous aroma of whisky came to me as I sat down on one of the two black horsehair chairs. Reason returned where panic had prevailed.

"Roland Chastelnau was not the victim!" I exclaimed; "he was his brother's murderer!"

Holmes said nothing. He was climbing the wooden ladder now into the lantern-room above us. There was a pause and then I heard his voice.

"It is as I supposed, though it was not obvious by daylight. The black metal shutters on the windows have been adjusted. The direction of the beam has been deliberately altered, not by much but enough to prove fatal. Any man trying to navigate the route back from the scene of the brothers' struggle to the Old Light by using this beam would have walked into the river estuary with a flood tide running. Not the quicksands, Watson, but the river, with its tidal undertow and currents."

Then I saw the whole mystery clearly. Roland Chastelnau had decoyed his brother to the mudflats by a warning gunshot. There was a struggle, in which Roland had either died or escaped only to drown later on. The evidence of that was conclusive since this afternoon. But to make assurance doubly sure, before he went down to the beach, leaving Abraham alone in the Old Light, Roland had moved the black iron shutters of the lantern in their grooves so that it shone several degrees or more in error.

No one who merely wound the mechanism, at the lower level, needed to climb to the top of the dome to check the iron shutters. The altered direction of the beam would not have been visible at all in daylight. To the Boston Deeps at night, it would be the usual distant glimmer. But whatever the outcome of the struggle on the beach, Roland intended that Abraham Chastelnau should never get back to the Old Light alive. The death which Holmes and I had avoided in the estuary at flood tide would have submerged Abraham if all else failed.

Roland Chastelnau, had he escaped whatever death overtook him, need only have returned to the Old Light and slid the thin iron plates of the shutters to their original position. Roland cannot have expected that Mr. Gilmore and his sexton should have seen the fight—or horseplay—on the sands, but even that evidence was conclusive of very little. From the facts available, Abraham Chastelnau's death would surely have been recorded as a tragedy of tide and darkness and of his own unaccountable miscalculation.

6

"With that, we have the whole story," I said, almost an hour later. By now the tide was rushing and swirling below us among the wooden legs of the barrack-room. Holmes looked at me thoughtfully.

"You are to be congratulated, Watson. It is your case, and you have marshalled the facts in such a way that I am quite sure Inspector Wainwright and our friend Lestrade will be among the first to commend you upon your conclusions."

There was something in his tone that I did not quite like, hinting a little too much at irony. Just then, however, I cared less about congratulations than the opportunity to sleep. There seemed to be no food in the barrack-room, other than cocoa made with hot water. However, I have long thought that a man can do without food for quite a while, provided he has sufficient sleep—and he may do without sleep for a time, so long as he is adequately fed. That being so, I made myself as comfortable as possible on the barrack-room bunk, which curved slightly to follow the wall of the lighthouse.

I was aware that Holmes was still moving about restlessly, and

I believe, before I fell into a deep sleep, that I was sufficiently conscious to know that he had made his way up the internal ladder to the lantern-room. I did not hear what he was doing; indeed, he could have dismantled the entire lighthouse dome without disturbing me. When I woke again, it was after midnight and there was no further sound of water on the sand below us. By his own standards, Holmes had shown extreme patience in allowing me to sleep for what must have been an hour or two.

"Watson!" I think it was the sound of the bunk creaking which provoked this summons. "I should be obliged if you would come and give your opinion in a small matter."

I sat up and looked for the shoes I had taken off. In a minute or two I climbed the ladder and was staring in some dismay at the dismemberment of the lantern-room clock-case. The mechanism was still functioning, so far as I could see, but Holmes had extracted several pieces of the wooden framework which were now lying on the log-book table.

It was plain that, as so often, he had not been to bed. His face was pale as parchment, but his eyes in their dark sockets were all the brighter for that.

"Tell me, Watson, if you were possessed of some small treasure in such a place as this, where would you choose to hide it?"

"I suppose that would depend from whom I wanted to hide it."

"From all the world—but most of all from your friends."

"Holmes, is this some matter to do with the clockwork mechanism?"

"No. Why should it be?"

"Very well. I should not leave it in the drawers or cupboards. There are not many of them, and it would quite soon be found. Perhaps I would hide it somewhere in the mechanism of the lantern, but that mechanism must be in motion twenty-four hours every day and seven days every week throughout the year. Moreover, according to Wainwright, the lantern and the reflectors are usually cleaned every few days or so; even the panes of the glass dome are polished."

"So far, you have only explained where you would not hide it."

"I should prefer a place where the mechanism which is never halted might conceal it. Since you have pillaged so much of the clock-case, I suppose that is where I should choose."

"Well done, Watson! We shall make a criminal investigator of you yet."

I looked at the pieces of wood, the clutter of screws and little bolts, anonymous items of brass and iron on the table. Though the machinery which regulated the reflectors was working constantly, there were convenient spaces within the wooden case, as there are in any long-case clock.

Holmes watched my eyes and read my thoughts.

"Put your hand up into the clock-hood, behind the dials and just below the drum that winds the clock-weight. You shall see what you shall see."

I felt—and found a narrow wooden ledge that ran round four sides of the interior of the case.

"There is a ledge an inch or so wide, but there is nothing on it."

"What purpose does it serve?"

"There is nothing resting upon it. It helps to brace the structure, that is all."

"Not of great interest?"

"I should hardly think so."

"Put your fingers under the ledge, where it runs along the rear of the case."

"It feels more like metal at that point, presumably to strengthen it. The other sides are made of wood."

"Now push upwards on the metal piece."

I did so, and felt that length of the ledge lifting clear. Holmes watched me closely as I brought it out.

"If I were to choose a hiding-place," he said thoughtfully, "I should choose also to make the object appear part of the structure of the building or the mechanism. An item that is regularly seen and therefore never examined. Something that, even if examined, would in this case appear as part of the clock-case."

I could feel that a man of modest ability as a carpenter might cut away as much of the wooden ledge at the rear as would accommodate the strip of metal I now held in my hand. Even someone who inadvertently lifted it out might think that it had been inserted merely to brace the inner support.

The length of corroded metal which now lay on the log-book table looked like a piece of scrap which had suffered from wind and weather. Corrosion had left the ends rough and uneven. It was a strut of some kind, six or seven inches long, an inch or so wide, and a little less than that in depth. It was dirty and darkened. To judge by three regular indentations, it appeared to have lost some screws which had presumably held it in place. It was too corroded to tell what metal it was made of. It might almost have been a neglected chisel with the end of its blade broken off. The rust of years had pitted the surface.

"I should hardly bother to hide that! It would disgrace the tool-bag of the most slapdash workman! One might almost think that the rats had been at its ends!"

"Precisely," said Holmes, turning it over. I now saw a groove across the back, about a third of the way down, where a cross-piece might have fitted it. Plainly, this had been no chisel. I imagined the missing piece in place. It might have been many things, but the image I had in mind was still in the form of a cross or, to be more accurate, a crucifix.

"How long has it been hidden there?"

Holmes shrugged.

"Not long, I should imagine. It might be a few years, perhaps a few months. Not before the Chastelnau brothers became keepers of the light."

Keepers of the light! Combined with the idea of a crucifix, his description had the sound of a religious order!

I looked again and saw that what I had thought to be holes for screws were merely three depressions in the tarnished and corroded metal. Holmes took from his pocket a small wash-leather bag. He withdrew the blue stone—the "Chastelnau pebble," that is—and placed it in each depression in turn. It fitted best at the head. Another, its hue resembling the mud on the beach and retrieved from Roland Chastelnau's pocket, filled a second depression where the cross-piece might once have been fixed to the upright. A third, of the same muddy appearance, rested lower down in the upright. The remaining two he placed at either side, where a cross-piece might have been. I felt how chill the night air was in that unheated place.

"Why was this village called Sutton Cross?"

Holmes looked at the pattern he had created.

"Because it was where the river could be crossed—forded—before a bridge was built. Or perhaps because it was here that an item of royal treasure was believed to be lost, found, and then lost again."

"Which item might that be?"

"According to one of the court parchments known as Pipe Rolls, when the tide and the quicksands overtook King John's baggage train in October 1216, he had been engaged in a long war with his barons. As Mr. Gilmore describes it, the king had commandeered treasure from all over the land. Among this was said to be the Chester Cross, a gold and sapphire pendant worn from a sash round the waist. It had formerly belonged to the Bishops of Chester. The cross was more than a thing of beauty, if we believe the chronicles. It had the reputation, when in the hands of a holy man, of performing small miracles of healing. There was a legend that it had been handed down from the time of Edward the Confessor."

"Are we to assume that this unprepossessing piece of metal is part of the Chester Cross?"

Holmes shook his head.

"Alas, no. I shall assume nothing. Imitations and fakes, masquerading as treasure trove from the baggage-train, were all too common after the disaster, according to the Pipe Rolls of the time. Yet I would give a great deal to know what either of the Chastelnau brothers assumed it to be."

I glanced at the window and saw that a half-moon was braving the horizon clouds of the North Sea.

Early that morning I took my story of the brothers' disappearance to Inspector Albert Wainwright at the police office in Sutton Cross. I had been over it in my mind and I knew it was the only explanation that fitted the facts. From having felt the cold fear of being lost in the soft mud at night with a tide rushing in, I knew how easily a victim might be decoyed into a river estuary. There had been no love lost between Abraham and Roland Chastelnau, yet it was surely Roland who contrived the death of his brother, not the other way round. It was Roland who had previously slipped those pebbles into his pocket and had adjusted the iron shutters before he left the Old Light. On the darkening beach, he had fired the shot which brought Abraham to him. There was a quarrel and afterwards, by accident or design, Roland was drowned. His brother, innocent or guilty of that death, even unaware of it, was drawn into the quicksands of the estuary as he followed the false promise of the altered lighthouse beam. How could it be otherwise on the evidence before us?

On Holmes's instructions, I had said nothing to Wainwright or the Freiston keeper about the curious strip of corroded metal and the pebbles. Perhaps these had been the cause of a fight to the death between the two brothers, but there was no evidence of it. Before such fragments could be evidence of anything, we needed proof of what they were.

7

Our last visit to the Reverend Mr. Gilmore was no less convivial than the first, although somewhat more frustrating. It was eleven o'clock on a sunny autumn morning. The brightness touched his churchyard yews to make a shadow pattern of garden geometry. Its reflection sparkled on the tide at low water. The rector's maid in her starched apron had brought a silver tray, upon which stood a cut-glass decanter of Blandy's Madeira, Solera 1868, three glasses, and three plates with slices of yellow seed-cake upon them. If Mr. Gilmore had distanced himself from Trinity College, Cambridge, he had certainly not forgotten its agreeable mid-morning ritual.

When the glasses had been filled with their sweet-smelling amber fluid, Holmes came immediately to the point.

"It must happen from time to time, Mr. Gilmore, that items are discovered which may be claimed as part of the lost treasure of King John. The sea having receded a mile or two since the year 1216, some of the debris might now lie quite shallowly underground."

The rector smiled the smile of one who has heard this story before.

"I doubt whether many such claims have been made good, Mr. Holmes. Certainly not in recent years. As I said before, most of the baggage-wagons and their contents probably lie buried under the fields and pastureland, inland from this village. A few items of jewels and metalwork, if they had fallen loose, might have been carried here and there by the tidal currents at the time of the disaster and left closer to the surface."

"And therefore might be found?"

Mr. Gilmore chuckled.

"And therefore might be counterfeit. In the later Middle Ages, from the time of King John to the coming of the Tudors in 1485, there are records of rewards paid in the Court of Exchequer to men and women who had found certain trinkets and surrendered them to the Crown. They did not amount to very much. The Plea Rolls tell us of a man receiving no more than twenty shillings for precious stones from a collar worn by King John himself."

"And there has always been a history of fabricated treasure?"

"To such an extent that after the disaster to the baggage-train, the scribe of the royal Patent Rolls was charged to make a careful inventory of all that had been lost. For some years subsequently, when it was claimed that an item was found, it was possible to check the description minutely against the entries in the parchments."

"And now?"

The rector smiled.

"At that time, Mr. Holmes, most of the land round here consisted of tidal mud-flats. Where we are sitting now, St. Clement's Church and the ground immediately about it was on a spit of land just above sea-level. At high tide, the church was on an island. In the reign of King John and his successor, Henry III, it would have been possible for fragments of wreckage from the baggage-train to be carried by currents. Scraps of wood may float and some items of jewellery are too light to sink far. But anything that was engulfed in the quicksands is not likely to have been washed out of them since."

Holmes nodded. His straight back and narrow shoulders reclined against the chair; the keen profile seemed to relax a little. He took his first sip from the glass of Madeira and said, "Mr. Gilmore, I would ask you to trust me."

"Great heavens, Mr. Holmes!" It was a burst of boyish amusement. "I am your brother Mycroft's friend, and I would certainly do more than that!"

"I will ask you to trust me and not to ask why. I will tell you this much. A man's life, let alone a family's reputation, may depend upon your discretion."

I had not the least idea what my friend meant. What man's life? From his bag he now drew a piece of folded yellow lint. From its soft covering he produced our slim length of metal with its corroded ends. From his pocket he took the leather pouch containing the five pebbles, which were all that we had so far found. Using the lint as a surface, he laid the upright across the table and shook the pebbles from their bag.

"I have gone so far as to clean a minute area of surface with carborundum, Mr. Gilmore. Unless I am much mistaken, the surface metal with which this strip is covered must be gold, though not of any great quality. I should like to know whether the object suggests anything to you."

The rector stared for a moment. He drew a reading-glass from the breast pocket of his black clerical jacket. Opening it, he continued to gaze at the pieces, his amusement giving way to perplexity. Holmes took the five pebbles and placed three in the indentations. The other two he positioned at either side where the crossbeam of a crucifix would have been. Mr. Gilmore put away his glass.

"One moment," he said.

He stood up and crossed to his tall break-front bookcase. Opening its glass-panelled doors, he took out a handsome volume bound in red cloth and stamped in gold. I saw that it had been issued by the Lincolnshire and Norfolk Society of Antiquaries to its members and had been published a dozen years earlier. He laid it down on the support of his oak bookstand, open at an illustrated page. Holmes and I joined him.

The page contained a steel engraving of a cross. It was done from a photograph but the subject was described as merely a reconstruction.

"You will see at once—" Mr. Gilmore drew his finger down the length of the engraving—"the mark of an inlay made by the maker's tool. It bears similarities to two lines on the piece that you have. Down the length of it and on either hand, the craftsman had embedded five stones. What they were was quite impossible to tell from a black-and-white engraving."

"What is the picture?" I asked.

Mr. Gilmore held the book open firmly.

"It is a facsimile of a twelfth-century bishop's pendant in gold, sapphire, and coral. The bishops donated it to the King's Treasury during John's war against the barons. It was said to possess miraculous powers. As with all such treasures, it carried a warning of the ill-fortune that would attend its loss. King John reached Swineshead Abbey, just up the road from here, on the day of the disaster to his baggage-train. When the news of it was brought, he fell into great distress of mind, followed by fever and heat. He died at Swineshead seven days later, robbed on his deathbed by those who attended him."

"And this?" Holmes indicated the pebbles and the metal upright. Mr. Gilmore shook his head.

"Impossible to say, Mr. Holmes. There have been copies, similar pieces, and downright fraud. The fraud, if it is one, may be medieval or Tudor as easily as modern. It may have been an attempt to impose upon the superstitious or the gullible five or six centuries ago by producing a miraculous relic. Just as Chaucer's Pardoner sold pigs' bones in a glass as relics of the Christian martyrs. Much would depend on how and where this remnant was found. When you are able to tell me that, I shall perhaps be able to pass better judgment. Until then, I will keep silence, as I have promised you."

"That is all?" I asked.

"No, Dr. Watson. I will say this. If anyone were to claim that this fragment had been found in the earth recently, I would think that it must be a fraud. It is a near-impossibility. If it has come to us in some indirect way, that may be a different matter."

"In what other way?"

"During six and a half centuries, Dr. Watson, an object may be lost, found, lost again, found again, lost and found once more. I should find that easier to believe."

"And what of any miraculous powers?" I persisted.

"Medieval people lived wretched lives and met early deaths. Typhus, scurvy, scrofula, bubonic plague, which are mercifully rare now, were common then. The healing of these widespread afflictions was the greatest object of their prayers. Heaven alone knows what may drive a man or a woman to pray for relief."

"You do not know of any cause that might have driven Abraham or Roland Chastelnau?" Holmes asked.

"Unfortunately, I knew neither of them well enough for that. Nor, I think, could anyone else answer your question."

Like so many local historians, Roderick Gilmore was not only delighted to provide us with information which might assist us but also to encumber us with a good deal that we could have done without. All the same, as we made our way through the churchyard yew hedges once more, towards the road that led back to the Bridge Hotel, I felt that our host had been suggestive rather than informative. Was there something he was holding back?

8

In the hours that followed, Holmes was kind enough not to remind me that so far as the strip of ancient metal and the "pebbles" were concerned, "my case" appeared to have run into the sand. I daresay he felt that with both the brothers dead, whatever evil possessed Abraham, according to the poor fellow's own account, was no longer a threat to those around him. My friend seemed content that I had provided a solution to the mystery of the Chastelnau brothers' disappearance.

That evening, as we sat at dinner in the hotel dining-room, the beam of the Old Light shot fitfully across the dark sea. The new keepers of the wooden lantern and barrack-room were now in place. Whatever part that remote beacon had played in murder or tragedy was over. Holmes looked up from his mutton chop, which along with potatoes, green peas, and a bottle of indifferent St. Emilion was the table d'hôte of the establishment.

"What is to become of our questionable relic?" I inquired, "The fragment of the Chester Cross—or not, as the case may be."

"I have given the matter a little thought," he said. "It should, of course, be yielded up to Her Majesty's Treasury, like all treasure trove. Far the best person to act as go-between would be Brother Mycroft. He knows these Treasury fellows and will save us a good deal of bother."

"Unless it should be a copy or a fake. In that case, you might keep it among your souvenirs."

He looked at me thoughtfully.

"You know, Watson, I believe that if it were not part of the Chester Cross, I should not care to have it among them. I have made it a habit to be selective. If it is genuine, on the other hand, it would be a symbol of faith and innocence, therefore out of place in such a menagerie."

I let this pass and watched the beam of the Old Light illuminate the horizon once more.

"There is one thing further," he said significantly.

"What would that be?"

He laid down his knife and fork and glanced into the darkness beyond the window.

"Whatever lies out there in the quicksands, this is your case, not mine. You have done it admirably and, as I say, I am sure Lestrade will commend you. However, were it my case, I should now feel it incumbent on me to present the findings to Miss Alice Chastelnau."

"Of course I shall! Once we are back in Baker Street, I shall set out the entire course of the investigation. Naturally, I cannot tell her precisely what happened to her brothers. No one could. In the circumstances it would be preposterous to accuse one alone of murdering the other. However, she may draw her conclusions privately from the evidence. Then I shall let the matter drop."

Sherlock Holmes tapped the table with his spoon and turned a little in his chair. The waiter came towards us, bearing a cheese board occupied solely by a large slab of farmhouse Stilton under a blue-and-white willow-pattern cover. When the man had gone, Holmes let the corners of his mouth turn down.

"It is beyond my comprehension why these establishments insist upon ruining a Stilton cheese by soaking it in port wine! As to the other matter, Watson, I fear that a letter to Miss Chastelnau and a private report will not quite do. At least I should think so if this were my case, and if I were as close as we are now to Mablethorpe. I would feel obliged to call upon the lady. I should break the news to her as tactfully as one may in a quiet talk—and as one cannot do in a formal letter."

It was difficult to argue against this, except in terms that would have sounded unchivalrous or downright caddish. Had Holmes not raised the matter in this way, however, I should have returned to London next day. I was still in medical practice. Though I left a locum in charge of my consulting rooms on these occasions, there were patients to be seen by me and hospitals to be visited.

"If you think it right," I said a little gloomily. "But I cannot stay in Sutton Cross for ever, waiting for an appointment with Miss Chastelnau."

He was undismayed by this.

"I do think it right," he said in a kindly tone, "and I do not think an appointment will be necessary. We are, after all, performing a service. It may be a greater service to her than can at the moment be supposed. The early morning train will get us to Mablethorpe well before lunch. The evening train will bring us back here before the dining-room closes. The day after tomorrow you will be back in London. Your grateful patients will doubtless applaud your return."

9

So it was that our pilgrimage to Mablethorpe began next morning, after an early breakfast. Holmes had sent a telegram to Miss Chastelnau, advising her of our visit, though how he could be sure the lady would be at home was not revealed. The three carriages of the stopping train from King's Lynn to Cleethorpe, pulled by something no grander than a shunting engine, rattled and jerked their way out of the little wooden platform at Sutton Cross. We traversed the expanse of the fens, their pastureland gathering the October rains in wide pools. After branching off the main line at Willoughby, a single track followed the flat coastline. Broad sands and paths among the dunes were fringed by tall grass and grey-leaved buckthorn with its orange berries. At a little distance out to sea, parallel with the shore, a series of sand-banks stretched in either direction as far as one could see.

I had no clear idea of what to expect from Mablethorpe. There was a church and two or three inns. Elegant houses, precisely of the kind that might contain a school for young gentlewomen, stood half-concealed in groves of fir trees and oaks. Elsewhere, brightly painted boarding houses and something approaching a promenade suggested all the makings of a popular seaside bathing-place or "resort." A brisk salty wind blew from the North Sea.

Holmes and I made the best of it, taking lunch at one of the inns, the so-called Book-in-Hand. Then we set out on foot towards what was once Miss Openshaw's academy. Nowhere in a place the size of Mablethorpe is far from anywhere else. The school house, at least, was very much what I had expected. It was a substantial family dwelling, classical or at least square-looking. Its crescent-shaped gravel drive entered between one set of stone gate-pillars and exited between another pair a little further up the suburban road. The gravelled way was flanked by laurel bushes and other shrubs. A front elevation showed us a house on three levels with a bay and two large sash windows on either side of its stone porch. It had no doubt been built in brick but was coated with pale stone rendering, painted white, as befitted the neo-classical ambitions of sixty years ago. With a long seat in a grey wooden summer-house on the lawn, it seemed precisely the residence to house ten or a dozen genteel pupils. I cannot believe that their instruction required anyone but Miss Chastelnau herself.

It seemed to me, as Holmes rang the bell, that there was very little sign of the young ladies. However, that was neither here nor there. A maid in cap and apron answered the door and Holmes announced us. Without hesitation we were admitted into the hall with its black and white tiling and an inner door of red and blue glass panels. From there we proceeded to what I suppose I must call the sitting-room of the headmistress.

Miss Chastelnau was evidently expecting us. She stood with her back to the bay window and her face in shadow. She was the same neat and restrained person who had visited us in Baker Street. Yet I sensed that her family tragedy had inspired her with anxiety rather than grief.

The sitting-room was just what I would have expected. The

sun filled its chintz curtains at the window, and on a small table stood a Chinese vase adorned with green dragon-handles. The hearth, where Holmes and I faced one another with Miss Chastelnau upright between us on a yellow settee in the Egyptian style, was lined with William De Morgan tiles portraying centaurs, the phoenix, and other mythical creatures of the ancient world. I thought afterwards that the entire room was a curious shrine of the non-existent.

As succinctly as I could, because that was kinder, I explained the details of my solution to the mystery of her two missing brothers. I added that there had, of course, been no inquest as yet. What its verdict would be I could not say. Miss Chastelnau sat quite still and listened in silence. When I had finished, she thanked me with every appearance of sincerity. If she showed little emotion, it was surely because she remained in that state of shock which precedes any outbursts of grief.

"And you, Mr. Holmes," she said quietly, turning to him, "thank you for coming to see me also."

Throughout all this, he had been sitting with his head lowered a little, as if reading the mythology of the hearth tiles. Now he was straight-backed in his chair and looking her directly in the eye.

"I fear you are in error, madam. I did not come here to see you, for that is Dr. Watson's business. I am here to see Mr. Abraham Chastelnau."

If a bomb had gone off in that ornamented and genteel room, it could not have produced a more stunned and silent aftermath than his words. I had not the first idea what he was talking about. Our hostess could only say, as if in a dream, "I do not understand you, Mr. Holmes."

"Do you not? Then I will explain."

"He is not here!" The desperate cry was so unlike her habitual composure that I felt the skin of my back creep with cold.

"If you mean," said Holmes, "that he could not be here without your knowledge, I will go so far as to accept that. I beg you, however, do not torment yourself by denials until you hear what I have to say."

She made no reply but stared at him, as if one or the other of them had gone mad. Holmes continued.

"We are asked to believe that your brother Abraham, at the allotted time of no later than 7:45 on Sunday evening, cranked up the chain of the lantern mechanism in the Old Light at Sutton Cross. At the same time, he must have wound up the clock and the governor which controls the mechanism in order that it should continue to run correctly. Somewhen soon after that, he was summoned by a gunshot from the darkened beach. We do not know precisely what happened there between your brothers but soon afterwards Roland Chastelnau died. We presume that he drowned, from whatever cause."

"I know that, Mr. Holmes," she said with quiet reproach.

"Abraham, it appears, attempted to return to the lighthouse. That should have been straightforward enough. However, it is alleged that Roland meant to ensure, whatever happened on the beach, that his elder brother should never reach the Old Light alive. Earlier that day, he had therefore adjusted the position of the iron shutters across the glass panes of the lantern dome. No one would have gone up there to check them, for the glass was cleaned that morning. No one would have seen the direction of the beam by daylight."

She was holding a pocket handkerchief to her mouth and her head was bowed.

"The truth, Miss Chastelnau, is best. The altered direction of the beam, shining through the darkness a little closer to King's Lynn and further from the Boston Deeps, was surely intended to lure its victim into the estuary and the quicksands. That would explain why his body was never found. If Roland had succeeded in such a plot, he had only to return to the Old Light as the tide ebbed and adjust the shutters to their original position. Unfortunately, he himself was drowned before the ebb. The misalignment of the shutters was therefore discovered by Dr. Watson and myself. That was intended to be conclusive evidence of Roland's guilt."

"Intended?" she cried, looking up suddenly. "I do not understand. What Dr. Watson has just told me is surely the truth."

"And I have to tell you that it is quite impossible."

"Why?"

"For two very simple reasons. Abraham could not have wound that clock at a quarter to eight, or at any time until after nine o'clock. Look at any simple grandfather clock, which the face of this one resembles. There are two keyholes which are covered when the hour hand is between the numerals for three and four—or eight and nine. The clock cannot be wound during those periods."

"It may have been done earlier!"

"When the mechanism of the Old Light was inspected on the following morning, the timer had run down, as it would do after eight hours. The chain would be too heavy for the man who had to crank it up again if it ran longer. Indeed, the skipper of a collier in the Deeps noted in his log at quarter past five that morning that the signal of the Old Light was no longer being transmitted."

"What has that to do with it?" she insisted.

"It has this to do with it, Miss Chastelnau. The indication of foul play was not that the beam of light failed after five o'clock but that it had not stopped before. Had the mechanism been wound as early as eight o'clock the previous evening, the hour hand would then cover the keyhole until after nine. Next morning, the mechanism would have stopped and the Old Light would have failed an hour and a quarter earlier than it did. Someone had returned to the Old Light and wound the mechanism an hour or more after Abraham Chastelnau went down to the sands in response to his brother's gunshot."

She stared at him now with a look of dread which came from trying to guess how much more he knew.

"What happened on the beach," he continued, "may be murder, accident, or misadventure. We can only be sure that Roland drowned, from whatever cause. Abraham lived and knew his brother was lost. He returned safely to the Old Light at about nine o'clock."

"Why was he not trapped in the river by the altered beam of light?" I asked.

"Because it had not yet been altered. Whatever the cause or the outcome of the struggle on the sands, Abraham believed that he might face trial and execution for his brother's death. He had not a single friendly witness to prove that he was guilty only of innocent self-defence, rather than premeditated murder. No one to prove that it was not he but Roland who fired the shot which signalled the beginning of the tragedy. Afterwards, he sat alone in the barrack-room, no doubt in distress and dread. He was alive and Roland was dead. He had very probably seen two figures on the church tower, witnesses of the struggle. The sound of the sexton's rook rifle confirmed it."

Neither of us spoke and Holmes continued.

"Who will believe him? He sees the stern-faced officers setting out from King's Lynn. He sees the dock at the assizes and the black cap put on by the judge who assures him that he will be hanged by the neck until he is quite dead. Worst of all, he sees the dreadful weeks in the condemned cell, hears the hangman's knock and imagines the last walk across the prison yard to the tall shed with its thirteen steps leading up to the waiting noose."

At last there was a sob from Miss Chastelnau. Holmes ignored her.

"The Old Light became a trap as the tide rose. He had only minutes to escape before the flood cut him off from the land. He went up to the lantern-room and wound the mechanism. It must run for as long as possible to conceal his absence. Then he altered the iron shutters to misdirect the beam of white light so that he might appear to have been its victim. Desperation sometimes breeds inspiration. You follow me? Those who inquired into the mystery would of course find the shutters altered. With luck, however, Roland would be found drowned. Abraham would have vanished. Where else was he but deep in the shivering sands, lured there by someone who had altered those shutters? What other man could have done that but his brother? Abraham would be searched for no longer. He did all this, and then he made his escape across the fens or the beach, as the tide filled the sandbank under the Old Light. He knew that the longer he was missing, the more certain it would seem that he had been decoyed into the quicksands by the river's edge and had died in their embrace."

"Suppose Abraham set the trap of the shutters for Roland?" I asked.

"Then Abraham need not have fled. Accidental death by drowning would be the verdict. Abraham need only slide the shutters back to their usual angle and there would be no case against him. This is something more."

"And what of the evil that he confessed to?" I asked. "What has he done?"

"I cannot tell you in his absence. I beg you, Miss Chastelnau, bring him in. I promise that I wish no ill to either of you and that I will help you if I can."

This was extraordinary! Had Sherlock Holmes tracked down a murderer only to offer him help?

The poor woman at the centre of the drama stood up and went to the door. Almost at once she returned, followed by a tall loose-limbed man with a ruddy complexion. He did not look like a fellow of great intelligence as his eyes flicked at each of us in turn. Holmes stood up and held out his hand.

"Mr. Abraham Chastelnau?"

Miss Chastelnau intervened, as if protecting a wild animal from those who hunted it.

"My brother watched you come into the hall and feared that you were police officers who had come for him."

"No," said Holmes calmly, "he need not fear that. Pray, Mr. Chastelnau, stand over here in the bay of the window. Face the light. Watson too, if you please. Have no fear, Abraham; my friend is a doctor. Perhaps he is the doctor for whom you composed your letter, and then could not bring yourself to send it."

I stared at Chastelnau's face. It was strong-featured but round. The jaw-bone and, indeed, the neck had been disfigured by small and inflamed lumps or swellings, long healed over. I would have expected to find similar marks on his chest and shoulders, had I examined them. The infections had come, suppurated, and healed over, but they had never disappeared.

"I believe, Mr. Chastelnau, that you have been a martyr to scrofula, have you not?" I asked.

"I have heard it sometimes called that, sir. I do not quite know what it might be."

"Your brother may have teased you unkindly?"

"He did sometimes, sir, but I would not kill a man for that—nor kill him for anything."

Sherlock Holmes intervened.

"Dr. Watson tells you that it is scrofula. But have you sometimes heard it called the King's Evil?"

"Mostly that, sir. I was taught how a king a thousand years ago, Edward the Confessor, was given power by the Pope to cure it. Afterwards, a king or queen had only to touch a man or a woman. They might have such a curse as mine taken from them.

Ornaments blessed by a king might do it. There was King Edward III. He could cure poor people by giving them a gold coin with St. Michael on one side and a ship on the other. An Angel, they called that coin."

For the second time since our arrival in Suffolk, I heard a few lines of Shakespeare quoted, this time by Holmes.

"The King cured, did he not, what the Bard calls strangely visited people? I daresay you are not familiar with the play of Macbeth.

> The mere despair of surgery he cures,
> Hanging a golden stamp about their necks,
> Put on with holy prayers."

"Who would look at me, as I am?" asked Abraham Chastelnau quietly.

"Because of the evil within you?"

"With the wickedness coming out through the sores, as I was taught, sir."

I could not let this mumbo-jumbo go on.

"I had better tell you," I said, "that what you have is not an evil curse but a chronic tubercular condition. It is not as grave as consumption, but it will produce hard red swellings which commonly suppurate."

"And what is all that, sir?"

"It is advice that you should seek a better diet, sunlight, exercise, and bathing. All those together will take you a good long way."

"And the Chester Cross?" Holmes inquired of Chastelnau. "If that is what it was."

Light returned to the poor fellow's eyes.

"I cannot tell, sir. It came from the oil-cake works in my father's time. It had been thrown to one side, left in a drawer with the pebbles. I took them all when we came away. I cannot say where it was from. I heard it was bought with the pebbles as tinker's magic for a shilling or two in my grandfather's time. We never knew where the tinker had it from. But I hoped it might be the very one His Majesty King John had blessed all those years ago. For then surely its touch might cure me."

Holmes led him to a chair and sat him down.

"Now, if you please, tell us the story of the sands."

Abraham Chastelnau knew what was meant but looked up at us without a qualm.

"Roland and I never got on, sir, but the cross and the stones was the worst of it. Trumpery, he called them. When we first went to the Old Light, he swore to throw them all into the sea."

"And that was why you cut a gap in the ledge at the back of the clock-case and slid the metal fragment in its place?" I suggested. Abraham Chastelnau nodded.

"And the pebbles I wrapped and pushed to the back of the table drawer. That Sunday night, I went to wind the mechanism of the clock and crank the chain of the lantern weight. It was just before eight o'clock. But when I opened the clock-case, I saw the metal piece had gone. I didn't bother to wind anything, but went to the table drawer. Four of the five pebbles had gone. He'd missed one of them because I always carried it with me for luck."

"And the letter?" I asked. "Surely he would have taken that?"

Abraham Chastelnau shook his head.

"No, sir, for he was no hand at reading."

"You heard the shot?"

"Just as I was looking in the drawer. I heard his gun and went straight down, not knowing what he might do. He always said I was a simpleton to believe such things; he'd throw them in the sea. It was dark and wet all round by then, no hard sand underfoot."

"You fought him?"

"I went for him to get the piece of the cross and the pebbles back. He'd got them in his hands. As we struggled, I said where was the harm in them. I'm stronger than he was and he'd been drinking. He did sometimes. I got the better of him and threw him down but I thought the pebbles fell. He tried to sling the piece of the cross towards the sea but it never went far. When we broke away from each other, I went down on my knees to find the stones and the metal. Roland ran off, along the beach with the tide after him and the drink driving him on. I found no pebbles, after all. I still ran after him, not to do harm, but he turned and raised the gun. I was the stronger and he knew it, but I daren't get near his gun—not even to save him. He drew further off and further off."

"Did he fire?" I asked.

"He kept making to. The distance between us seemed to grow. I tried to get closer, shouting at him to come back and not to be a damned fool, for he was in softer sand and almost to his knees in water. He might still have got back but then he fired in earnest. The sea was so far in, I hardly heard the shot above the surf, but I saw the flash. Something went wrong when he fired that seemed to knock him off his balance into the surf. The shot went well past me, but I jumped down and stayed down, for he might have reloaded the other barrel before this. When I looked up, I couldn't see him again, only the surf booming in. High tide and low tide there is miles apart. When it come in, that sea can move like an express train. With dark coming on, there was such water between us, all of a sudden, that I couldn't get near him nor see him. Only the surf. And that was all."

"Did you know that you were seen from the church tower?" I asked.

"I thought we must have been noticed when I heard the rook rifle. If they saw us fighting, not for the first time, and only one come back, they'd swear I'd choked him or chased him to his death. I'd never stand a chance. Better they should think we'd both gone into the sea, Roland in one of our fights and me on the way home. I went back to the Old Light, changed the shutters a little, wound up the chain, and then came away. I thought of everything, except the letter in the drawer."

"And then you came here?" Holmes asked.

"I lived rough on the fens for several days. I know how to do that. When my sister came to you in London, she didn't know I was alive. That's true. I kept clear almost a week. Then I heard they'd found the body. After that I came to her, having nowhere else to go."

From the settee, where she had been sitting with her face in her hands, Miss Chastelnau spoke at last.

"I do not own this house or much that is in it, but I have a little money. I would give it all to him. I thought if he could get to Hull, with no one looking for him because he was believed drowned, he could find a crossing to Amsterdam and be safe there. It would take only a few hours."

"But I could not do it," Chastelnau said. "What was there for such as I in a place like that?"

"Admirable," said Holmes sardonically. "Tell me, Miss Chastelnau, how long would your little money last in Amsterdam? What would happen to your brother when it was gone? He does not speak Dutch nor does he know the people. He has no work. What is there then, except the danger that before long an inquisitive observer may put two and two together?"

There was a silence in the ornate little room with its view of the sunny garden and the gravel drive. Then Miss Chastelnau spoke again.

"If you do not propose to betray us, what would you have us do?"

My friend turned to the young man first.

"Because my name is Sherlock Holmes, there are people who believe I set myself above the law. On rare occasions, that is true.

If I am to judge you now, I believe that what you have told us closely resembles the truth. I believe that you did not set out for the beach with murder in your heart. Your story of your brother having the pebbles appears to be true, for they were found in his pocket. Both barrels of the shotgun had been fired, though only one was reported as being used to summon you. He meant you harm, but he drowned without injuring you. Perhaps the post-mortem will find that he was in drink. These facts are not conclusive evidence of your innocence, but they are enough for belief. Yet, even so, they would be closely fought."

He got up from his chair and, as was his custom on such occasions in Baker Street, crossed to the window and continued.

"At the mercy of a skilled prosecutor, you would do badly before a judge and jury. As a matter of law, perhaps you have a case to answer. Yet, as a matter of justice, I shall not betray you."

Now he turned and spoke to both of them.

"A man travelling alone may be suspect when a couple is not. If you love your brother, Miss Chastelnau, travel across the Pennine hills with him to Birkenhead docks. Travel as a betrothed couple, if you wish. Take two berths on an emigrant ship. Single men and women are separated at either end of such a vessel but may associate for an hour or so in the evening. That will suit your purposes and your story. Among so many hundreds or thousands, you are unlikely to be remarked. The voyage to Australia under sail will take three months. By then, the Sutton Cross mystery will be stale news."

They both watched him, but neither spoke. Holmes continued.

"When you reach Queensland or New South Wales, the country you have left will have forgotten you. The one you have arrived in will know nothing of you and will not be looking for you. You can safely be brother and sister once more. You are both young enough to begin again. Such will be the last days of the old life and the first of the new."

Miss Chastelnau thought for a moment.

"There are only three girls in residence at the moment, Mr. Holmes. I have already communicated with their parents to explain the bereavement I have suffered. I have received an undertaking that they may all be transferred to the Abbey Close school in Lincoln. As for these premises, the lease has not long to run and the rent has been paid."

Holmes nodded. He opened his leather bag and took out an object wrapped in lint.

"Abraham Chastelnau, this shall be yours. It may be a holy relic or, for all I know, a tinker's trick. At least one of the pebbles is a sapphire and the metal upright is gold of a common quality, not in itself of great value. If it has lacked healing properties over the past centuries, may it assume them now for you."

10

So it was that we left Mablethorpe and Sutton Cross, returning to our quarters in Baker Street. The three months of an emigrant voyage passed and nothing more was heard or printed concerning the mystery of the Old Light. Several months later, an envelope arrived by post with my name upon it. It bore two lines of thanks from Alice Chastelnau. There was no address, but it had been stamped in Brisbane. I handed it to Holmes across the breakfast table. He read the lines and handed it back with a muted snort.

"Well, let us hope they will be happy. Curious, Watson, that you have surely noticed her partiality for Abraham over Roland and yet never remarked the possibility that she might not be his sister."

I was thunderstruck by this.

"How can that be?"

"Because she is perhaps his mother?"

"Impossible!"

"Put together the little pieces of the puzzle. She left home suddenly, at fifteen, for her health. Her father's new wife accompanied her to the seaside. Many months of convalescence followed, for a convenient touch of consumption. The two were visited by old John Chastelnau. Shortly before their return from the seaside, news was sent to Sutton Cross that Abraham Chastelnau had been born to the step-mother. Or was he?"

"Preposterous!"

"Is it? Suppose the mother remained in touch with the child and a little learning rubbed off. He may appear something of a Neanderthal, but do you not recall how he wrote 'physician' for 'doctor' and 'afflicted' for 'suffering from'? Not to mention his recollections of Edward the Confessor and Edward III."

"Absurd!"

"Very well, old fellow, you have only to go to the registrar of births, marriages, and deaths in Somerset House. Look up the name Chastelnau and, in this case, the mother's maiden name. I would not be surprised to find that it was also Chastelnau."

"I shall do no such thing. Even were it true, there are some things which it is better not to know—and certainly better not to hunt after."

He shrugged and sighed before opening the newspaper at a fresh page. He spoke from behind it.

"Very well. A hint to you, old fellow. I recall that in the lantern-room of the Old Light I congratulated you upon some little discovery and remarked that we should make a criminal investigator of you yet. It seems I was in error. There is a certain lack of morbid persistence in your method which must always be a handicap to your powers of detection."

III

The Case of the Portuguese Sonnets

1

In the archives of Sherlock Holmes, few papers have been more jealously guarded than those which touch upon blackmail or extortion. How strange it is that these should include a small collection of literary manuscripts and rare first editions acquired in the course of an investigation in 1890. They are items which Oxford's Bodleian Library or the British Museum or wealthy collectors like John Pierpont Morgan might have fought over in the auction rooms of the world.

To the present day, most of these treasures remain unknown to literature or scholarship. In the Baker Street files repose such lost works as the manuscript of Lord Byron's Don Juan in the New World, in the poet's own hand. Its stanzas confirm the great romantic rebel's ambition to make his home in the land of Thomas Jefferson. Among other manuscripts is The Venetian Nun: A Gothic Tale, written in 1820 by the notorious William Beckford, creator of the short-lived extravaganza of Fonthill Abbey. A further portfolio contains the monologue of a famous heretic facing the flames in fourteenth-century Florence, "Savonarola to the Signoria," apparently omitted by Robert Browning from his collection of Men and Women in 1855.

A shelf of rare editions, which Holmes acquired during the same investigation, was equally remarkable. He was particularly fond of a small octavo volume in pinkish wrappers. It bore the simple title of "Sonnets By E. B. B." At the foot of the cover was printed, "Reading: Not For Publication, 1847." Such was the first appearance of Sonnets from the Portuguese, written by Elizabeth Barrett to express her love for her bridegroom, Robert Browning, at the time of their elopement and marriage in the previous year. No more than three or four copies of the private 1847 edition have survived. It was intended for intimate friends, the printing arranged by Miss Mary Russell Mitford. Sherlock Holmes's copy bore a pencil inscription on the fly-leaf "For Miss Mitford, E. B. B." It was Mrs. Browning's reminder that this copy had been set aside for her friend.

How odd that half a century later, such a treasure should find its way into the pocket of a dead blackmailer.

2

The case occurred almost ten years after my first meeting with Sherlock Holmes. It followed a visit from our Scotland Yard friend Inspector Tobias Gregson on 24 April 1890. He was now in the habit of calling upon us of an evening, once a week, sharing a glass or two of single malt and passing on the detective gossip of the day.

In the course of conversation on this occasion, he mentioned that a man in a plaid overcoat was reported to have been found dying in a Chelsea gutter. The man in question was known to the police as Augustus Howell, of whom I had never heard. It appeared that he had been suspected from time to time of demanding money with menaces, but nothing had ever been proved against him. Gregson now told us that shortly before he left his office that evening, a report of the man's death had come in. It seemed that the gutter in which he lay was outside a bar in Kinnerton Street, Chelsea, and that the victim's throat had been cut. Between his teeth was wedged a gold half-sovereign coin. Several years later I was to learn, in our investigation of "The Red Circle," that in the underworld of Naples this is the traditional reward of a blackmailer or a police informer.

Our detective agency, as Holmes now liked to call it, had rarely received a complaint of blackmail. I had found this surprising at first because blackmail is surely one of the most common causes that drive a man or a woman to seek advice from a confidential investigator. However, the details that Gregson gave us on that April evening suggested that the more robust victims of extortion may scorn the services of a private detective and employ those of a professional assassin.

Gregson ended his brief summary of the message received by Scotland Yard with an important nod, as if to say, "So there!"

Holmes looked back at him and intoned, almost accurately, a line of Shakespeare from *Macbeth*.

"He should have died hereafter! Indeed, my dear Gregson, in Howell's case I can assure you he probably will continue to do so, as he has done many times before!"

"I don't think I follow you there, Mr. Holmes. How could the man be dead before this?"

Holmes lay back in his chair and began to guffaw with delight. Then he composed himself.

"A hint to you, Gregson. In a case that involves Augustus Howell, steer well clear of the matter. Let some other poor devil at Scotland Yard beat his brains out over it."

"I do not follow your drift, Mr. Holmes, but I should not have thought this a matter to be made fun of."

"Then you quite evidently do not know your man. Have you any idea how many times Augustus Howell has died in the last thirty years of his disgraceful career? At least four, to my knowledge. Notice of his death is generally followed by a post-obit sale of his effects at Christie's or Sotheby's. His announcement of his own death is a convenient method by which he escapes his creditors from time to time. However, if what you are told is true, it seems that someone may have settled accounts with him in a more conclusive style. Or perhaps he has merely performed his usual stunt with a little more melodrama, a touch more grand guignol, than usual."

"It can't be done, Mr. Holmes. Surely?"

"Can it not? No more than a year or two back, there was an obituary auction-sale of 'Howell deceased' at Messrs. Christie's in King Street, St. James's. It included paintings by Sir Joshua Reynolds and Thomas Gainsborough, as well as several by the late Mr. Dante Rossetti, whose agent Howell had been. That agency ended when Rossetti discovered that the man was pocketing money from collectors by mortgaging paintings which Rossetti had not done and would probably never do. Naturally, the purchasers all came upon the artist for the money that had been borrowed and spent by his agent. Gussie Howell had also purloined from the painter's studio Rossetti's sketch for the Venus Astarte. By imitating Rossetti's monogram on the canvas, he sold it as the definitive work at a handsome price to one of his more gullible connoisseurs."

Gregson was now paying attention.

"And the Reynolds, Mr. Holmes? And the Gainsboroughs?"

"For some time, Howell lived as man and wife with a woman in Bond Street, Rosa Corder. By profession she was a painter of horses and dogs. He trained her as what he called a facsimilist—in plain English, a forger. Between them they also produced copies of pictures for clients of questionable tastes. Some rather objectionable paintings by Fuseli were copied for sale, which was the cause of their landlord giving them notice."

"Well, I never did!" said Gregson thoughtfully. "I can tell you confidentially, Mr. Holmes, we do have records at Scotland Yard of Mr. Howell as a young man. A sympathiser with Orsini, he was, in the conspiracy to blow up the Emperor Napoleon III outside the Paris Opera. As the law stood then, there was nothing criminal in sympathising with an attempt. That was soon altered. I also remember from our Home Office records, in the time of Lord Aberdare, that Mr. Howell was the person who arranged for Mrs. Rossetti's coffin to be dug up from Highgate Cemetery. It was done at the dead of night in order that Mr. Rossetti's poems might be retrieved. Very rum business all round. Born in Portugal of an English father, was Mr. Howell."

"Indeed," said Holmes with a chortle, "and brought to England in the nick of time at sixteen, following a nasty outbreak of card-sharping in Lisbon and threats made with stiletto knives. I know him only at second hand, but even I have heard him called, with whatever justification, an arrant rascal, a filthy blackmailer, an impudent trickster, a ruffian, a polecat, a libeller, and a congenital liar. Take your pick, my dear Gregson! I once heard Mr. Rossetti recite a poem which he had composed after dismissing his former agent. It went something like this:

> There's a forger and scoundrel named Howell,
> Who lays on his lies with a trowel.
> When he gives-over lying,
> It will be when he's dying,
> For living is lying with Howell.

Poor fellow! You know, he is so utterly devoid of redeeming features that I rather have a soft spot for the rogue. There, but for the good fortune of my present occupation, go I."

"You would be a blackmailer?" inquired Gregson sceptically.

Holmes made a deprecating gesture.

"You would never convict him of blackmail. He is far too clever for that. It was Howell who introduced the young poet Swinburne to a genteel house of ill-repute in Circus Road, Regent's Park. Such gilded youths sported there on idle afternoons among rosy-cheeked damsels, in a manner lamentably reminiscent of the late Comte de Sade."

I was intrigued to see that Gregson, always the cocksure

man of the world, went suddenly and deeply red. Holmes continued.

"Howell and the fledgling poet exchanged letters, in which these rather childish goings-on were much discussed. At the peak of his fame, ten years later, Mr. Swinburne received a message from his former acquaintance. Howell had pasted all the poet's letters into a keepsake album. Having fallen into penury, he had been obliged to pawn it. Now he had not the money to redeem it. The pawnbroker had lost patience and proposed to offer it immediately for public sale. Within the week, Admiral and Lady Jane Swinburne paid a very large sum to buy back from the money-lender this chronicle of their son's youthful folly. The proceeds were no doubt shared gleefully between Howell and his accomplice pawnbroker. Now, make what you can of that, friend Gregson."

Gregson recovered himself.

"Strike me down!" he said thoughtfully. "As neat a piece of stitching as I ever heard of!"

"Precisely. On other occasions, where a client was difficult, Howell would encourage him by giving well-publicised readings from such compromising correspondence to groups of invited guests—until the author was minded to buy back his indiscretions. Do you really believe that, having gone to such lengths to conceal their son's folly, the Swinburne parents would enter a witness-box and reveal it? In any case, could you prove blackmail in the matter of the pawned letters? Was it not, perhaps, a friendly warning from Howell, by which the author of the letters might mend the damage done? And as for recitals of the correspondence, if you were to send me a private letter and I were to read it to others, it is certainly not the act of a gentleman, but it is hardly criminal."

"And have you known this person for long, Mr. Holmes?"

"I repeat that I cannot claim a close acquaintance, Gregson.

Indeed, though I have heard of him several times, I have not seen him for almost ten years. That was when I represented a client, Mr. Sidney Morse, in the so-called case of 'The Owl and the Cabinet.' Howell's name had always been pronounced 'Owl' by the cockney Pre-Raphaelite painters and poets. They made a joke of it."

Light was beginning to dawn behind Gregson's eyes.

"Was this matter of Mr. Morse also to do with Mr. Whistler, the American painter?"

"You are there before me, as usual, Gregson. In 1878, Whistler was going to Venice. He had sold to Mr. Morse a valuable Japanese cabinet, which had an upper and a lower half. Mr. Whistler left delivery in the hands of Howell. Mr. Morse came to Howell's address on a Saturday, paid for the cabinet, and was to have it after the weekend. The minute he left, Howell summoned a pawnbroker and pledged the cabinet to him for a considerable sum. The upper half went on a cart to the pawnshop, where Howell was paid. He promised to bring the lower half after the weekend."

"I think I see the trick," said Gregson suddenly.

"Perhaps you do. On Monday, Howell delivered the lower half to Mr. Morse. He claimed the upper half had been damaged in moving it. It had gone for repair and he would deliver it upon its return. Naturally he then informed Chapman, the pawnbroker, that it was the lower half which had been damaged and had gone for repair."

Holmes drew breath and suppressed another onset of laughter.

"Howell then disappeared with both payments, leaving each dupe with half the cabinet. Both men trusted Howell. Knowing no better, they thought that half a cabinet is no use to a thief on its own. How little they knew Gussie! The legal proceedings necessary to settle the matter lasted for three years. During that time, my services were retained by Mr. Morse. Mr. Whistler on his return was obliged to redeem the lower half of the cabinet from the pawnbroker, repaying the loan as well as three years' interest and restoring the furniture to its rightful purchaser. Mr. Howell hastily advertised his own death again and yet another post-obit sale of his effects was held."

Gregson looked almost overwhelmed.

"Oh dear," he said. "Oh dear, oh dear, oh dear!"

Holmes chuckled.

"One of the innocents at the sale was L. H. Myers, son and disciple of Frederick Myers of the Society for Psychical Research. The son was able to report to his father a celestial vision of 'Howell deceased' at Christie's sale-room. The lad was examining a locket, said to contain the hair of Mary Queen of Scots. He felt convinced that the shade of it was wrong. At that moment, a vision of the dead sidled up to him and said, 'I shouldn't bid for that if I were you, it's only Rosa Corder's.'"

And Holmes began to guffaw again, quite helplessly.

I could not see that such a maelstrom of dishonesty and extortion was an occasion for quite so much merriment. But just then there was a tap at the sitting-room door, soon after nine o'clock, and Mrs. Hudson's "Buttons" appeared with a telegram envelope in his hand.

"Wire for Mr. Gregson, gentlemen. No reply expected."

He proffered it to the Scotland Yard man and withdrew. We waited while Gregson read it. Whatever the message, it seemed to restore confidence in the inspector, who had just had the wind taken out of his sails, so to speak. He looked up.

"Well, doctor! Well, Mr. Holmes! Here's one for you. You can believe what you like about Mr. Howell. Here's a message that came in less than an hour ago from a duty constable at the Home Hospital in Fitzroy Square."

There was a twinkle in Holmes's eye as he inquired.

"Are you quite sure, that the wire has not been sent to Scotland Yard by Howell himself, masquerading as the duty constable? He is more than capable of that!"

Gregson glared at him—the only time I had ever seen such a thing—and continued to read.

"In Mr. Howell's greatcoat pocket they found a book, Sonnets by Mrs. Elizabeth Barrett Browning. An old copy, by the look of it. Nothing else of value on him. Also, the last words that the poor fellow was able to articulate, several times over, were 'Leaves of grass.'"

And so the sonnets came into the case, though as yet they meant nothing to me. But what had Howell to do with Walt Whitman?

"Leaves of Grass, by Mr. Whitman," I said quickly, for, having read and greatly admired the new American poet, I recognised the title of his work. "Does the message say whether Howell is now alive or dead?"

Before Gregson could reply, Holmes cut in.

"Whatever the answer, in the case of Augustus Howell, I fear it is very little to be depended upon."

And he chuckled again.

3

Gregson was mollified by another glass of single malt and a cigar. That should have been end of the matter. A fortnight later, however, we received two visitors of a very different type. A few days previously, Holmes had remarked to me that a Mr. and Mrs. Browning were coming to consult him at 2:30 P.M. on 8 May over a matter of some delicacy, which they had not detailed in advance. I gathered that they were the son and daughter-in-law of the two great poets of that name.

The famous Robert Browning had died only the year before, but the equally famous Mrs. Elizabeth Barrett Browning had been dead for almost thirty years. The present visit of their descendants to us might seem a coincidence, after the discovery of the Sonnets in Howell's pocket. Sherlock Holmes, however, was not a great believer in the law of coincidence. He lived in a world of cause and effect.

Mrs. Hudson knocked on the door at the appointed hour and announced, with a look of self-conscious formality, "Mr. Robert Wiedemann Penini Browning and Mrs. Fannie Cornforth Browning."

I recognised, as any reader of the newspapers might, the distinctive names of Robert Browning's son. He was universally known as "Pen" Browning, an easy-going young man who had taken up painting and sculpture rather than poetry. I found him slighter in build than I would have expected. At thirty, he had almost the look of a man who might not yet be fully grown. His face was still youthfully round, though with full dark whiskers and thinning hair. His was quite a contrast to the bold head and profile of his late father. Fannie Cornforth Browning appeared several years his junior. She was a fine and handsome woman, rather plump and with the blue eyes and red hair of a Titian painting. She had been, as I understood from the newspapers, American by birth and English by upbringing.

When the introductions were over and the Brownings were seated, it was Pen Browning, if I may so call him, who took the initiative.

"Mr. Holmes—Dr. Watson—my wife and I have lately had occasion to approach Inspector Gregson of Scotland Yard. He can do little for us but he has suggested that we should consult you. It is a complicated and delicate matter. I fear that it concerns the death of a man called Augustus Howell, whose manipulation of the truth and downright chicanery had begun to threaten my parents' reputation and our own peace of mind."

"I am sorry to hear it," said Holmes deferentially—he had put on his black frock coat for the occasion—"I know of the man Howell, of course, and I know of his reported death. I also know from Mr. Gregson that a copy of your mother's poems was found with his body."

Pen Browning nodded.

"He had been a complete stranger to me until I received a note from him. He suggested that he was prepared to sell the volume of poems to me—and a good deal else concerning my parents—for a very considerable sum of money. Indeed, I was to have met him on the following day. He said he was an agent of some kind and authorised to do so. He claimed that he had private papers in his possession, confidential papers emanating from my parents, which he was commissioned to put into a public auction on behalf of their owner. The volume of Sonnets itself was an extremely rare private edition of 1847, three years before general publication. It was his approach which brought me to London last month. You may perhaps know that Mrs. Browning and I live most of the year in Venice."

"Indeed," said Holmes. "The Palazzo Rezzonico on the Grand Canal, I believe?"

"Correct. My father bought it and bequeathed it to me. You may also know something of the late Jeffrey Aspern's life in Venice?"

Holmes looked a little surprised.

"Who does not know of Jeffrey Aspern? A precursor of Edgar Allan Poe, who left Virginia in 1818 and lived so much of his life in Europe. The friend of Byron and, I believe, briefly of Shelley during their last years in Italy. Does not Edward Trelawny in his *Recollections* have something to say about their meetings in Venice and Ravenna?"

"And still more in his private papers."

"Most interesting," said Holmes enthusiastically. "I cannot pretend to be a literary critic but I have always considered that Aspern's early promise remained unfulfilled. However, his 'Juanita' lyrics will live as long as poetry is read. His dates, if I remember correctly, were 1788 to 1863. He certainly outlived Lord Byron and his English counterparts. Like William Wordsworth, he lasted too long, for a romantic poet, and he worked past his best."

"You are remarkably well informed, sir." Pen Browning looked at Holmes and then glanced quickly away again as though coming to the painful part of the matter. "You know that Aspern's former companion, Juanita Bordereau, died last year as a very old woman?"

"I had read a notice of her death in the papers. She was quite ninety years old, I believe."

"She became Aspern's young mistress in 1820. The worse he treated her, the more devoted to him she seemed to become. After his death, twenty-seven years ago, she was joined at the Casa Aspern in Venice by her younger sister, Tina. They lived there until last year, as a pair of elderly spinsters. The house lies on a small canal in a quiet backwater."

"Indeed," said Holmes again. His eyes invited Pen Browning to continue.

"Since her sister's death, Tina Bordereau has left the house empty and returned to America. The estate is a complicated one, for there was no marriage between the poet and his mistress, and no children. Everything is in the care of executors and agents. Yet the Casa Aspern apparently contains treasures of great literary value, as well as secrets capable of creating an insupportable scandal. I am told that in the locked drawers of a Napoleonic escritoire there lies the whole unpublished correspondence of Lord Byron and Aspern."

The eyes of Sherlock Holmes narrowed in astonishment. Pen Browning continued.

"There are also said to be manuscripts of poems by Byron which have never seen the light of day. I have even been offered by a dealer the chance to purchase the manuscript of an unpublished novel of 1820, supposed to have been bequeathed by Byron to Aspern when his lordship left Venice on his final and fatal voyage to Greece. It is The Venetian Nun: A Gothic Tale, by William Beckford, the so-called "Abbot of Fonthill." The only known copy to survive, it had been presented by the author to Byron. Goodness knows what more there may be. Worst of all, for me, there are said to be unknown poems and letters of my father's and of my mother's. That is what brings me here."

"Remarkable," said Holmes tolerantly.

"There are alleged to be letters written by both my parents. These may be rough drafts but they are none the less compromising. They include intimate letters to one another. Also my father's private letters to close female friends written by him after my mother's death in 1861. He was very close to Miss Isa Blagden while in Florence, as was my mother, and the attachment continued long after his bereavement. They exchanged letters sometimes every day. The same was true in London during his attachment to Miss Julia Wedgwood, also after my mother's death. Such women were an intimate part of his life. There was nothing vicious or improper in these friendships—hardly even indiscreet. Yet it is now suggested by the agents that some of these Casa Aspern letters, containing expressions of private affections, are already in the hands of dealers."

He paused, as if watching us for incredulity. If so, he found none.

"I fear," said Holmes, "that a letter becomes the property of the person to whom it is addressed, though the right to publish it does not. However, the contents may be made known."

"Such stories are lies, Mr. Holmes, or at the best misinterpretations. How any such papers could have reached Aspern—let alone the Bordereau sisters—I do not know. Domestic dishonesty is unlikely, but chicanery may well be the answer. A housemaid may have a follower. In truth, he cares nothing for her but a great deal for access to the house, to documents which he may steal and sell. Something of that sort. As for Jeffrey Aspern, of course my father, and indeed my mother, knew him. I do not think they found him *simpatico*, and I am sure they would not have entrusted such papers to him knowingly. Of Robert Browning's poetry, there is said to be a rejected prologue to *The Ring and the Book* among the Aspern papers, and also dramatic monologues excluded by my father from his great collection of Men and Women in 1855."

He paused once more.

"Pray continue, Mr. Browning!" The impatience had vanished from Holmes's eyes.

"I doubt if the Bordereau sisters knew the half of what was there. They were not connoisseurs of poetry but, if you will forgive me, money-grubbing harpies! They lived a secluded life after Aspern's death and I never met them. My father, of course, lived in Italy until 1861 and had certainly known Aspern in his later years. My father also returned to us in Venice for part of each year and died there in December."

"And you have seen none of the material which is said to lie in Aspern's escritoire?"

"Not as yet. I was first informed of it by a hint from the notary, Angelo Fiori, who had acted at one time for the Aspern estate. Fortunately his sister is a family friend who nursed my father in his last days. It was through her that her brother communicated with me."

Holmes glanced at his pipe, but forbore to light it in the presence of Fannie Browning.

"Forgive me, Mr. Browning, but how would so many private papers of your father's come to be in this collection unless he gave them to Jeffrey Aspern or the Misses Bordereau? Could a housemaid and her follower account for all that you have described? In any case, surely Aspern himself was dead before most of your father's letters to female friends, of which you speak, could have come into his hands."

"Exactly so, Mr. Holmes. Perhaps they have simply been stolen by an intruder and sold to the Bordereau sisters. Perhaps they are innocent letters misinterpreted in some way. I am at a loss to say. After Aspern's death, the sisters were notorious as dabblers in innuendo and defamation. Lice on the locks of literature, as Lord Tennyson puts it! On one occasion, my father used that very phrase to describe them. He never liked Juanita Bordereau. He thought her meddlesome and troublesome. She was scandalous in her youth; and when she became too old to create scandal, she encouraged it in others. That was how he summed her up. For many years, she had been a collector of documents and any rare editions which had a whiff of sensationalism. William Beckford and the like. Then it seems her tastes became more depraved. She employed scouts, if I may so call them, to attend the sale-rooms or to negotiate privately."

"But she did not negotiate with you or your father, I take it?"

"She would have known better. However, I have been visited by two of these scavengers since my father's death, asking me if I would care to buy back certain papers. I sent them about their business. I see now that it was perhaps not wise to do so. And now Juanita Bordereau is dead. Tina Bordereau has shown no interest in the papers nor in Jeffrey Aspern, except for the money that could be made. Since the death of her sister, she has put the whole business into the hands of agents, whose job it would be to dispose of them at the best price. This is regardless of what damage may be done to the feelings of the living or the reputation of the dead."

"And, of course, the present agent—or one of them—was Augustus Howell?"

Pen Browning lowered his head and nodded.

"I had come to London in order to negotiate with him, but at first he wrote and intimated that I was too late. A good many of the worst items were already in the hands of the auctioneers or the valuers. He explained that he was not empowered by Tina Bordereau to halt their sale. I must buy at public auction."

"He would not negotiate with you?"

"Eventually, he made a concession, as he called it. He would agree to make what he called 'a special price' if I would buy the papers 'sight unseen' before the auction. In other words, with no idea of what I might be getting. Even that seems impossible, now that the wretched man is dead."

"So he would lead us to believe."

"And so you see my predicament, Mr. Holmes. The matter is in the hands of Tina Bordereau, who is heaven knows where and has no interest but money. Before long, these so-called papers will be released to the world."

Holmes walked across to the window and looked down at the traffic of Baker Street in the spring sunshine. Then he turned back.

"Mr. Browning. Before we squander any more of your time or, indeed, your money, I think we must clear the decks a little. You should return to Venice as soon as convenient."

"We are to travel next Monday," said Fannie Browning quietly, "subject to your advice."

"Excellent. The sooner the better. If you wish it, my colleague and I will follow as quickly as we are able. By the end of next week at the latest. As I say, you should return beforehand. At the earliest opportunity, we must get sight of these documents."

"But how?" she exclaimed. "They are scattered among any number of unscrupulous dealers."

"Madam," said Holmes coolly, "when a poisonous cobra has embraced you, it is of no use to struggle with its coils, to fight against its fangs, or stab it here and there. You must sever its head from its body and the coils will fall away soon enough. The Casa Aspern is the head of this conspiracy. That is where we must strike, before it is too late."

"I wish it, Mr. Holmes," Pen Browning broke in passionately. "I would have you act to guard my father's reputation and my mother's. I have inquired a little after this man Howell since I have been in London. I can find only that he boasted of having dived for treasure lying in the wrecks of sunken galleons and of having been sheikh of an Arab tribe in Morocco. He is a braggart and probably a liar. I do not want my father's character to lie in the hands of such a man or those who now continue his work."

"That is commendable indeed," said Holmes. "I believe this is an occasion when speaking ill of the dead may be permitted. He was a thoroughgoing scoundrel—but an effective one."

"Then I would have you go to Venice, to the Casa Aspern if you can, Mr. Holmes. Destroy that nest of deception and slander. You have detective skills and I have not. Believe me, they are needed."

"All this must be done before someone of Howell's type succeeds Howell," Holmes spoke reassuringly, placating the young man. "Who has authority there?"

Pen Browning looked uneasy.

"At present, there is an interregnum. The house is briefly in the hands of the Venetian notary, Fiori, on behalf of Tina Bordereau. She shows no interest in the papers beyond their commercial value. It was only her sister, after all, who had been the poet's great love. Before some other person intervenes or the auction houses hold their sales, I believe it would be possible to negotiate with the friendly notaio. It might be agreed that you should, on my behalf, examine such of my father's papers as are said to be in Aspern's escritoire."

"And then?" Holmes asked warily.

"Mr. Holmes, the love of Robert Browning and Elizabeth Barrett was a great and noble passion, a redemption from sickness and death. It must not be sullied by trash or trade. If I have to pay, I must pay."

Holmes stared long and thoughtfully. Then he spoke.

"Allow me until noon tomorrow to make the necessary arrangements."

"Indeed I will, Mr. Holmes."

Pen Browning was on his feet now, and so was Sherlock

Holmes. Our visitor was shaking my friend's hand with a warmth beyond anything I had expected of him. It was plain to Mr. Browning—as it was to me—that wild horses would not prevent Holmes setting out for Venice as soon as berths could be booked in the wagon-lit of the continental express. There was justice to be done to the memory of a noble man and woman, but that was not all. Holmes's nostrils were twitching to inhale a few molecules of the very same air that Lord Byron and Robert Browning had breathed—and, of course, to fight his now invisible adversary, the late Gussie Howell.

For my own part, I felt subdued by what I had heard. Once we were alone, I could not conceal it.

"This is a bad business, Holmes, however we go about it. Once those papers have been scattered over the earth, there will be no holding back the scandal. Whatever the truth, the wise world will say that there is no smoke without fire."

He was brooding over the pages of the evening Globe and now looked up.

"I will repeat for your benefit, Watson, that the man who would kill the serpent must sever its head. That is the one sure way—and it is the one I shall follow."

I was still not greatly reassured.

4

It was several days later when our train crossed the long railway bridge from the desolate landscape of Mestre to the enchanted island of Venice in its lagoon. Pen Browning was on the station platform to rescue us from pandemonium, briskly commanding the porters and dismissing the officials of the fever hospital, until our bags were accommodated on a launch and ourselves in his gondola.

We had declined his offer of rooms in the Palazzo Rezzonico, in favour of Danielli's Hotel. It would be best, as Holmes put it, to remain "independent." Moreover, Pen Browning was a gifted exponent of the female nude in painting and statuary, which was reputed to have led to domestic disagreements. Fannie Cornforth had been brought up in the strict American Puritan tradition. It would not do, Holmes remarked, to become a party to family quarrels and find ourselves obliged to take sides.

Pen and Fannie Browning had left London three days ahead of us. Since his arrival in Venice, Pen had accomplished almost everything. An inquiry from the Palazzo Rezzonico had been addressed to Signor Angelo Fiori, the notary for the Aspern estate, whose sister Margherita had by great good fortune nursed Robert Browning senior. Fiori cabled at once to Tina Bordereau, informing her that Italian law would require a valuation of the entire Aspern estate before matters could proceed further. He received his instructions within the day. After her sister's death, she had confided to him that she had never been in the least fond of Venice and had long wanted to get away from it. She was even less fond of Jeffrey Aspern, though she had never met him. While it was clear that she would do nothing to help us, her attachment to Aspern's papers remained financial rather than sentimental. Let the estate be valued as soon as possible.

While the gondola rolled side to side in the swell of the Grand Canal created by passing steam launches, we floated between marble palaces and gleams of reflected sunlight. Pen Browning described the latest unproductive negotiation with Tina Bordereau. Angelo Fiori, however, would allow Holmes to see such papers as remained in the Casa Aspern, by appointing him as "assessor" or "valuer" of the questionable material. Miss Bordereau agreed after being warned by Fiori that it would never do for her to sell as genuine what afterwards proved to be fraudulent.

"It's as well you never had the two sisters to deal with, Mr. Holmes," said Pen Browning. "They'd have led you to your ruin, getting all your money and showing you nothing. They haggled like fishwives. They always tried to combinare, as the Italians call it, to make a special price! When that failed, they would wheedle you like stall-holders. 'Perhaps we could find some way of treating you better,' they would say. But you always came out of it worse! As for Aspern, he was one of those fellows at whom such women as Juanita Bordereau flung themselves—and they soon thought that he treated them very badly. I daresay he did."

By such means, we found that we had only Angelo Fiori to deal with. It was now arranged that we should visit the "Palazzo Aspern," as the dilapidated house was absurdly called by the gondoliers, whenever we wished. A housekeeper would be there to arrange whatever we needed—and, of course, to ensure that we did not steal any of the contents. However, any doubt as to our good characters was soon laid to rest, for Miss Bordereau's benefit. At our first meeting, Signor Fiori confided to me that he acted on our behalf after receiving a testimonial to our honesty and integrity written at the request of Mr. Browning by "Signor Lestrade" of Scotland Yard. The name of that famous institution was our "Open Sesame!"

The warmth of the Venetian spring was tempered by a sea breeze across the lagoon, which stirred the net curtains at the windows. Our evenings were spent eating ices or drinking coffee after dinner at Florian's in St. Mark's Square. It was agreeable to pass the twilight away among music and chatter under the lamps, to hear smooth footfalls on polished marble and watch an afterglow of sun touching the low domes and mosaics of the famous basilica.

On our first morning, the gondolier took us into the quiet and shaded domestic waterways, which rather recalled Amsterdam. We came to a clean quiet canal with a narrow footpath running along either bank. The front of the house was of grey and pink stucco, about two hundred years old. A stone balcony ran along its wide façade with pilasters and arches at either end. Holmes pulled at the rusty bell-wire, and the summons was answered by a maid in a shawl.

We entered a long, dusty hall and followed our guide up a high stone staircase, passing fine architectural doors in a building that seemed empty and abandoned. There were brown paintings in tarnished frames. Above us, the stone shields with armorial bearings still retained vestiges of the paint applied to them centuries ago. The floors were so empty and the walls so bare that it was hard to imagine anything of value in such a place. Harder still to think there could be an answer here to the riddle of Augustus Howell, unless he was alive to supply it after all.

"Surely," I had said to Holmes in the train, "he may have announced his own death on previous occasions, but he never claimed to have been murdered."

My friend made no reply but continued to read his Baedeker.

Now we were in the upper rooms with a view of rough-tiled roof-tops and the sunlit lagoon in the distance. There was a garden below us, or rather a tangled enclosure whose stone walls hid it from the world. How could anyone, let alone the Bordereau sisters, have lived in this desolate place just a year ago? What squalor it must have been!

Our guide took out a bunch of keys and unlocked the door ahead of us. It opened on to yet another dusty room with straw-bottomed chairs and rush mats on a red-tiled floor. Its window reflected a cooler light from a northern sky. Almost the greater part of the far wall was taken up by a tall escritoire of dull mahogany, larger than many a wardrobe. Its style was that of the First Empire of Napoleon Bonaparte with brass eagles and regal ornaments. This was surely Jeffrey Aspern's famous "secretary," containing, as his famous poem Old and Young describes it, "the arid secrets of a soul's decay." Its tiers of locked drawers and the cupboards on either side seemed a suitable receptacle for tales of illicit passions or furtive criminality. On a writing-table, which formed the central part of its design, lay a single key to its drawers and cupboards.

"Please," said our guide with a wave towards the writing chair, "you will sit and I will be here if you need me. The key will open all."

I was astonished to hear her speaking in very good English, albeit with an accent.

"I was for some time a translator at the hospital," she said with a smile. "Angelo Fiori is my cousin. The papers of Jeffrey Aspern that were here have nearly been lost twice. The old Miss Bordereau hid them between the mattresses of her bed when she was dying. She called my cousin to add a clause to her will that they were to be buried with her. Perhaps she was a little ashamed of them. It was never done. The young Miss Bordereau burnt a few of them in the kitchen fire on the last night she was here, but the rest are in the drawers. There are also the rare books, but you will find those in the side-cupboards and on the shelves."

"Thank you so much, signora," said Holmes with a gracious half-bow. "You have also met Mr. Howell, I believe?"

She smiled, but there was a hint of concern in her eyes.

"He was here more than a month ago. He went back to England. I did not see him again."

"He left no message of any kind?"

"I do not think so."

She went out without closing the door, and we could hear her busying herself in the next room.

Despite the first heat of the Venetian spring, Sherlock Holmes was still dressed in his formal suit. From the waistcoat of this he now drew a powerful lens, laid it on the writing desk, and set to work. Using the key, he opened the lower drawers. The first contained nothing but dust and chips of wood. The second yielded a few scraps of paper of the most ordinary kind.

He tried the lowest and deepest of the main drawers. Then, with a muttered syllable of satisfaction, he lifted out a decayed olive green portmanteau, which nonetheless looked as though it had been dusted in the past few months—possibly by Tina Bordereau. Underneath this was a folio correspondence box, cased in leather and stamped in gold with Aspern's name.

Holmes sprung the two catches and brought out its contents. He also opened the cupboards to either side of the escritoire, revealing shelves lined with volumes that were almost new and, at the worst, only a little worn. I was not surprised that there should be notebooks and folders of papers. What I had not expected was that so much of the treasure would consist of printed books, most of them of comparatively recent date and in multiple copies. It was a little like a publisher's stockroom. They were still rarities, of course, first printings often inscribed by their authors. I noticed Dante Rossetti's *Verses* printed as late as 1881. The bulk of the volumes were the works of John Ruskin, William Morris, and Algernon Charles Swinburne, as well as Rossetti. There were three rare printings of Robert Browning's poems. Two were inscribed by the poet to Jeffrey Aspern, dating from the 1850s. The third, *Gold Hair*, published after Aspern's death, was inscribed to Juanita Bordereau. How much had the author disliked her after all?

Holmes opened the gold-stamped and leather-bound correspondence box. Here, if our information was correct, lay Jeffrey Aspern's letters from Lord Byron, Robert Browning, and William Beckford, as well as other literary treasures. The papers had been neatly arranged in portfolios, and I would have said this had been done recently, for the covers appeared much newer than their contents. Those papers that I could see looked tarnished by time, but the black ink was far less "rusty" than I had expected.

Holmes stood up, walked to the window, and held a paper to the north light.

"I believe that the usual iron-gall ink of the 1820s has been adulterated by indigo to make the script darker. So far as that goes, what we have appears genuine and is not contradicted by any date in the watermark."

"What is the writing?"

"A corrected page from the manuscript of Canto 6 of *Don Juan*. John Pierpont Morgan would pay a small fortune to add the complete work to his library, in the author's own manuscript. According to the list of papers, it is in Byron's own hand. Notice the date at the top, '1822.' The formation of the first '2' makes it look almost like '1892,' does it not?"

"Very like."

"A forger would have taken care to make both figures '2' look alike. None of us signs a name or writes a line in the same way twice. A perfect forgery may be too consistent, too perfect, as if it has been drawn rather than written. Here you will see in the first line Byron has written, 'There is a Tide. . . .' The letter T in both cases has a loop at either end of its cross-piece. Each letter in the line has a gap before the next one. That is almost too consistent, a cause for suspicion. By the fourth line, however, the poet's pen is flowing freely, rather than hesitating. Every T is joined to the following letter, lacking the loops but sprouting a confident tail."

"And that is all?"

"Far from it, old fellow. However, Lord Byron is the most forged of all the English poets. The appetite for new discoveries is insatiable. In 1872, Schultess-Young foisted on the world two sets of Byron letters said to have belonged to his aunts. They were obvious impostures and the manuscripts were not available for inspection. Nineteen others in his book were examined in manuscript and proved to be the work of De Gibler, who called himself Major Byron and claimed to be the poet's natural son. He had been exposed long before, because the paper on which the letters were written was watermarked ten years after the writer's death!"

Holmes was in his element among so much high-class dishonesty. He sat down at the writing table and adjusted the range of the magnifying lens.

"When a manuscript is examined closely, it is possible to see minute breaks in the line, where the writer has lifted pen from paper. In a genuine copy, as here, there are relatively few places where the pen has been lifted. A forger of modest talents will stop more often, in order to compare his copying with the original. There may also be signs of counterfeiting, when a letter in a word has been patched, as they call it, to make it a more accurate imitation, leaving a feathery appearance."

"And by such clues forgery is detected?"

"Among many others. A true craftsman, of course, will know what I am looking for and will take care to provide me with it. Indeed, a counterfeiter who practices an author's script for long enough can produce a flowing imitation. In that case, we must use other methods of detection. Perhaps the date of ink or paper, sometimes the provenance of the work. I think we may assume that this is a genuine page of Byron's manuscript."

He examined a letter of some kind and then chuckled as he quoted two lines of Don Juan.

"This note was written upon gilt-edged paper,
With a neat little crow quill, slight and new!

We need have no doubt about these two pages. They have been known as a forgery for almost eighty years."

I looked over his shoulder at the narrow page of script, the paper yellowed and the ink rusty. I read the first words, which looked mighty like Byron's hand that had written Don Juan. "Once More, My Dearest. . . ."

Holmes smiled.

"It poses as a letter from Byron to Lady Caroline Lamb. Unfortunately, it was forged by Lady Caroline Lamb herself in 1813 as a means of stealing his portrait. The story is well known. She was insane with love of him, the man whom she called mad, bad, and dangerous to know! She forged this letter in his handwriting, authorising her to go to his publisher John Murray and demand the famous Newstead miniature of the poet. She got the portrait, and he got her letter back from Murray."

Under Lady Lamb's copy of his signature, the poet had

written, "This letter was forged in my name by Lady Caroline Lamb," and he had signed the postscript.

"The two Byron signatures are very much alike."

"Lady Lamb might have made a competent forger in time. However, look at the letter 't' again. In Byron's hand, the cross-stroke extends over the next two letters. She extends it still further. It is a fatal mistake, when forging, to exaggerate such foibles. She also varies her style twice by adding a strong up-stroke before the main down-stroke of the 't.' That is a grave error. A writer who makes a 't' with a strong down-stroke may embellish it, but will hardly precede it with a strong up-stroke. The up-strokes of normal script are light, whereas the down-strokes are strong. Where the pressure of a nib is of uniform strength throughout, as it is here, you may suspect facsimile copying or forgery. In short, however like the two scripts may appear to be, Lady Caroline Lamb's effort raises too many questions to be acceptable."

"How did such a document come into Jeffrey Aspern's hands?"

"It must be from Byron. No doubt on the occasion, a few days before his death, when he bequeathed such treasures to his friends before leaving Venice for Greece."

Despite Aspern's reputation as the recipient of a rich hoard of Byron's correspondence, a good many documents in the leather box were questionable. There was a further forgery, if one can call printed material by that name, again the work of Lady Caroline Lamb. It had been published in 1819, purporting to be a new canto of the poet's Don Juan. Holmes read the opening line.

"'I'm sick of fame—I'm gorged with it—so full. . . .' Heaven preserve us, Watson! It does not even sound like Byron!"

Then he paused. He had put aside this pastiche and was looking at a sheaf of papers that were clipped unevenly together. His face was grave and yet his features were tense with excitement.

"And here, I believe, is the legend of Lord Byron in the United

States! For a good many years before going to fight for Greece against the Turks, it was said that he had determined to make a life for himself as Europe's ambassador to the New World. Who better than an American poet like Jeffrey Aspern to receive his confession?"

He ran his eyes down a sheet of wizened paper, its ink once again rusted by time. Then he passed it to me. I read it with astonishment and a chill in the spine at the thought that I was holding a sheet of paper which the greatest of the romantics once had held and that I must be one of only three or four people to read these lines since Jeffrey Aspern had received them from Byron all those years ago.

Ravenna, April 25, 1821

My dear Aspern,

So you and Murray would have me write a modern epic! You know my opinion of that second-hand school of poetry. But what would you say to my hero's visit to your own country? "Don Juan in the New World"? When anything occurs in it to betray my ignorance of your native Virginia, pray revenge yourself upon the manuscript as freely as you like. If you can observe that condition, let our man take a turn in the footsteps of Thomas Jefferson.

Upon the Virgin land is Juan set
A place of beauteous slaves and tropic morals.
(I don't much wonder that Bob Southey funked it
Or that his women had a score of quarrels.)
Juan lay fast in Venus' toils, whose jet
And agile limbs wore little else but corals.
Pillowed he lay, on skin as hot as Hades,
Treasured by those who sported like true ladies.

Sing, Muse, of Coleridge and the Susquehanna,
(I won't sing Southey since he came in first).
Who knows, from Philadelphia to Savannah,
Which of Juan's conquests would have pleased 'em worst?
Both Senate's wives and maiden queen Susannah
Juan's nocturnal catalogue rehearsed.
O Lords of Golden Horn, stand ye in wonder
To see our hero steal your Sultan's thunder!

Could not you and I contrive to meet this summer? Could you not take a run here with Miss B.—or alone if need be?

Yours ever & truly,
Byron.

I read it again and stood in disbelief. If this meant what it said, the portmanteau in front of us contained an "American epic," written by Byron while still in Venice but corrected by Jeffrey Aspern to give it the authenticity of Virginia and Georgia. Who could forge such a thing? Not Augustus Howell—but Aspern himself!

Yet there was nothing in the document, at first glance, to suggest that its substance was counterfeit. The writing and the style were surely Byron's—as surely as Lady Lamb's were not. The paper appeared identical to other documents of that age which are known to be genuine. The black ink had "rusted." Perhaps most important of all, two stanzas of Byron's poem were embedded in a letter to Jeffrey Aspern, among whose correspondence they had been found. This surely established their provenance beyond question. The style was Byron's, if anything ever was.

If all these facts were so, might not the sheaf of papers, in the portfolio which Holmes was examining, contain one of the great undiscovered literary treasures of our time? Even while Byron led his amorous hero through the gallantries of Seville and Cadiz or the harems of Turkey in Don Juan, his eyes were already raised to the distant prospect of Washington and the Delaware.

I looked at Holmes.

"Can it be true?"

"I should not think so for one minute."

I was utterly deflated. I felt what the forger's dupe always feels at first. With all my heart I wanted these lines to be Byron's own. A cold douche of scepticism was profoundly unwelcome. I had expected my friend's excitement to turn to enthusiasm. Too late, I saw that his exhilaration was not that of literary discovery but of unmasking a villain. I continued to protest.

"It is entirely convincing."

"Augustus Howell has a peculiar gift of being entirely convincing. He owes his success to it. Because he has planted this among Aspern's correspondence from Byron, it will carry all the more conviction in the sale-rooms of London or New York."

"How much is in that collection of papers?"

"Enough to kindle a good bonfire."

My surprise turned to dismay.

"The paper is of the right date—1822?"

"Almost certainly."

"The ink has rusted over the years?"

"It would appear that it has."

"It is Byron's writing."

"Deceptively like."

"The handwriting, the ink, and the paper are those of seventy years ago. That cannot be Howell. He was not alive seventy years ago."

"Precisely. Therefore it is a recent forgery."

With that, he took the letter from my hand and walked to the window again. Holding the page of manuscript horizontally, he tilted it a little this way and that, catching the light on its back and examining the surface with his glass. I felt a certain annoyance at such self-confidence.

I could not tell what he had discovered by scrutinising the surface of the paper. However, he now put it down abruptly, turned to the escritoire, and began to pull every drawer clear of its slot. I thought we had already emptied the furniture of all that might be of interest. Now he was looking for scraps. He searched the recesses, as if for some secret compartment. He turned each drawer upside down and shook it, scattering the last fragments of paper, dust, and wood-chippings onto the table. Not satisfied with this, he continued to rummage in each of the cavities where the drawers had been. At last he gave a sigh of satisfaction and retrieved a small slip of paper. I could see quite easily what he had found—a receipt from a London ironmonger.

"It behooves us, Watson, to become snappers-up of unconsidered trifles."

The receipt was stamped by Kinglake & Son, High Holborn, for three shillings and eight pence. Its date was "12 November 1888." Why should anyone keep a common receipt of this kind for such a length of time and in such apparent secrecy as this? Perhaps, after all, it had not been hidden but had merely fallen from the back of the drawer and been lost behind it. Only Augustus Howell could tell us, and he must be presumed dead. Then I saw that there was writing on the back of the receipt.

"1 oz. galls, 1 oz. gum arabick, 1 oz. iron sulphate to oxidise, 6 cloves, 60 grains indigo. Add 30 oz. boiling water/stand 12 hours."

"How soon can we make sense of this?"

"I have already done so. It is a recipe for making iron-gall ink which, I imagine, no one has bothered to do for many years. Logwood and then blue-black replaced it long ago. When I have a reply to my wire, sent to the Vacuum Cleaner Company in St. Pancras, we may have a complete explanation."

"But you have surely not sent such a wire?"

"It is remiss of me," he said impatiently. "I should have known how this would turn out. Trickery—and shoddy trickery into the bargain! We will go to Thomas Cook the courier at once and despatch a cable. Meantime, be good enough to look at the so-called poem of Lord Byron you were reading. Hold it at the window. Let the light fall upon the back of the paper at an angle and tell me what indentations you can make out."

I stood in the window and held it at various angles, studying it through the magnifying lens.

"It is a little creased here and there; so it should be after seventy years!"

"Look for a pattern."

"There is a very slight pattern impressed on it."

"Indeed there is."

"It appears to be the impression of a grid, a series of horizontal and vertical lines."

"They suggest, do they not, that the paper has rested for some time on top of such a grid? And that means nothing to you?"

"I can't say that it does."

"Then the sooner we reach Messrs. Cook, the sooner we shall have an answer."

5

By that evening, we had a reply from St. Pancras. The so-called Vacuum Cleaner Company had been a novelty a year or two earlier with its new carpet-cleaning device, though the device itself was not new. Holmes, with his insufferable fund of arcane knowledge, assured me that it had been patented in America as early as 1869. The device had originally required two servants to operate it. One worked a pair of bellows to create a vacuum, and the other held a long nozzle which sucked up dust.

My friend, intrigued as always by such eccentricities, had quoted to me an article on the subject in the Hardwareman of the previous May. This promised a cleaner operated by a motor instead of bellows. Though I had heard these "vacuum" contraptions spoken of, I had never seen one of them.

As we sat with our coffee at one of Florian's tables in St. Mark's Square, Holmes offered his explanation.

"The indentations which you observed, Watson, were those created by the paper lying on a wire mesh."

"Very likely. What has that to do with a vacuum cleaner?"

"To acquire so clear a pattern, the back of the paper must have been supported for some considerable time on a wire screen, held in place by clips or pegs. In addition, the gentle application of a vacuum tube would suck it back against the mesh, for as long as was necessary. Soft paper, such as this, was always made of rags and takes the impression of metal very easily."

"But that would not alter the apparent age of the paper, surely."

"Certainly not. What it would alter is the apparent age of the ink."

"By the use of a vacuum?"

"Cast your mind back to the formula on the ironmonger's receipt," said Holmes patiently. "It is a prescription for the manufacture of a small amount of iron-gall ink, used by Jeffrey Aspern, Lord Byron, and their contemporaries in the 1820s. It was long ago superseded. Therefore, ask yourself why anyone should want iron-gall ink in November 1888."

"You did not need to send a wire to a vacuum cleaner manufacturer in London to learn about black iron-gall ink!"

He looked surprised.

"My dear fellow, of course not. A pair of bellows may produce a vacuum without the assistance of a cleaning device, though with more effort. The wire was merely sent to inquire whether these benefactors of man and womankind had recently supplied one of their excellent machines to Mr. Howell of 94 Southampton Row, London West Central."

"And the answer?"

"They had not."

"Then you were wrong!"

"Not entirely. They had supplied a machine to that address. However, the customer gave his—or her—name as Mr. Aspern."

He snapped his fingers for the waiter and ordered more coffee.

"Black iron-gall ink sinks very slowly into such paper as this. As it does so, it goes rusty by reason of oxidation. If it remains black, then it cannot be of any great antiquity."

"As any schoolboy might deduce."

"One moment, if you please! The purpose of a vacuum applied to the back of soft rag paper, long and gently while the ink is still damp, is to draw the fluid more deeply and quickly into the paper, to accelerate the ageing process. All things considered, I believe we may conclude that Byron never intended Don Juan to follow in the footsteps of Thomas Jefferson. However, I think we have followed those of the Bordereau sisters and their forger very closely indeed."

6

On the following morning Holmes received a note, or rather a press cutting, from Gregson. Without comment, our Scotland Yard man had forwarded a paragraph cut from the previous Thursday's edition of the Winning Post and Sportsman's Weekly, published for racing men by Robert Standish Siever in Pall Mall.

> We are informed that the smartest mover in the village, "Gussie" Howell of Southampton Row, has gone to his reward. His mortal remains were interred on Wednesday at Brompton Cemetery, attended by his creditors and the belles of Piccadilly in garters of the friskiest black silk. His elegy by the bard "ACS" is currently circulating among the cognoscenti and reads as follows.
>
> The foulest soul that lives stinks here no more,
> The stench of hell is fouler than before.
>
> A toast to his memory will be drunk by the swell mob of Romano's in the St. Leger Bar on Friday at 6 P.M.

"Truly dead this time," I said.

"A pity," said Holmes coldly. "I might have obliged him to be useful to us. After that, he could have died as often and as soon as he liked."

It was an hour or so later that we came across a final batch of papers. The letters bore dates between 1845 and 1855. There were also a number of poems, written in manuscript on octavo sheets of paper. I picked up one of these, covered in a neat and purposeful hand, devoid of the loops and curlicues of Lord Byron. It was a speech—or rather a dramatic monologue. I soon gathered that it was supposed to be spoken by the fanatic reformer Savonarola, his adieu to the council of Florence which had condemned him to be burnt.

Savonarola to the Signoria
24 May 1498

I drink the cup, returning thanks.
(The rack that turns one cripple in an hour
Draws a man's throat to nothing with the pain.)
So let them hear me first and last,
The Florentines that keep death's holiday. . . .

"Robert Browning!" I said excitedly. "It can only be he. I am no expert, but I would recognise the style anywhere as being his! This is surely the poem, or one of them, that was discarded from Men and Women before publication of the book in 1855."

"You are of course quite right, friend Watson," he said rather languidly.

"I am right that we have found Browning's lost poem?"

"No! That you are no expert."

I was considerably put out by this and continued to read a few lines of the condemned man's speech, which made me all the more hopeful.

Ah, sirs, if God might show some sign,
The very least, to be God's own,
The certainty of bliss with hell beneath,
What man stands here who'd not endure my flame?
Or buy my place in pain with all he hath?
But God being not, not in that sense, I say,
Let this unworthy flesh His proxy stand. . . .

"The tone and the style. . . ."

"Confound the tone and the style! Any mountebank could work those up."

Holmes was now scrutinising the neat and level lines of verse through his glass.

"Very well," I insisted. "What of the penmanship?"

"Plausible," he said grudgingly. "This is the work of an expert who has studied and practised the author's writing until he can produce it flowingly. It has been written with speed to make it convincing. See how the pen has just joined the last letter of one word with the first of the next. See here, the slight connecting stroke of 'throat' and 'to,' then here again with 'of' and 'bliss.' Such tricks indicate skilled counterfeiting, where the pen seems to be in motion almost before it touches the paper."

"Precisely as it would do in a genuine document."

"It is a forgery. You may depend upon that."

"What of the ink?"

"It would not be iron-gall, of course; this is merely blue-black made with indigo, and that alters far less."

"Then ink and penmanship appear to stand examination?"

"One moment."

He began to check through a bundle of these octavo manuscripts and then set several of them aside. The pages were of a size usual in correspondence. They were far less yellowed than the Byron samples.

I noticed several rough drafts of letters, the hand identical to Savonarola but with crossing-out and insertion. I saw a first draft of a letter from Robert Browning to Elizabeth Barrett. It came from their courtship in 1846, while she lay a prisoner and an invalid in her father's house. I cannot betray the secrets of that correspondence, when letters passed between them every day. I will just say that it was full of reverence for his dearest "Ba," as she signed herself in replies that called down heaven's blessings upon him.

It was monstrous to think that such intimate memorials of their devotion were destined to pass under the auctioneer's hammer, merely to gratify the greed and curiosity of the public. Who knows what had already been hoarded in sale-rooms across the world in anticipation of this? Holmes turned to me.

"I think we must have young Mr. Browning here. I shall have him sent for."

He went to inform our guardian, Angelo Fiori's cousin, and gave instructions for Pen Browning's immediate attendance. While we were waiting for him, Holmes took from beside him a neat black attaché case, no more than eighteen inches by ten. He unclipped it and took out the polished steel components of Monsieur Nachet's Combined Simple and Compound Microscope. This was the most powerful instrument of its kind; yet it could be dismantled or assembled in a few seconds, thanks to a milled head on its tubular stem, by which the body of the microscope might later be detached and the dismembered instrument packed away neatly in its case.

From his bag, he also retrieved a metal right-angle set-square. I cannot count the number of times I had witnessed the scene which followed, usually at the work-table in Baker Street. Holmes, tall and gaunt, sat with his long back curved, gazing into the mysterious world of the powerful microscopic lens. One by one, he took the papers he had selected, all of them adorned by the strong neat lines of Robert Browning's script. After scrutiny, he set each page down carefully with its lower left-hand corner in the angle of his set-square. At first he frowned and then his face cleared. When he had examined the last of them, he straightened up and turned in his chair.

"I believe we have the rascal, Watson! Empty every cupboard. Collect every book from every shelf. I believe they will tell us whatever else we need to know."

I began to remove books by the armful and stacked them on the bare table. As I did so, Holmes took them one by one, trying each of his chosen documents against the blank fly-leaves of the volumes. Or rather, he tried them in many cases where the fly-leaf would have been—had it not been cut out! Someone had used the blank leaves as writing-paper—but might not that have been Robert Browning? Presently, Holmes put the manuscripts aside and subjected the books themselves to the lens. Each was opened and exposed to its powerful scrutiny.

He did not choose a particular page but opened each volume at random. I noticed the earliest printing of Lord Tennyson's Morte d'Arthur in an edition of 1842, Mrs. Browning's Sonnets of 1847 and her Runaway Slave of 1849, Robert Browning's Cleon and The Statue and the Bust, both published in 1855, as well as Sir Galahad by William Morris and Dante Gabriel Rossetti's Sister Helen, both having been issued in 1857. He looked closely at the first few but dismissed the rest with hardly a glance.

7

It was while Holmes was still examining this collection of rare editions, with the exclamations of a man who has been proved right after all, that Pen Browning arrived alone. He looked with some surprise at the tubular steel of Monsieur Nachet's compound microscope. Holmes swung round but without getting up.

"Mr. Browning! Pray be seated!" He indicated one of the straw-bottomed chairs. "First I will tell you what you already know. You and your parents' reputations have been in great danger, since their secrets and confidences have somehow been distributed to the auction houses of the world. I believe we may now say that the danger of blackmail or embarrassment is past."

For the first time in our acquaintance, the young man smiled.

"I am truly your debtor, Mr. Holmes, if that is so."

"I have no doubt that it is. First, however, you must indulge me by answering a few questions."

"I will gladly do that."

"Very good. You remember nothing of your mother's Reading Sonnets of 1847 because the edition would have been issued long before you were born."

"I know that my father had doubts about publishing the poems at all, even after they had been given to the world in 1850. He said to me several times that people should not wear their hearts upon their sleeves for daws to peck at. He said it again when it was suggested that his letters to my mother during their courtship—and hers to him—should be published after his death."

"Very interesting. Now I must ask you one question that is most important. I beg that you will consider carefully before you answer."

"Indeed I will."

"When your father made a fair copy of a poem, and while the ink was still wet, did he use a sand-box to dry the ink in the old-fashioned method? Or did he use blotting-paper as many people have done for the past thirty or forty years?"

Pen Browning looked surprised, but the answer came readily enough.

"Neither. My grandfather had held a post in the Bank of England and had used a brass sand-box, shaking fine sand onto the ink and then shaking it off again. In Florence, we still had the brass box. I played with it as a child. It was never used otherwise."

"And blotting-paper?"

"When I was a little boy, I sat with my father while he made fair copies of his poems. He never used blotting-paper, for fear that it would cause a smudge and that he must begin again. I do not recall that he ever possessed any. Indeed, he said that a poet must be like a medieval scribe and set out his pages in the sun to dry. That was easily done in Italy."

Holmes handed him the manuscript of Savonarola.

"Would you look at that, please? It is dated 1855. Is it your father's?"

"It appears like his writing. I do not know the poem. It may well be his."

"Would you look at the last lines and tell me what you see?"

"Nothing. Unless that they are dimmer than the rest. He would not have allowed that in a fair copy."

"Would he not?"

"The appearance of a poem was a work of art to him, like a painting. He was very particular about the look of it."

"But the person who wrote this was not particular, was he? Moreover, your father did not use blotting-paper, as you say. This page was written out complete and then blotted. The upper lines of ink had dried and darkened progressively by then. The later lines were still wet and the ink was drawn away, leaving them dimmer."

"Is that all?"

"No, Mr. Browning, it is not nearly all. Under microscopic examination, it is possible to see that the fainter letters are also feathered in their outline from the pressure of being blotted. There is even a microscopic wisp of what appears to be white blotting-paper."

Pen Browning's face clouded with unease.

"I have told you what I remember, Mr. Holmes, but no one can swear that my father may not have used blotting-paper on one particular occasion. Perhaps this was not a fair copy."

"Perhaps it was not, Mr. Browning, but it was blotted and dated 1855. Curious, is it not, that blotting-paper was not manufactured commercially until 1857, and only then in the United States? Moreover, until 1860 it was made of pink rag, and only after that from white."

"And is that all?"

"It is not," said Holmes a little impatiently. "The pages of the poem, like most of the manuscript copies on this table, are not quite square. Take my set-square and try to make a right angle at the bottom left corner. You will see that there is a slant to many of them, rather than a straight line, and that many others are a little too narrow for octavo. It is often difficult to cut straight at the beginning when one cuts a blank fly-leaf from a book."

Pen Browning's mild face looked up uncomprehendingly.

"I do not understand, Mr. Holmes."

"I daresay not. These pages are the fly-leaves which have been cut from books on this table, perhaps six months ago. During the time you have been on your way, I have matched most of them with the stubs left in the books from which they were cut. Our forger had imagined he would return here with ample time to cover his traces. Mortality has caught him out."

"Why would my father, or anyone else, want to write a poem in 1855 on a fly-leaf cut from. . . ."

"Cut from his poem Cleon printed in that year?"

"Yes."

"He did not do so. The book itself is a forgery. Like the rest of these volumes and the inscriptions within them."

I interrupted at this point.

"I think you had better explain that, Holmes. How can a book be a forgery? Cleon is one of Robert Browning's outstanding poems, and it is included in Men and Women."

"More precisely then," said Sherlock Holmes, "whatever it may claim on its title-page, this copy of Cleon was not printed in 1855, nor in 1865 nor in 1875—nor probably even in 1885. It would have been a physical impossibility. Would you care to make use of the microscope?"

My friend unceremoniously tore a page from the "1855" copy of Cleon. He positioned it on the stage of the microscope and adjusted the lens. Then he made way for the young man to sit down at the table.

"Ignore the printing, if you can, Mr. Browning. Look at the paper itself. What do you see?"

"Nothing, except that it is magnified and therefore appears more speckled than paper normally is."

"Will you please concentrate on the pale yellow specks? Some of these you can ignore for the moment. One or two, however, will show what appear to be rather like fine hairs. Do you see them?"

"Yes," said the young man uncertainly, and then, more confidently, "yes, I do."

"Leaves of grass," said Holmes magisterially. "The words used by Augustus Howell as he lay dying, whether or not his throat was cut."

"The poems of Walt Whitman!" I said at once.

"I think you may take it, Watson, that this has nothing to do with Mr. Whitman. It has everything to do with esparto grass, of which paper-makers in England nowadays use a great deal. I choose the word 'nowadays' advisedly. Until 1861, paper in England always consisted of rags. The cotton shortage caused by the American Civil War made this impossible. Other ingredients were then substituted."

"In other words. . . ."

"In other words," said Holmes finally, "the Sonnets printed in 1847 at Reading—as well as the 1855 copy of Cleon—and the manuscript of Savonarola dated 1855—all of them are on paper not manufactured until Thomas Routledge of Eynsham Mills near Oxford first used esparto grass in 1861. Indeed, in my view, the true reason that your father could not have been the author of Savonarola is that he was already dead when it was written. The same applies to the so-called rough drafts of his letters to your mother. By trickery or dishonesty, something of the genuine letters reached a forger who has built most shamelessly on that in an attempt to enrich himself."

There was silence in the tiled room with the bright sun outside and the quiet splash of a gondolier's oar in the shady waters of the canal. Pen Browning looked cautiously at Holmes.

"Let me have this clearly, sir; you are talking of. . . ."

"Fraud," said Holmes exuberantly, "on an outrageous and preposterous scale. Indeed, though esparto grass had been available since 1861, I would suggest that this is a very recent fraud, committed within the past few months. More specifically, those who committed it could only do so in safety once your father was dead."

"But you talked of 1861, Mr. Holmes, almost thirty years ago. My father lived until last December."

"Very well," said Holmes patiently. "If you will look through the microscope again, you may be able to see similar specks in the paper. However, they lack the fine hairs of the esparto leaves. These other specks are traces of chemical wood. During its manufacture, this sheet of paper with its date of 1855 has passed through a mill where it was in contact with such pulp. However, the first use in England of chemical wood in paper for printing was in 1873. In the form we have it here, it was unknown to us until about five years ago. Taking all the evidence, including the likelihood that had your father still been alive he would have denounced the poem about Savonarola as a fraud, the date of this manuscript is almost certainly not six months ago."

"And the letters, Mr. Holmes?"

"They are written on the same paper. The forger—or impostor in the case of the letters—was prepared to take a chance. Having acquired forged copies of these books which had been accepted as genuine in their dates, he thought himself safe in cutting out fly-leaves on which to compose forged documents."

"Can you be certain that so many of these books are forgeries?"

Holmes sighed.

"I will tell you what I am certain of, Mr. Browning. The rare 1847 edition of your mother's Sonnets contains traces of chemical wood and, on that evidence, must have been printed more than thirty years later. Her poem The Runaway Slave, in what purports to be a first edition of 1849, contains a modern form of the letters 'f' and 'j' cast as type for the printer Richard Clay in 1880 and never used before then."

Pen Browning looked dumbfounded; there was no other word for it.

"It is a conspiracy, Mr. Holmes! Nothing less."

Holmes brushed this aside.

"Among the other rare editions, the paper used for the so-called first edition of Tennyson's Morte d'Arthur in 1842 has the 1880 type as well as esparto grass and chemical wood. The same is true of Mr. Swinburne's Dolores, which purports to be a first rare printing of 1867. There are multiple copies of all the volumes to be found on these shelves and in these cupboards, ready to be slipped into book auctions. A small fortune if they could be sold as genuine to J. P. Morgan and his rivals. However, Lord Tennyson and Mr. Swinburne are still alive, therefore they must wait a little. Your parents were, for the forgers, conveniently dead—as indeed was Lord Byron. Even if a manuscript forgery was skilful enough, it was important that whoever was supposed to have written it was no longer alive to deny the claim. Meantime, such treasures of Byron and Beckford, of Elizabeth Barrett and Robert Browning, would make a fortune for the criminal. This, believe me, was only a beginning."

"And Mr. Howell?"

"We are advised by that estimable racing paper The Winning Post and Sportsman's Weekly that he has indeed been gathered to his fathers."

"With his throat cut?"

"I should take the liberty of doubting that. I think it more likely that when he was taken into the Home Hospital in Fitzroy Square—with pneumonia, shall we say?—he seized the chance of putting about a story that would deter his creditors once and for all. Unfortunately for him and, I imagine, rather to his own surprise, he then succumbed in reality to this pneumonia. I rather think he is now beyond justice of the sort administered by judges of the Central Criminal Court."

"It was not revenge of some kind?" I asked.

Holmes shook his head.

"As for the coin wedged between his teeth, you may forget the underworld of Naples. More probably, the loyal fingers of Rosa Corder or some other classically minded acquaintance placed it there to pay Charon the ferryman for the crossing of the Styx into Hades."

"And the cutting of the throat was an incision in the trachea to the bronchial tubes to assist his breathing?" I asked sceptically.

"It would not be unknown."

Pen Browning interrupted.

"What of the volume of Sonnets in his pocket?"

"I believe that was there," said Holmes quietly. "However great Howell's avarice, it was mixed with a very large dash of vanity. Hence the stories of having dived for treasure on a sunken galleon, having been sheikh of a Moroccan tribe, and indeed of being attaché at the Portuguese embassy in Rome. Perhaps he knew that his last moment had come, and he certainly knew that those who had attended him would have found the '1847' Sonnets in his pocket."

"That would convict him of nothing."

"There is a certain type, Mr. Browning, whose greatest pleasure is in boasting of his tricks. He is like the murderer who taunts the police with 'Catch me if you can.' He puts his neck in the noose and snatches it out again."

"And Howell?"

"'Leaves of grass,' which I can well believe were his last words, was not a reference to Mr. Whitman but to the Sonnets. Esparto grass. The world had been tricked. But where was the fun unless, before he died, he could tell the world how cleverly it had been tricked?"

"He was not murdered after all?"

"His killer was far more likely to be a meek and merciless little microbe, thriving on the fermentation in his lungs, than the agent of a Neapolitan criminal gang. The story of underworld vengeance has too much of Gussie Howell about it to be believed."

8

After that, Sherlock Holmes was not inclined to remain in Venice "to no purpose," as he said. It was impossible to book a wagon-lit for the next day's Grand European Express to Calais and London. On the following day we were more fortunate. By then the fate of Augustus Howell was beyond question. His death had been attended by such drama of his own making that they had held a coroner's inquest on him. The report in the Continental edition of The Times reported a verdict of death from natural causes.

"How are the mighty fallen!" Holmes exclaimed as he closed the pages of the newspaper. "Poor Gussie Howell! To die of natural causes after all!"

It was the evening before our departure, and we were sitting at a table outside Florian's, with the sunset casting fire across the outlines of basilica and palaces. We were waiting for Pen and Fannie Browning, whom Holmes had insisted should be our guests before we left for home.

"There is something amiss in their household which I cannot quite put my finger on, Watson. It is probably the incompatibility of Puritan principles and nude female models under the same roof. I sense that the young Brownings' marriage is 'but for a two months voyage victualled,' as Shakespeare puts it. I would therefore prefer to meet on neutral ground."

That evening, under the lamplight and the soft echoes of the wavelets by the canal steps, Holmes offered his final advice in response to questions from the youthful Pen Browning.

"You have a clear course before you now. You or your attorney must let it be known that whatever manuscripts are in the hands of auctioneers or vendors, purporting to be written by your parents, have been proved fraudulent. You may call me to witness if necessary. You must make it plain that those who dabble in such things are parties to a criminal fraud, carried out solely for the purposes of deception. That will put a stop to most dealings."

"It may not stop publication."

Holmes set his coffee cup down and looked thoughtful.

"Unfortunately, the good old-fashioned remedy of taking a horsewhip to the scoundrel who publishes falsehood in this manner has been rather at a discount for some years. Now it must be a matter of threatening in advance to bring proceedings for libel against whom it might concern."

"But surely," said Pen Browning quickly, "it is no longer possible to libel the dead."

Despite the difficulty which this presented, I saw that the young man was no end pleased in "putting one over" on the Great Detective. Holmes smiled at him indulgently.

"It is quite true that, at Cardiff Assizes in 1877, the excellent Mr. Justice Stephen ruled that the dead have no remedy against civil libel since they are no longer juristic personalities. Criminal libel, however, that is to say defamation so offensive as to threaten a breach of the peace, is another matter and carries with it prison sentences long enough to deter all but the most resolute liars. There is your remedy."

It was plain that young Mr. Browning's knowledge of English law stopped far short of this. He was chastened but grateful.

"Well then, Mr. Holmes, there is only one more question. I must decide whether the letters of courtship between my parents should be published or burnt. About five years ago, my father burnt almost all his letters and manuscripts. He was in London at the time, in Warwick Crescent. He brought down an old travelling box of my grandfather's and threw papers by the handful onto the fire in the front room. I saw the whole of his correspondence with Thomas Carlyle go up in flames."

Holmes prompted him.

"And the letters written by your parents during their courtship?"

"He could not do it. He knew that he ought to destroy them, but he could not. They were kept where they still lie, in an inlaid box. Not long before he died, he gave this box to me and said, 'There they are. Do with them as you please when I am gone.' But what am I to do?"

"When the time is right, you must publish them," said Holmes at once. "Not now, but in five or ten years. If they are anything like the two people who wrote them, they are noble and passionate, faithful and understanding, the exchanges of lovers who would die for one another. They must not perish, for there is too little of that sort of thing in the world. Publication will smash the forgers once and for all. Such creatures of darkness cannot endure the light of the sun."

Pen Browning looked up, as if startled by this.

"I believe you are right," he said firmly.

The letters were published nine years later, and whatever fakes or forgeries may have lingered were extinguished by their beauty.

Next day, Holmes and I returned to England. He would accept no fee from Angelo Fiori on behalf of Pen Browning.

Instead, he asked only for the "worthless" manuscripts of Don Juan in the New World, The Venetian Nun, and Savonarola to the Signoria, with a set of the false "first editions," including the 1847 Sonnets of "E. B. B." They were given a place in what he called his "Cabinet of Curiosities." By an irony of time, some of the books were to become more valuable than the genuine first editions which they had claimed to pre-date.

Yet Holmes knew the difference between true gold and fool's gold. As the express left Venice, he opened a copy of Robert Browning's "Roman Murder Story," The Ring and the Book, which he had picked up from a book-stall at the last moment. It so absorbed him that he sat up all night reading and closed the last page of its twelfth book about ten minutes before our train pulled into Charing Cross.

IV

The Case of Peter the Painter

1

On a morning in early December, three years before the Great War, Mrs. Hedges brought us the unusual story of a yellow canary. By this time of the year, the branches of the great elms and beeches were bare. Beyond Clarence Gate, on my morning walk, the avenues of the Regent's Park echoed to the scuffling of pedestrians striding through drifts of dried leaves, as if they were wading through the shallows of a holiday beach.

When the rain began that morning, at ten minutes before ten o'clock, I had just returned to our rooms, stopping only at my tobacconist for two ounces of Navy Cut. Sherlock Holmes had still been at the breakfast table in his dressing gown when I set off. Now he was rigged out in a tweed suit with a belted Norfolk jacket. As I entered the sitting-room, he drew aside a corner of the Paddington Gazette and looked at me from his arm-chair.

"You had not forgotten, Watson, that the mysterious Mrs. Hedges is to call upon us at ten-thirty precisely?"

"No," I said, a little irritably, "I had not forgotten."

I sat down at the table in the window and began to rub the moist tobacco leaves, crumbling them into my leather pouch.

Holmes and I had reached that stage of our history when the clatter of omnibus engines in the street below had begun to eclipse the more homely beat of hooves and the grinding wheels of the hansom cabs.

"Good," said Holmes in a tone that irritated me somewhat more. "I am glad you had not forgotten. The romance of crime has grown stale of late, Watson. Villainy is at a discount. Let us hope that Mrs. Hedges can bring a challenge into our too-sedentary existence."

I thought that was most unlikely. Mrs. Hedges had been recommended casually by John Jervis, the new young curate of St. Alban's Church, Marylebone, a stone's throw from Baker Street. Mr. Jervis with his scrubbed nails and shining face had presumed, on a very slight acquaintance, to send a note recommending the lady to our attention and suggesting that an appointment at ten-thirty on the morning in question might be convenient. He described her as a worthy woman who was in some difficulty over a matter concerning a yellow canary. And that was all. It scarcely sounded likely to restore to our lives the drama of major crime. In that, not for the first time, I was to be mistaken.

It was a measure of our present idleness that Holmes had welcomed the young curate's suggestion.

"Depend upon it, Watson, there is nothing so indicative of true villainy as the commonplace. The song of a yellow canary is quite capable of heralding the arrival of gangsters of the most atrocious kind."

He spoke more truly than even he could possibly have known. For the moment, I sat and rubbed tobacco while the sky darkened. Then the rain swept along Baker Street in a winter storm for half an hour. As suddenly as they had darkened, the heavens cleared again. A little before ten-thirty, Holmes got up and stood at the window, his tall spare figure veiled from the outside world by net curtains. He was gazing at a wooden bench outside the florist's shop.

"It appears to be a characteristic of our working classes, Watson, that their greatest fear is not of murder or highway robbery, but that they may be late for an appointment at which such things are to be discussed. Hence, they are always early. Unless I am mistaken, our visitor is already in attendance. See there." He reached for his ivory-rimmed opera-glasses, which were kept on a bookshelf conveniently close to the window, and unbuttoned their case. "A worthy woman of the less fortunate class, as Mr. Jervis promised. Do you not observe?"

I studied the figure sitting on that public bench. If this were she, Mrs. Hedges was the type who is about forty-five years old but has been made by toil and deprivation to look more like fifty-five. Her dress of polka-dot cotton, her white blouse, boots, and dark-blue straw hat secured by a pin of artificial pearl, spoke of thrift, hard work, and economy. She also wore a dark outdoor coat which had seen better, not to say more fashionable, days.

"Mr. Jervis told us little enough," said Holmes quietly, "but by the aid of strong glasses and at comparatively short range one may deduce a little more. Mr. Jervis may hail from Marylebone but I fancy that the slums of Whitechapel or Stepney are this lady's parish."

I laughed at him.

"How can you tell?"

"Observe the sky. A glance at its movements suggests that the clouds and rain are moving eastwards at about five miles an hour. Our visitor has escaped the rain. Her coat you will see is quite dry. The umbrella she carries is not even unrolled. The welt of her boots is a little damp from walking in Baker Street where rain has already fallen. Yet there is no drop of water on the uppers nor even a mark where a drop has dried. Therefore she did not arrive in Baker Street until after the rain stopped ten minutes ago. She evidently came by omnibus as a matter of economy, since we have heard no sound of a cab drawing up. Moreover, it cannot have been raining at the point where she boarded the bus for her journey, shall we say forty minutes ago? That would put her just clear of the oncoming rain from the west. Let us say she was some three and a half miles to the east or south-east of us. I believe that would place her at Whitechapel or possibly Stepney. Had she come from the west, she would have been rained upon, probably twice."

"And what if she came by the underground railway?"

"I think not. That journey would have been quicker, which means she would have caught the rain at one end of it or the other."

We drew back from the window. At half-past ten to the minute, there was a knock at the sitting-room door. Our landlady Mrs. Hudson announced Mrs. Hedges. Sherlock Holmes was on his feet at once. In a couple of strides he was shaking our visitor's hand and simultaneously gesturing her to a buttoned lady-chair which was now at one side of the fireplace.

"Mrs. Hedges! How good of you to come all the way from Stepney to see us. My name is Sherlock Holmes, and this is my friend and colleague, Dr. John Watson, before whom you may speak as freely as to myself."

For all his bonhomie, she was a nervous type.

"I hope, sir," she said quietly, "it's no inconvenience. It was Whitechapel, rather than Stepney, to tell the truth."

Holmes glanced at me with a look of reproach, which said, on behalf of Whitechapel, "Oh ye of little faith." Then he spread out his hands, gallantly dismissing any suggestion that her arrival might be an imposition.

"Pray be assured, Mrs. Hedges, that no service we can do you will be an inconvenience."

"Not Whitechapel, precisely," she continued awkwardly. "Houndsditch, more like. Perhaps I should tell you a little. . . ."

Holmes gave her a nod of reassurance and another deprecating gesture. My heart sank, for I felt he might be in the mood for sport.

"Let me see if I can deduce a little, Mrs. Hedges. That is, after all, the profession of a criminal investigator. You have come from Houndsditch and that is all we know, beyond the fact that you were evidently a seamstress until you retired from that occupation because, as is sadly so often the case with sewing, you suffered a loss in your near-sight. You are plainly left-handed and you have a little girl who has lately suffered an infectious disease. She is not at present attending school. The poor little mite is a nervous child and apt to be lonely."

"You could not know so much, Mr. Holmes, sir! Not even Mr. Jervis knows about my little girl. Though, to tell the truth, it's the canary that began it."

Holmes paused, then laughed gently at the unease in her face. "There is no black magic here, my dear Mrs. Hedges. A certain quickness in the movements of your fingers, a fine mark imprinted on the left forefinger and thumb, a fuller development of the left-hand musculature would suggest something more than fireside stitching. You do not wear spectacles just now, so it seems evident that you do not require them all the time. Yet there are the marks at the bridge of your nose to indicate that you require glasses for close work. Were you still systematically engaged in it, the marks would be more definitive. Therefore you have retired from an occupation which, in anything but the best light, damages the near sight."

He could be as charming sometimes as he could be misanthropic at others, usually more charming with a poor seamstress than with a peer of the realm or a captain of finance. With his guessing game, he had certainly charmed Mrs. Hedges. Now that everything had been explained, she relaxed—and even smiled. Holmes smiled back at her and continued with the same reassurance. The game had been played to good purpose.

"After all, Mrs. Hedges, I deduced nothing about the yellow canary. As to your little girl, there are still two fair hairs adhering to the darker wool of your outdoor coat. You would hardly see them where they are. They are shorter than your own and of a lighter hue. They have adhered to the material a little above waist-height. That is where they would have attached themselves had they been brushed from the head of a child who is some twelve inches shorter than you. Or had she clung to you very determinedly just before you left her. That suggests you have been obliged through circumstances to leave her on her own."

Mrs. Hedges shook her head in admiration, pleased now but wondering. Holmes continued.

"The two strands of hair are on your outdoor coat. This indicates that you brushed her hair shortly before leaving home. By then, it was much too late for her to go to school today. Yet the Education Act would require her attendance there, except in the case of a communicable or other disease. I could be more elaborate, but I really think we must proceed to business."

Again Mrs. Hedges relaxed a little.

"Louisa," she said at last. "Our Louisa is just gone eight years old. Whooping-cough was what she had. They won't have her back until the doctor signs a certificate."

Holmes touched his fingertips together and became the listener.

"And what is it that troubles you?"

Our visitor looked at him doubtfully.

"The foreigners, Mr. Holmes. They moved in at the back four weeks ago."

"At the back?"

"Yes, Mr. Holmes. We live at Deakin's Rents in Exchange

Buildings, in what they call a cul-de-sac off Cutler Street that runs off Houndsditch. It's no use pretending it's a palace, one room up and down at the front and the same at the back. At the back we look straight out on the opposite backs of the fancy-goods makers and tailors in Houndsditch. Their windows ain't ten feet from ours. In between us, each of our tenements has a yard with a privy and a bit of paved space about ten foot square, for a washing line."

"Yes," said Holmes quietly, as Mrs. Hedges outlined the domestic arrangements of her poverty, "I understand. Please continue."

"Well, sir." She leant forward now, anxious that he should miss no word. "In consequence, the back upstairs window of each tenement overlooks the yard next to it as well as its own. When you see other people in their yard, it's about the only time you do see them, now that so many are foreigners. Russians and Germans, I should think."

"Those in the tenement adjoining yours are Russian or German?"

"About a month ago," said Mrs. Hedges, "some new people moved in there, German or Russian, as I say. Them being at the very end of the row, only us overlooks their yard."

"I understand."

"Not a family. About eight or ten of them just come and go. I never know who's stopping there. There's one plays music in the house—and in a club they go to, in Jubilee Street."

"Have they bothered you?"

She shook her head.

"Not at first, sir. I'm at work all day, so's my man Harry. I don't do close work any more, but I help with packing. He works down Millwall docks. The long and the short of it is—Louisa has to be indoors on her own just now."

"And they have bothered her?"

"About three weeks ago, a man—Russian, perhaps—came round one morning. He offered my girl a threepenny bit if she'd run an errand for him. She was to go down to the bird-shop in the Commercial Road and buy a canary for him. It had to be pure yellow with no brown on it. If they hadn't got such, they was to tell her where she might get one, and she was to go there instead. They hadn't got a pure yellow in Commercial Road, as it happened, but she found one in St. Mary Axe."

Up to this point, Holmes had treated her visit good-naturedly. At the account of the yellow canary, he was alert and attentive. He drew out his small black notebook and began to make jottings.

"And how long was she away upon this errand?"

"I should think perhaps an hour and a half," said Mrs. Hedges, "perhaps a little longer even. Next day, the man it turned out was called something like Mr. Lenkoff came round again. He asked Louisa if she wouldn't mind going and getting a cage and some seed for his little bird, from the same shop in Commercial Road. So she did. Later that week he asked her to go again for some seed and to get him a twist or two of tobacco. Promised her threepence for herself again. Not wishing to disoblige, she went."

Mrs. Hedges paused, and Holmes looked at her as keenly as if she was revealing a plan to rob the Bank of England.

"Pray continue, madam. Take your time. Omit no detail. This is most, most interesting."

His keenness seemed to disconcert her a little, and I caught a glance of alarm.

"Two things happened, sir. On the evening of the day when the bird was bought in the morning, the lady on the other side of us found a yellow canary in her yard, like it was lost or someone had let it out. She took it in and cared for it. But still the next day, and the next, Mr. Lenkoff sent my little girl for bird-seed. My friend kept the little bird because she thought they put it out unkindly. Deliberately."

"Perhaps it was not the same bird?"

Mrs. Hedges almost guffawed at the absurdity. "There ain't that many yellow canaries round Deakin's Rents! Anyhow, Louisa swore the one she bought had a white and blue ring on his leg—sort of pedigree—and so had this one. Why should they want bird-seed and a cage for a canary they hadn't got any more?"

I intervened at this.

"You cannot be certain that it had not escaped of its own accord."

Mrs. Hedges sat back and folded her arms.

"That's true, sir. But why go on buying the seed? See here. They could buy birds or not, for all I cared. Even if they let them go free, that was their business. I got plenty to worry me apart from that. But I swear they were up to something else. What if this was some plan to steal my Louisa?"

"Louisa was too useful to them as she was," said Holmes softly. "That was three or four weeks ago and they have not harmed her, you say. What happened next?"

"I arranged for Louisa to stay all day with my sister-in-law in Altmark Square or at home while I was out. That was the finish of running errands for them. But then I came home last Friday and the back drain-pipe next to our little yard had gone."

There was a slight flush in Holmes's customary pallor, and a pulse beat visibly in his cheek.

"Be very careful, Mrs. Hedges, I beg you. Let me have this from you in precise detail."

Her bounce had gone now, and I thought she looked a little frightened.

"Well, sir, there's a water-pipe goes down from each tenement at the back, from the rain-water gutter on the roof to the drain in the yard. Halfway down, it goes into an iron box with water from both tenements. Then it goes in a single pipe to a drain in their yard, just the other side of our party wall. That pipe had been there in the morning and it was gone by that evening—though it was dark then and we didn't see until next day. By that time, it was raining. Both yards was collecting water, and it was rising round our back-door step."

"Did you ask Mr. Lenkoff what had happened?"

"My Harry did. Mr. Lenkoff said it was all right. The pipe was leaking and the London council had taken it away. When I asked the council's man, he said they hadn't taken anything away. What's more, the lady on the other side of us said she'd heard a noise most of that Friday, as if someone was using a hacksaw on iron. That drainpipe would have been too long for them to take indoors without cutting it up. My Harry happened to look down into their yard next evening and saw one of them carrying something from the privy to the house. It was round and heavy. He swears that it was a two-foot length of the pipe. I don't know what their game is, Mr. Holmes, stealing for scrap, I daresay. And I'd take an oath they were trying out my Louisa with that errand lark. We should have come home one evening and found her gone—sold in Russia or somewhere."

Quite unpredictably, after her earlier self-assurance, Mrs. Hedges began to weep. I understood now why our young curate had been discreet in passing her on to us. Holmes stood up and put his hand on her shoulder, glancing at the notes he had taken and clipping the pencil back in his breast-pocket. He was not much experienced in comforting the distressed, but he did his best.

"I beg you not to upset yourself, Mrs. Hedges. I believe you may put child-stealing absolutely from your mind. You say that your upper window is the only one with a view of the little yard at the rear of this adjoining house?"

"It is, sir."

"And you and most of the other people living around you would be out at work during the day?"

"Just about every one, Mr. Holmes."

"It is as I supposed. The object of the errands was that your little girl should be away from the scene for as long as possible. I doubt if they meant her any harm otherwise. The less she saw, the less she threatened them. However, you are quite right to take every precaution for her safety."

"And the drain-pipe, Mr. Holmes?"

My friend paused. "That, I think, is a matter for the police. If you will leave it to me, it shall have immediate attention. I fancy that my friend Inspector Lestrade of Scotland Yard may find the missing drainpipe to be of considerable interest. Concern yourself only with the safety of your little girl. I do not believe she is in any danger. However, for your own peace of mind, it will be better not to leave the child in the house on her own."

2

"Considerable interest!" Mrs. Hedges was off the premises now and I was able to vent my scepticism. "Inspector Lestrade will find a stolen drainpipe to be of considerable interest? He will find it to be no such thing! It is a matter for the local constable and the council!"

After seeing Mrs. Hedges to the door, Holmes was now lounging on the sofa, a pipe-rack within reach, balancing on the edge of his hand a stout bulbous-headed walking-stick, as though this was an aid to thought. The December sky had darkened again, so dramatically that it had been necessary to light the gas.

Without taking his eyes off the balanced stick, Holmes said, "Unless I am greatly mistaken, Watson, we may stand on the verge of a considerable criminal conspiracy. It may well be a story that parents will tell their children for many years to come."

"A yellow canary and a stolen drainpipe?"

"A drainpipe stolen and sawn into two-foot lengths. Now why should that be?"

"They could not carry it to a scrap-metal dealer in any other form. What more common crime is there than for thieves to rent premises, strip them of all that can be sold and move on? These scamps will have flown the coop by now."

"I daresay. However, it occurs to me that heavy iron drain-pipes have another purpose, especially when those who steal them are criminal Anarchists. Read a little political history of the past century, my dear fellow. The assassination of Tsar Alexander II and the attempted assassination of Napoleon III. You may then concede that a two-foot length of cast-iron drain-pipe packed with explosive and blocked at either end will make one of the most efficient bombs that the criminal world has yet devised."

3

It was two days later when Inspector Lestrade paid us an evening visit in response to the story of Mrs. Hedges, which Holmes had forwarded to him. The Scotland Yard man with his "bulldog features," as Holmes called them, was sitting before the fire with us, a glass in his hand. He was in philosophical mood.

"I must acknowledge you were right, Mr. Holmes, when you said the birds—except for the canary—would have flown by the time our inquiry was made. So they had. Nor do I think they will be back, which is the best news for Mrs. Hedges and her little girl. These scoundrels have been a little in front of us all."

"A little in front of you, to be precise," Holmes said coolly.

Lestrade shot him a glance, shook his head, and lit the cigar which had been offered him.

"We could make very little of them. They appear to have been Russian, rather than German, but then so is half the population of that area. They call themselves Anarchists but, to tell the truth, their real enemies are the brutes who persecuted and ill-used them back in Russia. A few of them may be criminals born. The rest have no cause for a quarrel with us."

"Precisely," said Holmes, "and the born criminals are those who now seem to have slipped through your fingers."

This bickering ran on for a moment or two, then the whisky took its effect. Before the evening was over, my two companions had settled back into a discussion of the late Dr. Crippen, hanged three weeks earlier for the poisoning of his wife. Lestrade had played a part in tracking him down. Holmes rode his latest hobby-horse, insisting that Crippen was unjustly executed—indeed, wrongly convicted. He had never intended to kill Belle Elmore with hyoscine, merely to render her unconscious while his young mistress Ethel Le Neve was in their house. Rather than put Miss Le Neve in jeopardy by calling her to the witness-box, he had saved her and taken a terrible penalty upon himself.

It was well past nine o'clock and we were deeply immersed in this debate before a well-laid fire. Holmes had just reached for the poker when there came an extraordinary hammering at the front door of 221B Baker Street, accompanied by repeated ringing of the door-bell. My friend was out of his chair and down the stairs before our landlady, Mrs. Hudson, could reach the hall. He had guessed, correctly, that this was no caller of hers. We heard voices and then the tread of two men on the stairs. Holmes entered, followed by a uniformed constable.

"A visitor for you, Lestrade."

"Mr. Lestrade, sir? 245D Constable Loosemore, Paddington Green. An urgent message, sir, relayed from Commissioner Spencer, Scotland Yard. A suspected major safe-robbery is in progress in the City of London."

"Where?" asked Holmes sharply.

Loosemore handed a police telegraph form to Lestrade.

"Exchange Buildings, sir, back of Houndsditch. They think it must be a safe-breaking. Constable Piper, the beat officer, put through a call to Bishopsgate police-station after complaints from local residents. Bishopsgate called Scotland Yard. Officers are on their way from Bishopsgate, but the commissioner understands Mr. Lestrade has a current inquiry in Houndsditch. If you could be found, sir, he would be obliged if you would attend to co-ordinate the investigation at Houndsditch itself."

Lestrade did not look as if he welcomed this diversion from a warm fireside and a glass of hot toddy on a cold December night. Holmes, however, was already half-way into an Inverness cape.

"There's only a police van available," Loosemore explained, "but that's at the door. The driver says he can have you at Houndsditch in twenty-five minutes."

"Come on, Lestrade!" said Holmes cheerfully. "Watson and I have a stake in this inquiry as well. We must go, whether you do or not. Much better make up your mind to it, old fellow."

The three of us were presently following Constable Loosemore down the stairs to the street. Holmes, just behind me, said, *sotto voce*, "It will be no bad thing, Watson, if you have remembered to pack your service revolver in your overcoat pocket."

"I have," I said aloud. "I have no intention of venturing into the alleys of Houndsditch at this time of night without its protection."

The police motor-van was no more than a "Black Maria" commonly used for transporting prisoners from the cells to the criminal court, two benches facing one another down its length. There was little view of the city outside as the motor clattered down the Euston Road and City Road, until it stopped abruptly in Houndsditch. We scrambled out at the back into a dark and cavernous thoroughfare. Most of its tall buildings housed jewellers and fancy-goods merchants on the ground floor with warehouses above. Yet if Houndsditch seemed menacing in the darkness, the cul-de-sacs which ran off it were far less welcoming.

The only blaze of light was down Cutler Street, where a gin palace called the Cutlers' Arms was doing a busy trade.

In Houndsditch itself there were three lanterns showing, from officers who had already arrived. The man who approached us was Constable Piper. He saluted Lestrade.

"Mr. Lestrade, sir? We had a report just after nine o'clock from Mr. Weil, owner of the fancy store at number 120, just over the road there. He and his sister live above the shop. There's noises from somewhere at the back of the building, sir. Drilling and sawing, and someone using a crowbar on brick. I couldn't see anything out of the ordinary when I walked round there, but after I came away the noise started again."

"How many men have you got?" Lestrade demanded.

"I left Constable Woodhams and Choat to watch the front here and went straight to Bishopsgate. Sergeant Bentley and a constable came back with me. Martin and Strong from the plain-clothes patrol are coming along. There's seven of us all told."

"Enough to deal with common robbery, in all conscience," said Lestrade irritably. He shivered in the cold wind of the December night. If the dark street was eerie, that was precisely because there was at present nothing to be seen or heard of the suspects. Yet they must still be somewhere close at hand.

Sherlock Holmes walked across to the window of Harris the Jeweller, next to Mr. Weil's premises. At the rear of the shop stood a large and efficient-looking safe with an electric light shining above it night and day. Anyone who tried to attack the lock must do so in full view of the street. Holmes turned back, hands thrust deep into his overcoat pockets for warmth. However much hammering and drilling there may have been earlier, there was no sound of it now. I said as much.

"No, sir," said Constable Piper, "the noise stops the minute anyone goes near Mr. Weil's counting-house. It's the safe next door they're after, I'll be bound."

Lestrade looked about him.

"We'll take a good look at the back alley-way. Sergeant Bentley and you men, come with me."

Our bulldog set off with Sergeant Bentley and five constables following, leaving Piper to watch the front. Holmes and I followed at a little distance, denying Lestrade the opportunity to tell us to keep back. The Cutlers' Arms was immediately ahead, down the side street, and its glaring gas-lamps blinded us to all else. Having reached it, Lestrade turned right into Exchange Alley, whose tenements ran along the back of the Houndsditch shops and warehouses. It was very probable that safe-breakers would make their attempt from the rear of one of these cramped dwelling houses.

In this cul-de-sac of Exchange Buildings, several of the dingy tenements were decrepit in the extreme, lightless and apparently deserted. My abiding memory is of a damp cold in the air and a chill street-wind between tall shabby buildings. At the far end, the alley was blocked off by a tall packing-case warehouse. We reached its wooden doors without hearing any sound of drilling or sawing. There was only the same cold and eerie stillness. Then, as we faced the doors of the packing warehouse, there was a shout from somewhere on our right and a little behind us. I guessed it came from one of our men who had got through the ground floor of a deserted tenement into a yard at the back, sharing a wall with the rear of the Houndsditch shops. The cry came again.

"They were almost through! There's only the inner wooden lining of the jeweller's wall left!"

Holmes and I turned round. It was so dark that one could not readily identify anyone. There were figures moving quickly, but visible only as silhouettes against the harsh gaslight of the Cutlers' Arms at the far corner. In quick succession there was a flash here and there, a crack and a snap. I felt a sudden blow that sent me sprawling on the cobbles. It was not a bullet but a mighty shove from Sherlock Holmes.

"Get down!" he shouted—and not for the first time he may have saved my life at that moment.

Several more shots came in quick succession, reverberating in the darkness between the tall buildings. My revolver was in my hand but I dared not fire. I could see only silhouettes against a glare of gas. Which were Lestrade's men and which the robbers? Worse still, the disturbance had brought out a crowd of spectators from the public house. To fire now would almost certainly mean hitting one or other of them. For twenty or thirty seconds, the obscure alley of Exchange Buildings was a scene of commotion and chaos. Where were the gunmen and who were they firing at? I picked myself up and walked cautiously forward. My presence as a marksman had been of no use but as a medical man I might now be in demand.

If anyone had told me that in such a brief burst of gunfire—less than half a minute—five policemen could have been shot, I would not have believed it. Yet by the light of our lanterns I saw Constable Choat lying motionless outside the doorway of a tenement that had looked deserted. Constable Tucker staggered out through the same doorway and fell, almost across his comrade. Sergeant Bentley was lying on his back on the cobbles with his head on the pathway. Constable Bryant leant against the wall of the tenements. He was, at any rate, still alive. Constable Woodhams had been on his feet when I first saw him but now he fell on the cobbles, as if his legs had given way under him.

Because our policemen do not carry guns, it is rare for criminals to do so. I had never heard of any robbery in which an entire gang had been armed, as seemed to be the case here. In my first examination of the wounded, I found that Choat had been shot six times, through the body and the legs. Tucker was wounded over the heart. Sergeant Bentley was shot through the throat and unconscious. For these three men, the only hope was a hospital. Woodhams was shot through the thigh and could not stand. Bryant was injured in the left arm and chest but less severely. I looked about for Lestrade. He had been hit in the shoulder but the bullet had lodged in the thickness of his overcoat and he had escaped with superficial injuries.

I ordered the survivors to alert the nearby motor-ambulance at Bishopsgate, for Sergeant Bentley and Constable Choat. Even before that, a hansom cab was flagged down in Houndsditch. Its passengers alighted and the driver took Constable Tucker to St. Bartholomew's hospital at his best speed. I gave my attention to the injuries of Bryant and Woodhams.

Such was the disorder and confusion in that half-minute of gunfire. Though we did not know it at the time, one of the criminals had shot another—Gardstein—in error. His companions managed to carry him away, but he died on the following morning and a doctor who was called to attend him brought the police to his bedside. Two young women, the only other occupants of the house, were arrested.

4

Such were the events of that night, confused and unexplained. However, there had not been a newspaper story to rival the "Houndsditch Murders" for many years. Safe-breakers who shot their way to freedom in this manner had been quite unknown. Holmes was with Lestrade for most of the following day, and when he returned to Baker Street in the evening it was with a story that even then I had not expected to hear. He threw himself down in his chair, as if it were too great an effort to remove his unbuttoned overcoat.

"A bad business, Watson, and the press do not yet know the half of it."

"What they know is bad enough."

He shook his head.

"No, my dear fellow. This outrage may be a precursor to civil war, a war against us all, the Anarchists against the world. Lestrade, thank God, is not badly hurt. I have sometimes been critical of his abilities but he never lacks pluck. His sergeants and I have spent much of the day in the tenement at Exchange Buildings, behind the Houndsditch jewellers. It seems the criminals had made themselves very much at home there. The remains of a fire were still smouldering in the grate when we arrived."

"What was their plan?"

"They were cutting through the wall of the outside privy, which is a party-wall shared with the rear of the jeweller's showroom. The hole they had made in the brickwork was diamond-shaped and about two feet square. They were so nearly through it that one can reach in and touch the matchboard lining of the jeweller's back room, just where the safe stands against it. That was why we heard no more drilling or hacking at the brickwork. In five minutes more they would have been in the showroom, though concealed from the street window by the bulk of the safe. They were so accurate in their measurements that they could have touched the rear of the safe without stepping through the wall."

"But how would they have opened the safe?"

Holmes stood up, shrugged off his overcoat and stooped to warm his hands before the fire.

"They certainly did not propose to pick the lock. How could they, with the strong electric light illuminating them to the street? However, a gas pipe runs through the tenement. We found that they had tapped it, using black tape and a rubber tube sixty-three feet long, still in place. It was more than enough to reach the back of the jeweller's safe. When they fled, they also abandoned three diamond angle-pointed drills, a large cold-steel chisel, three crowbars, and a combination wrench and cutter. This collection was enough to burn or hack a hole in the rear of the safe without being seen from the street. The light illuminating the front of the safe as it faced the window would eclipse the glow of the flame as they cut through the back."

As we sat that evening in the quiet of our Baker Street rooms, it was hard to imagine that the horrors of the previous night were anything but a bad dream. Holmes went on to describe how an urgent call that morning had brought Scotland Yard men to a house in Grove Street, a mile east of Exchange Buildings. In an upper room, a young man lay dead upon a blood-soaked mattress. He was George Gardstein, a young Russian Anarchist gunman and one of the police-murderers. He had been accidentally shot in the darkness by one of his own friends as he struggled with Constable Choat, receiving a bullet aimed at the policeman.

"Gardstein would have certainly been hanged," said Holmes philosophically, turning from warming his hands at the fire, "had one of his companions not saved us the trouble. When his pockets were turned out, there was a seven-cartridge magazine clip for a 7.65-mm pistol, a drill, a pair of gas-pliers, welder's goggles, and a key to fit the new lock which they had put on the door of the tenement to prevent unwelcome interruptions of their work."

"Damning evidence," I said reassuringly.

His lips contracted.

"And yet not the most interesting. The true discoveries, my dear Watson, were a violin and a small oil-painting of a Parisian street scene, showing considerable skill. It bore a signature that is not unknown."

"Was Gardstein a painter—or a collector?"

Holmes shook his head again and sighed.

"For several years I have made it my business to be an unobtrusive listener to talk in the political clubs of Whitechapel and Stepney. Few people had met or even seen George Gardstein. Like all the Anarchist leaders, he is a 'name,' as they call it. In this case he is Poloski Morountzeff, a revolutionary and a fugitive from the police in Warsaw. In that city he is better known as a robber and murderer."

"And what of the painting?"

He stood up and yawned.

"That, my dear Watson, is the work of a man who is far beyond Morountzeff and his kind. A man who might be a leader of nations if revolution should ever enthrone the philosophy of Anarchism or Communism. His name sends a shiver down the backs of Kings, Kaisers, and Tsars. He warms the blood of political debaters and cut-throats alike. He is Peter Piatkoff, and he is known in the Anarchist underworld as Peter the Painter. Oh, yes, he might have made his name as an artist, but he is too pure for that. In the name of the stern justice of a virtuous republic, he would cut a throat as readily as you or I would slice an apple."

"Another Robespierre!"

He looked at me as if I had not understood.

"Robespierre wanted only France. Piatkoff will settle for nothing less than the world."

"And he is here, in England?" I asked uneasily.

Sherlock Holmes smiled to himself.

"He is not here—but he is coming. Oh, yes, he is coming. And when he comes, England will know all about it. My information is recent and particularly reliable."

I was more than a little unnerved by this. Holmes seemed to take a strange pleasure in his promise. It was as if he anticipated single combat of some kind, alone against a terrible enemy. I went to bed and slept badly. There was something in the air—or rather in the manner—of Sherlock Holmes, which disturbed me. It was rare indeed that in any of our cases he had thrilled to the prospect of a personal duel. But now I was reminded of the dreadful day when he went to meet his fate at the hands of Professor Moriarty, remarking that the world could no longer hold both of them and that if his own life must be forfeit to destroy his enemy, he would think the price well worth paying.

5

Two days later, I came down to breakfast to find Holmes already there and unusually cheerful. As I sat down, he put aside his knife and fork, extending his palm.

"And what, Watson, do you make of this? I fear I purloined it yesterday in Morountzeff's room. Lestrade and his merry men had overlooked it on their visit."

I saw a round lead bullet for a muzzle-loading rifle, which I recognised from my days of military service.

"A twelve bore!" I said at once. He chuckled.

"Well done, Watson! It was not at all what Lestrade and his sergeants expected to find. Because they did not expect it, they overlooked it."

"But what does it mean?"

"Evidently Gardstein and his friends are looking for rifles of any sort. So far they have been content with revolvers. After all, you cannot carry rifles through the streets of London without causing comment! Yet rifles mean something quite different to handguns. They can be used to defend a strong-point. They will do it with a terrible accuracy which revolvers lack. Lee-Enfields are the easiest to come by and our opponents are clearly in the market for them. But if they are prepared to defend—or even to attack—strong-points in this manner, then the revolution is probably much closer than we believe."

This did not reassure me in the least. Holmes, however, was in excellent spirits. He glanced through the newspaper and then said, "Here is something for your scrapbook, my dear fellow!"

It was a report of the incident on Friday night, the terrible night-time drama of Exchange Buildings and Houndsditch. Holmes waggled his fork at me with a little impatience.

"The third paragraph in the editorial, old fellow. This is precisely what I had hoped to avoid."

> A curious coincidence in the terrible events of Friday night was the presence among the police officers in Houndsditch of the well-known consulting detective, Mr. Sherlock Holmes. Scotland Yard will say only that Mr. Holmes chanced to be in company with Inspector Lestrade at the time and was in no way connected with the case. Most of our readers will surely hope that this is not the truth. Our nation and our society are under attack by the scourings of Europe's political gutters. We have tolerated too much for too long on our own soil. If Mr. Sherlock Holmes were to purge England and the civilised world of such unprincipled villainy, the civilised world would rally to him and he would earn the sincere gratitude of all decent men and women. If Mr. Holmes has not been invited to exterminate this menace, let that invitation be issued now.

I laid the paper down. Never had I read an editorial which adopted so strident a tone.

"A little strongly put," said Holmes brightly, "but then I have not been invited to do anything except to have dinner this evening."

"Where?"

"I was remiss in not mentioning it last night. By the by, I shall be a little late home. Lestrade, sensible fellow that he is, has decided to call upon the advice of Brother Mycroft in this case. Our friend is in deeper water than is usual. Even the Political Branch at Scotland Yard has not been able to help him much. Mycroft, on the other hand, lives, moves, and has his being in the world of politics and conspiracy. He keeps an eye upon it, on the government's behalf."

"An eye upon Russia?" I inquired sceptically. Holmes smiled.

"Mycroft is particularly fluent in the Russian language, and deeply read in Russian history and culture. His translations of the poetry of Alexander Blok are, I understand, highly regarded. I have also agreed to do what I can for Lestrade. In consequence, Brother Mycroft is giving us dinner in a private room of the Diogenes Club. Please, do not wait up."

And that was all. After he had gone out, I was left to wonder what labyrinth we were invited to explore. By the time that evening came, I was ready for an early dinner. Then I took down a volume of Sir Walter Scott from the bookshelf—The Heart of Midlothian—and was presently far away in the North, the Edinburgh of a hundred years since and the drama of the Porteus riots. The narrative carried me along so easily that at the end of every chapter, I resolved to read just one more before the early night that I had promised myself.

It was, I think, gone eleven o'clock when I first heard the noise in the street outside—or rather on the outside wall of the room. Something like an empty tin-can hit the wall of the building with a clang and clattered back into the street.

"Mr. Hoolmes! Mr. Share-lock Hoolmes!"

A first blow of the knocker on the front door was followed by a second.

"Mr. Hoolmes, it is I—You know who I am!—and I know you for a lackey and a lick-spittle! A craven flunkey of your monarch and his ministers! An oppressor of the people, one who must share the fate of his paymasters!"

It was so preposterous and unexpected that for a moment I sat and was not sure what to do. There was a pause, and I thought the bawling lout had gone on his way. Perhaps he was disconcerted at getting no response. Perhaps he thought it was the wrong house, though the address of Sherlock Holmes was certainly no secret. The curtains were closed. I moved carefully towards them and, at the side, made a tiny gap which gave me a view of the street below by lamplight.

The man was still standing on the far side of the roadway, outside the unlit florist's shop. He was not in the least the ragged trousered fellow I had expected. His smart black overcoat had what looked like an Astrakhan collar and he carried a broad brimmed hat in his left hand. There was something in his right hand which looked like a stone. He was tall, neatly and quite expensively dressed. His hair was dark and trim, he had fine whiskers, his features were more aristocratic than not, indeed his nose was beaked almost to the point of disfigurement.

"You know me! You know me, Mr. Hoolmes. When I tell you the name Piatkoff, you will know. You cannot answer? That you are a friend of tyrants, I have known. That you are such a coward, I did not think! A policeman's lackey!"

I had been completely caught on the hop, as they say, dragged from the comfortable pages of Scott's novel to face this ruffian. I tried to remember what Holmes had said about Piatkoff the previous night. At that moment, the fellow's long right arm hurled the stone with the power of an out-fielder returning a cricket ball towards the wicket-keeper. There was an impact and a sound of glass falling on the floor below. I thought of Mrs. Hudson but just then dared not take my eyes off this hooligan. He was lounging against the opposite wall now, not the least concerned for the disturbance he had caused. Lights had sprung up in two windows opposite and, at this quiet time of night, the din would surely attract a policeman on his beat.

I remembered that, among his souvenirs, Holmes had a police whistle which he had acquired during our pursuit of Dr. Neill Cream, the Lambeth poisoner. I pulled out the drawer below the bookcase to rummage for it. By then, however, someone in the opposite house was shouting into the night to draw the attention of the Baker Street constable, who must therefore be in view.

I went back to the window, astonished to find that Piatkoff, or whatever his name might be, was still leaning against the florist's wall as if he had not a care in the world. I had a terrible fear that perhaps he carried a revolver in his overcoat pocket and was waiting to shoot any policeman dead, as his compatriots had done on the previous Friday night. However, he was cleverer than that. With his Bohemian broad-brimmed hat on his head he waited a moment. He was evidently able to see something of which the policeman who strode towards him in helmet and gleaming waterproof was unaware.

The lighted interior of a red double-decker motor-bus was coming down from the Regent's Park towards the Metropolitan underground railway, like a ship illuminated in the darkness. The man waited until it was almost level and the policeman was hardly twenty feet away. Then, in two or three steps, he came forward and sprang onto the moving platform at the rear of the bus, as deftly as if he had practised for this moment all his life. He and the constable stared at one another as the distance between them widened. I could not be sure, but I believe he dropped off again as the bus stopped at the railway station, which was just in sight. The policeman had seen the last of him.

I thought of Holmes's last instruction to me: "Do not wait up." I was in no mood to do anything else. He came in a little before midnight, full of Mycroft's ideas, though curious about the broken pane of glass in the downstairs window. I told him my story and he became more subdued, though caring nothing for his own safety.

"We had not counted on his arriving so soon," he said at length, "though of course if they plan some spectacular violence he was bound to be close at hand. Our people have been watching him in Paris. Indeed Monsieur Hammard, the Chef du Service at the Sûreté, has a private line to the Assistant Commissioner at Scotland Yard on such matters. Brother Mycroft assures me that Piatkoff was last seen in Paris not a week ago. For he really is a painter and had two pictures hanging in an exhibition which opened in a private gallery near the Quai d'Orléans."

He sat quietly for a moment like a gaunt brooding bird and I knew, by instinct, that he did not wish to be interrupted. At last he let out a long breath.

"I will not deny that this changes matters somewhat. I shall speak to Mycroft tomorrow morning. The greatest service you can render, my dear fellow, is in identifying Piatkoff as he now is. If Lestrade will put a vehicle and two plain-clothes officers at our disposal, you and they may tour Houndsditch, Whitechapel, and his likely London haunts. See if you can pick him out, Watson, for you may be the only person who can. His appearance is seldom the same on any two occasions, but he will hardly be able to change it so often. Even his confederates in London cannot be sure of his identity during his recent masquerade in Paris. If we can pick him up and follow him, he may lead us to the heart of the entire conspiracy in London."

Grave though the situation had become, there was little more to be done that night. I slept with my revolver close at hand, but I did not really suppose our enemy was likely to make an early return to Baker Street.

6

On the following morning, there was a further unwelcome development. The late edition, which a few days earlier had been so quick to report the presence of Sherlock Holmes at the police murders in Exchange Buildings, was after us again. There had just been time to include a garbled "Stop Press" account before the paper was "put to bed." Whatever secrets we may have held were secret no longer.

ANARCHIST DISTURBANCE IN BAKER STREET
"PETER THE PAINTER" IN ENGLAND

Late last night the international Anarchist Communist leader, who goes by the name of Peter Piatkoff or "Peter the Painter," brought the threat of revolution to the very doorstep of Mr. Sherlock Holmes, the well-known consulting detective. The man who calls himself Piatkoff shouted abuse from the street for at least ten minutes and threw various objects, causing damage to a ground-floor window. He fled at the

> approach of a policeman on the beat and escaped on a motor-bus. The prophet of revolution and the defender of our liberties appear well-matched.
>
> Piatkoff is described as tall and thin with prominent features, dark hair and whiskers, wearing a dark overcoat with Astrakhan collar and a broad-brimmed felt hat of "Rembrandt" design.

"Which will make him almost indistinguishable from a hundred thousand other men in our city," said Holmes philosophically.

I felt a little heat at the newspaper's familiarity.

"The whole thing is written with tongue in cheek," I said, "a piece of damned impertinence and a handy tip for Piatkoff! His friends will be reading the paper this morning, even if he is not."

Holmes continued to butter his toast before spreading marmalade.

"I have not the least doubt that he and they will be reading it."

Soon afterwards, he left to give his assistance to the nation, as represented by his brother William Mycroft Holmes. For many years, the ungainly but brilliant Mycroft had dominated the British Civil Service, as the Chief Adviser on Inter-Departmental Affairs. Wherever there was trouble, Mycroft was soon on the spot. As his younger brother Sherlock had once remarked to me, "Not only is he an adviser to the British government, on occasion he is the British government."

I was left to cool my heels for an hour or two while the brothers made arrangements with Lestrade for my tour of Holborn, Houndsditch, Whitechapel, Mile End, and wherever else we might find Piatkoff or tales of Piatkoff. Within half an hour there were stories enough. To the Anarchist Communists, if not to the world of art, his arrival was nothing less than a messianic event.

My companions, who arrived at Baker Street that morning in a nondescript cab, were Sergeant Wiley and Constable Parks of the Plain Clothes Division. In their grey flannel suits and bowler hats, their neatly cut hair and clipped whiskers, they might excite the suspicion of the criminal world by their uniform ordinariness. However, that was no business of mine. The cabby, who, for all I knew, might be another plain-clothes officer, drove us briskly down the length of Baker Street and then eastwards towards Holborn and the poorer districts of the city.

Except for the dreadful incident in Exchange Buildings, I knew absolutely nothing about the geography of Anarchism in London's East End. My companions were better informed. I had only to keep my eyes "skinned" as we passed down street after street, repeatedly, throughout the day. It was impossible to let me out of the vehicle, for fear that I should be recognised by someone who had seen me on the night of the shootings. Dark though it had been, I had spoken to a considerable number of people in the dreadful aftermath, as I did my best for the injured and the dying.

Fortunately, my companions were well informed. In the wastes of the Mile End Road, with its drab commercial premises and the narrow streets of dockers' terraced houses running to either side, Sergeant Wiley called a halt. We had stopped by a hemp merchant's warehouse to pick up a shabby young fellow whom I would have avoided at all costs. In his brick-red windcheater jacket and his corduroy trousers, a careless scarf flapping at his neck, this idler proved to be Sergeant Atherton of Scotland Yard, in plain clothes suited to this habitat. It was no surprise to me after the shooting of five policemen that officers were active in the area, disguised as boot-blacks, pedlars, and street-hawkers.

We turned off the main highway and dropped Atherton in the narrow thoroughfare of Jubilee Street to the north. Between the terraces of little houses was what appeared to be a dilapidated church hall. In reality it was, as a board announced, "The Hall of the Friends of the Workers." This had been founded by the most famous Anarchist of all, Prince Kropotkin, during his long exile in England. It had a reputation for preserving anonymity. Even with his pseudonym of George Gardstein, Poloski Morountzeff was never known here as anything but "The Russian."

The building was dilapidated, but the gossipers gathered inside and outside its doors every day. That afternoon, we again picked up Sergeant Atherton, or, Volkoff, as he was known in the club. He met us several streets away and confirmed that the sole topic of conversation among his comrades had been the arrival of Peter the Painter and the triumph that was to come. Men and women who associated at the club were by no means all in support of assassination, but every one of them seemed to hail Piatkoff as the leader of a promised revolution.

Of Piatkoff himself there was still no further sign. Our driver turned his horse's head from Whitechapel to Houndsditch, then to High Holborn. For the rest of the day, we pulled up at various cab-stands, as if waiting for a pre-arranged fare. At length we were drawn up near High Holborn, almost at half-past four with the lamps lit in a growing fog. I was watching the slow parade of pedestrians who sauntered past the illuminated shop-fronts with their lavish displays behind plate-glass windows.

We had been there almost ten minutes when I noticed a man moving more quickly and purposefully than the rest. He was walking away from us on the left-hand pavement. A broad-brimmed artist's hat covered his head and the collar of his dark coat bore a strip of Astrakhan. I could not be sure that he was our quarry. As Holmes remarked, the coat, the hat, and the man's height matched thousands of others.

Just then he began to cross the street and in doing so naturally turned in our direction to see that the way was clear. For about ten seconds I saw his face—the time was long enough. The steady eyes, the pointed nose, even the dangerous flush at the cheek-bones, were those I had fixed in my mind the evening before. He reached the far side, turned away from us again and almost at once entered a smartly equipped shop with its window brightly lit. Before I spoke to Sergeant Wiley, I looked up to see which shop this might be. The name was there in polished brass, set into mahogany: "E. M. Reilly & Co.—Guns & Rifles."

My escorts were under orders not to approach the subject. He was likely to be armed. I could not say whether Sergeant Wiley or Constable Parks carried a gun, but such a thing is rare, even on plain-clothes duty. In any case, Holmes had insisted that a man suspected of being Piatkoff was not to be seized immediately. He was of more use at liberty, leading us to the rest of the conspiracy. Acting on my information, the sergeant and his constable now stepped quietly down from the cab, went separate ways, and closed in upon their prey from opposite points of the compass.

That was the last I saw of the drama. It would never have done for Piatkoff to recognise me—if he could. Much to my chagrin, the day now ended with a drive back to my club, the Army and Navy in St. James's Square, where I dined alone. Winter had come with the darkness. The breath of muffled passers-by beyond the dining-room windows condensed into clouds of mist. At half-past nine, another cab took me to Baker Street, where I slid my latch-key into the lock of 221B just as the clock of St. Mary's, Upper York Street, struck ten on the cold and foggy stillness of London's sooty air. Mrs. Hudson's maid had put up the gas, and there was a welcome fire in the grate—but of Sherlock Holmes there was no sign. He had dined again with his brother Mycroft, and I was content to pour myself a glass of whisky and reach for The Heart of Midlothian.

About twenty minutes later, I heard voices and footsteps on the stairs. Holmes came in first, with Lestrade just behind him.

"Ah!" said Holmes, sliding his stick into the rack and taking the inspector's coat, "our sleuth-hound Watson is here before us. We have heard from Mycroft of your invaluable piece of detection today, old fellow. My congratulations."

He poured a measure from the decanter into each of two glasses and handed one to the inspector.

"He is our man, Watson, and you have tracked him down. Single-handed, last night and today, you have put Piatkoff within our reach."

"Then had Scotland Yard better not arrest him while he remains within your reach?"

Lestrade had been bursting to say something important and now took his chance.

"Watch him, Doctor! Shadow him. Those are the orders. Not just orders from the higher ranks in Scotland Yard. Not even from Mr. Mycroft Holmes. They come from the Home Office and the Home Secretary himself—Mr. Winston Churchill."

I needed no account of this Home Secretary in Mr. Asquith's government. At the Colonial Office and the Board of Trade, he had already shown a refusal to let problems stand in his way. "Do not argue that there are difficulties," he told his protesting subordinates; "the difficulties will argue for themselves."

"The duel between Churchill and Piatkoff is something of a personal matter," Holmes remarked, "but Winston, as his minions call him when he is not present, is determined to have the entire bunch of Anarchists in his bag. His instructions are that nothing is to be done to alert them until we can get them all. Anarchism is what he describes as the hydra of revolution. If you merely cut the head from it, it will sprout twenty more."

"Then what has happened?" I asked.

Lestrade gave a satisfied smile.

"Sergeant Wiley had a chat, as you might call it, with the manager of E. M. Reilly. Their customer did not call himself

Piatkoff, but Schtern. Despite that name, he claimed to be a Frenchman. According to the Home Office files, over which Mr. Churchill has given us free range, Piatkoff sometimes uses the name Schtern in Paris and is known to most of the underworld simply as The Frenchman."

"More to the point," said Holmes impatiently, "their customer purchased three Enfield rifles, muzzle-loading but deadly accurate, to be delivered as a parcel in the name of Schtern to 133 Jubilee Street, Stepney."

"But that is the same street as the so-called Anarchist Club!" I said.

"It is better than that—it is the Anarchist Club. If we can keep absolute surveillance there, we may have them all before any harm can be done."

Lestrade knocked his pipe out and looked up.

"With revolvers or handguns, they can only be sure of hitting their targets at close range. With rifles, a first-class marksman can hit a target a hundred yards off. Rifles, gentlemen, are the stuff of assassination. Mr. Churchill has now taken measures over the Prime Minister's movements between Downing Street and the House of Commons, as well as the appearance of the King and Queen at the opening of parliament in the New Year. We know that Gardstein and his friends already had ammunition for rifles. Now, it seems, they also have the weapons."

"Only because you allow them to buy rifles from a gunsmith!" I said with some little indignation.

To my astonishment, Lestrade tapped the side of his nose, though he did not exactly give me a wink.

"As to that, Doctor, this is one occasion when you really must allow us to know our own business best."

Holmes said nothing, and at last Lestrade, standing up, wished us good night. At the door, however, he turned back.

"When you read the paper tomorrow morning, Doctor, you

will see the face of your Peter the Painter from last night, as our plain-clothes men saw him close up this afternoon. You must let me know what you think of it—as a work of art."

I could hear him chuckling all the way to the foot of the stairs. I tucked The Heart of Midlothian under my arm and stumped off to bed, muttering "Blasted impertinence!" or something of the kind. Holmes made no reply but continued to gaze in deep thought at the dying fire.

7

I felt, as I believed I was entitled to, that I had been treated with something less than the consideration I deserved. Next morning I found that, once again, Holmes was at breakfast before me. I was about to make a protest of some kind when I looked at him and saw how ragged his face appeared. I swear that he had not been to bed all night. Despite that, there was no sign of nocturnal activity in the sitting-room. Thinking about it afterwards, I thought I had smelt something like the hot acrid and metallic smell of a soldering iron in a workshop.

All this was put out of my mind as I laid down my knife and fork for a moment and took up the Morning Post. There, on an inner page, a face stared out at me. It was the twin of the one I had seen two nights earlier, shouting abuse across Baker Street as a tin-can and a stone hit the house. Above the sketch, in bold type, was the inscription "Peter the Painter."

"That is he!" I exclaimed.

"Is it?" said Holmes listlessly. "Only you can tell, my dear fellow, you and your two plain-clothes men."

"They have got him to a T!" I insisted. "He will hardly be able to stir out of doors in London without being recognised!"

His fork was idle and he showed none of his usual morning appetite.

"One thing of which you may be certain, Watson, is that as soon as our artist's drawing appeared in the newspaper, the fugitive changed his appearance beyond recognition."

He was right, of course.

"Far better," Holmes added, "had Lestrade and his boobies kept this to themselves for the time being." At the word "this," he stabbed the face in the newspaper with his finger. Then he left his breakfast unfinished and went to the window, watching the street below. I thought it best to let the matter drop. With a show of great attention to the day's news, I finished my toast and marmalade and drank my coffee.

Ten minutes passed in silence. Then he turned from the window and reached for his waterproof, drawing it on and buttoning it.

"I shall be with Mycroft today," he said, crossing to the door. "We are required to give an account of ourselves to Mr. Churchill and his advisers. I see that you and I have no immediate engagements of any other kind. However, it is possible that you may receive a call from Mr. Chung Ling Soo. If so, be good enough to ask him to leave a card with his present address and assure him that I will communicate with him forthwith."

Mr. Chung Ling Soo! What madness or nonsense this might be I could not tell, and Holmes did not say. It was evidently some case that he had picked up and neglected to mention. It hardly seemed worth bothering about, by comparison with the threat from the Revolutionary Anarchists.

As Holmes went down the stairs, I stood up and replaced him at the window. There was a cab waiting outside and he was about to step into it. I now saw that he was in the company of two Army officers. I recognised from my own military service that their lapels and hat-bands proclaimed one to be a colonel and the other a brigadier. Whatever game Holmes and his associates were playing seemed too rich for my blood, as the saying goes.

I kept an appointment for lunch in the refectory of the London Hospital with my friend and colleague Alfred Jenkins, who had been a lieutenant with me in Afghanistan—and who had pursued his military career as surgeon major for several years while I was invalided out after Maiwand. When his time was up and he returned to civilian life, he had been offered a senior post as surgeon at the London Hospital.

As we were eating our steak and kidney pie, a colleague of Jenkins came up and sat down beside us.

"We've got him!" he said excitedly. "There was great competition, and he's as handsome as Adonis—a very beautiful corpse." The acquisition, I discovered, was the body of Poloski Morountzeff, who had gone by the name of George Gardstein. His corpse was of great importance, because few people had met him or had any idea what he looked like. In order that he might now be identified, it was necessary for his remains to be preserved intact for a further three months. The task of accomplishing this had been awarded to the London Hospital, who had arranged to keep him in a formaldehyde-fume preservation-chamber with glass windows. His eyes had been carefully opened, while a policeman photographed his face for a life-like poster which soon appeared on public display.

When I returned to our lodgings, Holmes was already there. He was not very communicative beyond saying that Lestrade's men had been watching the East End. They had picked up the trail of Piatkoff, who, contrary to Holmes's expectations, had evidently not changed his appearance as yet. Possibly, as I remarked humorously, he was not a reader of the Morning Post. Holmes stared back at me, unsmiling. He remarked that Piatkoff had been seen in Jubilee Street. He had been watched by Atherton, alias Volkoff, at the Anarchist Club, where other members present had at first seemed so in awe that no one spoke to him. Then he had conversed at random, not as if he had a rendezvous with anyone.

No carter's van had called at any address in Jubilee Street to deliver rifles. For all their cleverness, Mycroft Holmes and the pursuers had lost the scent of that consignment. I stood up, stretched, and wished my friend good-night. I noticed, as I did so, a carte-de-visite on the sideboard. It showed a tiny head-and-shoulders photograph of an expressionless Englishman in a suit and hat, under the inscription: "Memorandum from Chung Ling Soo: Marvellous Chinese Conjuror." Written underneath were the words, "Wood Green Empire until Saturday. Always a pleasure to see you in the stalls." What on earth Holmes wanted with a stage conjuror I did not know and, at that moment, I did not care.

8

If Sherlock Holmes and his brother had an idea of what was going on, they seemed in no hurry to do anything about it. Then a few mornings later, I went down to breakfast and once again sensed a smell of solder or hot metal in the sitting-room. It did not seem to emanate from the room itself. Holmes had it on his clothes. But where had he been that night? Who had he been with and what had they been doing? He certainly looked, once again, as if his head had never touched the pillow.

I thought perhaps I should become my own detective, but I did not suppose I should get very far. Even Scotland Yard had accomplished little. Thanks to an innocent couple who came forward because they wondered what had happened to their lodger, the CID had located Poloski Morountzeff's workroom. The chemicals found there, chosen for the manufacture of bombs, he had explained away to the credulous landlord as a formula for his patent fire-proof paint. There was a supply of rifle cartridges, though no rifles, and clips of ammunition for a Mauser pistol. Morountzeff had been well-behaved, an ideal lodger, who sometimes locked his rooms and travelled to the Continent.

During the next week, thanks to such "information received," the City of London police arrested three men and two women. Fedoroff, Peters, and Duboff were charged with the Houndsditch murders, Sara Milstein and Rosie Trassjonsky with conspiring to assist them. Unfortunately, it seemed that the informants against them were more attracted by the rewards offered than by any allegiance to the truth. When the evidence was examined, all the defendants were set free. Murder could not be proved against the three men, much less against the two women.

It was difficult to establish the identity of any of the suspects. The internal security system of the Anarchist movement discouraged the use of names. Where necessary it still preferred to allude to "The Frenchman" or "The German" or "The Russian." For every man who knew the sobriquet of "Peter Piatkoff," there seemed to be a thousand who knew "Peter the Painter." What was not known could not be betrayed, even under police questioning.

A few names were known to the police, among them such men of violence as Fritz Svaars and Yoshka Sokoloff. They had not been caught, as Holmes remarked with a sigh, and it seemed likely that they were in Russia or France by now.

Such was the situation when I went to bed a few nights later and, somewhen after midnight, had that unusual sensation of waking from a dream within a dream. After what seemed like several minutes, but was probably more like ten or twenty seconds, of dreaming about dreaming, I was fully awake. It was almost four o'clock in the morning and, so far as I knew, Sherlock Holmes was in bed and asleep. He had certainly retired before midnight. Now, however, I heard voices in the sitting-room below me.

I had missed whatever they were discussing, but I was quite clear in my mind that one of the voices was Sherlock Holmes and another was his brother Mycroft. There were at least two more, probably four but I could not be sure. I did not recognise these other speakers, though one of them had a very distinctive tone of voice. His words were spoken rather slowly but emphatically and, at times, with something like a growl. The voice was rather slurred on occasion, as if the tongue might be a little too large for the mouth. When this visitor concluded a rather lengthy remark, another speaker whose voice was unfamiliar to me addressed him as "Winston."

I began to wonder whether I was not, after all, still dreaming. What were the government's most senior civil servant, Mycroft Holmes, the Home Secretary, and someone who knew the Home Secretary well enough to call him "Winston," doing in our sitting-room at four o'clock in the morning? The discussion was less intense now. They dropped their voices and I could make out only a rumble of talk.

Instinct told me that it would not do to walk in on their debate. On the other hand, I must be dressed and ready in case my presence should be necessary. I was just fumbling with a collar stud and tie when a board outside creaked and Holmes, perhaps seeing light under the door, tapped gently as he entered.

"I heard you moving about," he said quietly. "I fear there is trouble boiling up near the Anarchist Hall in Jubilee Street, or rather about two hundred yards away. It seems as if we may have an insurrection on our hands. If Sergeant Atherton's information from the underground is correct, the aim is to kill as many of our officers and officials as possible, and of as high a rank as possible. In other words, assassination under cover of a general outbreak. Rifles for the one, pistols for the other."

I began to unscrew my trouser-press.

"What will you do?"

"Major Frederick Wodehouse of the War Office is here. So is the Home Secretary—Wodehouse picked up Mr. Churchill from his house in Eccleston Square on the way. Nothing is to be said, at this stage, about either of them. It would not look well for the military to be involved."

"And you will go with them?"

His profile, in the gaslight, looked leaner and tauter than ever I had seen it.

"This minute, old fellow. We also have a captain of the Scots Guards in attendance. Theirs is the nearest regiment, at the Tower of London. This is likely to be more than the police can deal with. We have no more room in the motor, so you must follow on as quickly as you can. Take a cab from the Metropolitan line for Stepney police station, just off Commercial Road. Ask for directions there. The desk sergeant will know where we are."

With that he was gone. I heard footsteps and voices going down the stairs from our sitting-room to the front door. Then I took out my watch and looked at it. The hands were at just five minutes past four. Ten minutes later I was walking up Baker Street towards the rank at the underground railway. A single cabby was dozing on his perch. He was awake and alive in a second.

We did the journey to Commercial Road in less than half an hour, through a ghost-like city of empty streets and half-lit avenues. I told the cabby to wait and went up the steps, illuminated by the blue police lamp. Inside, it was as though I had stepped into the foyer of the Alhambra theatre five minutes before the curtain went up. This was plainly the headquarters of the operation, police officers pushing this way and that. I found my way to the sergeant's desk and was answered in two words which would soon travel round the world.

"Sidney Street."

I was not given the number of the building but, if even half of what Holmes had told me was true, I should not need one. My cabby drove the half-mile through Stepney, past the deserted

Anarchist Club, down Hawkins Street—and then no further. A helmeted constable stepped out into the roadway ahead of us, swinging his bulls-eye lantern side to side to bring the cab to a halt. As he did so, I noticed in the beam of light that snow had begun to fall. There were no tracks of other wheels to be seen.

"No way through, sir." The policeman's face was at the window. "The road ahead is blocked off. If you want to drive west, you must turn back and go down to Commercial Road."

"I am a medical man, Dr. John Watson. I have a rendezvous with Mr. Sherlock Holmes. I understand he is with Major Wodehouse and Mr. Churchill."

"That's different then," the policeman said, opening the cab door. "I shouldn't wonder if you were needed presently."

I paid off the cabby and followed the policeman through the thin drifts of the falling snow. I had not brought my medical bag with me, but just then I could see—or hear—no reason why I should need it. Nor had I packed my revolver in my pocket.

Perhaps it was the snow which gave Sidney Street its sinister appearance as the clocks struck five. More probably it was the sight of a formation of men standing absolutely motionless in a side-street and uttering no sound. If this was the Anarchist Communist revolution, it seemed just then to be a remarkably silent affair.

Sidney Street, as we came to its corner, was at least forty feet wide. Its terraces of plain red-brick working men's houses faced one another. The block of eight houses which was now the centre of attention, Martin's Buildings, was named after its owner and had been built ten years earlier. Each house had about ten rooms located on several floors. At the rear they overlooked a jumble of yards, sheds, and alleyways. At the front, the windows had a clear view across the street but only restricted visibility along its length. Immediately opposite the house which had become the focus of interest was a yard with a wooden fence and gate. Its paintwork dimly proclaimed "Isaac Dickholtz, Coal Merchant and Haulier." On either side of the street, some of the houses had little shops on their ground floors with grilled windows and shabby black paint.

Further off, at the next road junction north, stood the tall buildings of Mann and Crossman's Brewery with a yard and stables to the rear. The van gates also opened opposite Martin's Buildings. In the other direction, the Rising Sun public house, which we were now approaching, occupied the next corner site on the other side of the road. The flat roofs of the Rising Sun and the cooling tower of the brewery both offered a vantage-point, looking respectively north and south along the thoroughfare towards 100 Sidney Street. There was still no sight nor sound of a gang of Anarchist assassins.

In the dim lamplight of the early morning, the large but silent body of dark-clad police cutting off the thoroughfare at either end was concentrated in two side-streets, out of view of the windows of houses in the middle of the block. As to the suspect house itself, there might be fifty armed gunmen ready to fight to the death—or one—or none.

Just as we drew level with a back lane, running along the rear of the houses, I saw three figures. Two of them were uniformed police officers and between walked a young woman, barefoot in her underclothes, her white petticoat immediately visible.

"They are evacuating the other houses in Martin's Buildings," said Sherlock Holmes, just behind me. I gave a start for I had neither seen nor heard him approach. "The Home Secretary is here with Major Wodehouse, but that is for your ears only. We do not want every reporter in London getting under our feet or betraying his presence to the enemy, for he would immediately be at risk."

"How many gunmen are there?"

He drew me towards the street corner outside the bar-room

windows of the Rising Sun, on the opposite side of the street from Martin's Buildings.

"No one knows. We have the names of two: Fritz Svaars and Yoshka Sokoloff, otherwise known as The Limping Man. They are not in Russia after all, it seems, and both are very efficient shots. Others who will try to come and go may keep up an impressive fusillade. Piatkoff, if he is in there, will be their commander."

"And the police?"

"Lestrade is on his way, but this is a matter for marksmen and the police have none. Twenty or thirty constables have occupied the houses on the far side of the street, as well as the vantage-points of the brewery and the flat roof of the Rising Sun. Several of their men are armed, but that will not do."

"And Mr. Churchill?"

Holmes chuckled.

"He has taken command from the Commissioner of Police, as he always meant to do. Major Wodehouse tells me that 'Winston likes a straight fight.' A telegraph has gone to the Secretary of State for War requesting the immediate release of a detachment of the Scots Guards from duties at the Tower of London. That too is for your ears only, though they will be here within the hour."

As we groped our way up the dimly illuminated staircase of the Rising Sun to the darkness of its flat roof, I thought of the repercussions of Scots Guards and straight fights, if this should prove to be a fuss about very little. As we came out into the open air, a city clock across the quiet streets struck quarter-past five. It crossed my mind that at this time of year it would hardly be light much before eight.

Close at hand there were three small groups, engaged in quiet conversation. One of these included Major Wodehouse and the Home Secretary, who was dressed in his long coat with its velvet collar and cuffs and his tall hat of black silk. From the gruff confidence of Winston Churchill's voice and his face as I had seen it in a magazine photograph, I had imagined a much taller man. Yet, though he was burly in build, I guessed that Sherlock Holmes topped him by almost a foot.

For the next hour or so we were pestered at intervals by the landlord, who had hoped to hire out his flat roof to newspaper reporters at a sovereign a time. Major Wodehouse's aide told him briskly to "cut along" and leave us to our business. It was no part of the plan to have the press in attendance before there were events to report. Mr. Churchill's instructions were also positive in another matter: there was to be no battle until the sky was light enough for us to see who we were shooting at and to make it more difficult for our opponents to enter or escape from the houses on the far side of the street.

"It will be the easiest thing in the world, sir," interposed Holmes, "for those opponents to break through the ceilings of the upper rooms and travel from one house to the next. In the roof spaces there may be no proper dividing walls and, if there are, they will be no more than a single thickness of brick, easily broken through. If that happens, the battlefront will be eight houses long."

"Quite so, Mr. Holmes," the Home Secretary said gruffly. "I am obliged to you for your very salutary reminder." Mr. Churchill then stepped behind the shelter of a chimney stack and presently I noticed the faint glow of a cigar, concealed by the brickwork from the street below.

We had a bitter couple of hours, waiting for the sky to lighten. At intervals, the landlord appeared with tots of rum and sandwiches of ham or tongue. Finally, when the steeple clocks had struck seven, the Home Secretary said, "Very well, gentlemen, let us proceed. Everyone, unless instructed otherwise, will remain under cover and out of sight."

He descended the stairs, followed by Major Wodehouse and his aide, then by Captain Nott-Bower, who was Commissioner of the City of London Police. Holmes and I had been bidden to bring up the rear. I could not say what use we might be; but when my friend went down, I kept him company. In the saloon bar of the public house, Lieutenant Ross of the Scots Guards in his greatcoat and cap was already in attendance. Though it had taken some time to rouse the Secretary of State for War and obtain permission, a detachment of the regiment, including two sergeants who were musketry instructors and nineteen private soldiers, had volunteered for this duty. Lieutenant Ross had come on ahead, and the volunteers were on their way.

In the street, the snow had turned to slush. Our party moved quietly along the far side, out of view of the windows of 100 Sidney Street, behind which might lie an entire Anarchist gang or a single gunman. We crossed over to the exposed side, where Major Wodehouse, Holmes, and I drew into the shelter afforded by the stone pillar at the gate of the brewery's stable-yard. To my astonishment, the Home Secretary remained with head and shoulders in view, his identity plain, staring up at the closed curtains of Martin's Buildings. He spoke sideways, confirming an instruction. At this, a uniformed constable walked across and banged on the front door of 100 Sidney Street. There was silence. The policeman stooped, retrieved a handful of small stones and threw them at one of the upper windows.

It was at this moment that I saw the slow and sinister protrusion of a rifle barrel from the slit of a partially opened upstairs window. Had they been hand-guns, the chance would have been doubtful, but a rifle fired by a trained shot could scarcely miss Mr. Churchill at this short range. There was a flash of fire from the gun barrel and a crack that reverberated like thunder between the two rows of houses. I expected to see the Home

Secretary fall, but he ducked his head and then straightened up again, still standing against the wall close to us. Why did he not keep down?

Now there was a second rifle barrel, protruding from a gap in the adjoining casement. I have read often enough the cliché of a man whose heart was in his mouth with fear, but I never knew the truth of it more certainly until that moment. A second crack and a spurt of flame from a rifle barrel came in Mr. Churchill's direction. It was often said afterwards that he had to be compelled to take cover, and this, I believe, was the source of that story. A third rifle snout appeared, and again there was a bolt of fire and a crack that made the ears ring.

Like a stage magician, after three rifles had missed him at such short range, the gruff figure in the long coat and tall hat turned and walked the few yards to shelter, close to our stone pillar. It was as if the gunmen had recognised who he was, which was quite possible, and were determined to silence him at all costs. For this they paid a heavy price, by giving away their positions and numbers to the firepower which now faced them. Had they held their fire on seeing the Home Secretary, they might have escaped in the darkness or perhaps even shot their way out before the Scots Guards were in position.

A few minutes later came the crash of a first fusillade from our side. Bullets streamed from the first of the Guards as they hastily scrambled into place. They were aiming from front rooms at street-level, where they shot from behind overturned sofas, or else had climbed up among the chimney-stacks. The windows from which the Anarchist rifles had fired at first were now smashed to pieces. Their net curtains were in shreds and one of them was on fire. Then there was a command to the Guards of "Cease fire!" though our ears still rang with the echoes. Presently a further sequence of shots was exchanged, the gunmen this time keeping up the greater rate of fire. I saw one of the constables go down suddenly, among a group who were too close to the far side for their own good. "Jack, I am done!" he cried to his comrade as he spun and fell. He was taken to hospital at once and happily survived his wound.

After the first rifle shots, the weapon of the assassin, our opponents' fire came from handguns. They laid down a barrage with which we could not at first compete. I could make out the long barrels of their Mauser automatic pistols, firing two shots every second. But while their hand-guns might be deadly in intensity, they were less accurate than the rifles which their marksmen had used at first. Why had they abandoned those? As it was, their rifle barrels had merely revealed their positions. They had drawn a ferocious fire into the two upper windows of Martin's Buildings, possibly killing half of those within. Had it been the Home Secretary's intention to make them show themselves by offering his familiar figure as a target?

The events that followed during the next few hours were printed large in every newspaper across the land. What schoolboy did not know of "The Siege of Sidney Street" and the famous part played by the Scots Guards and Winston Churchill? Even as it progressed, the crowds and the pressure grew behind the police cordons at either end of the street, raising cheers every time our men fired back. It seemed impossible that this was the heart of London on a peaceful weekday morning, when office clerks and shop walkers were on their way to work and schoolchildren trudged to their classes. All had now played truant to watch the drama.

Holmes and I remained under cover for the moment behind the gate-pillar of the coal-merchant's yard. What struck me most of all was the way in which many of the inhabitants of the street went about their normal lives as the two sides exchanged fire and the bullets sang round them. An old woman with a shawl over her head crossed the street a little further down to fetch her washing, as indifferent to those bullets as if they had been the falling snow-flakes.

In the coal-merchant's gateway a young journalist, the first I had seen that morning, was standing beside me leaning on his stick. He gave a lurch and almost fell as the stick was neatly cut in half by a bullet which we neither saw nor heard—and which was within inches of ending his life and depriving the world of the genius of Sir Philip Gibbs. A piece of stone flew from the corner of the wall beside me as a shot nicked it, and another fragment bounced from the metal helmet of a startled policeman. Before long, a reek of burnt cordite hung in the damp air and the acrid tang of it scorched one's throat. The sharp cracks of the service rifles were answered by the snaps of pistols from the besieged Anarchists. This was the point at which we were ordered to remove ourselves to safety.

It was not a time to indulge in irony, but I could not help noticing, above the level of the gunmen's positions, an attic floor running along the eight houses of Martin's Buildings. In its window was a sign showing, of all things, the Union Jack flag on a large card with the slogan of "Union Jack Tailoring." Much tailoring would be done that day!

Before long, the press had arrived in numbers, greatly to the satisfaction of the landlord of the Rising Sun, who was able to hire out his flat roof to the reporters after all. Captain Nott-Bower of the City Police stood beside us, watching the front of the besieged houses while his inspector organised a cordon at the rear. It was intended that there should be no reinforcements for the Anarchists and no escape. That, at least, was a matter of opinion in the confusion that existed. These were men capable of fighting the police through sewers and over rooftops, if necessity demanded. In Russian uprisings they had already done so.

Only now were the reporters allowed to know that shots

coming from the houses on our side were fired by the Scots Guards and that the Home Secretary was directing the operations. I overheard an exchange between Mr. Churchill and Lieutenant Ross, the latter asking whether it was intended that his men should presently storm the houses opposite.

"Nonsense!" said Churchill's gruff and emphatic voice. "Do you not see how easily you might trap yourselves in a bunch on those narrow stairways and confined passages? That is just what they would like you to do. I should prophesy the most grievous losses among your detachment. You have only two sergeant-instructors and nineteen men. You cannot afford to lose a single one. No, sir, you must fight it out where you stand."

In truth, the Scots Guards were no longer standing. At either end of the street, newspaper boards had been thrown flat and guardsmen were using them to lie upon as they directed rifle fire against the windows. The Anarchists emptied their pistols repeatedly. From time to time we glimpsed the hand which held a gun as the grimy shreds of lace curtain were edged aside. Once I saw the side of a face, when the man who had fired drew back behind the wall. To have stood behind the curtain in the window opening would have been certain death, as the guardsmen's bullets streamed in.

This inferno of small-arms fire was now so intense that most of the time it was almost impossible to make one's voice heard. The revolutionaries were either using the shelter of the wall of the window-casement when they fired, or shooting from far back, at the rear of the room, with no hope of an accurate aim. They dodged from window to window. One was shooting from so high up that I believe he must have been standing on a chair or a step-ladder.

I had been so absorbed by this that I had not noticed Holmes move away. Now I turned and saw him approaching again.

"I have been talking to Wodehouse," he said. "The Home

Secretary is sending for a field-gun and its crew from the Horse Artillery in St. John's Wood. That will never do. This is London, not Moscow or Odessa."

Still we saw nothing of the gunmen, except a hand with a gun at the corner of a window or a glimpse of eyes or chin as the net curtain blew aside. One of their bullets smashed through the brewery gates and there was a smell of escaping gas. Holmes scanned the attic floor of Union Jack Tailoring, above the windows which the gunmen were using. I doubt if any other pair of eyes was raised that high. There had been no movement there and no sign of life.

"I shall not be long," he said.

I could only assume that he was going to find Lestrade, who was still not to be seen, and possibly to seek out Mycroft Holmes in case he had made the journey from Whitehall.

"I wondered why Holmes should care about Moscow or Odessa?" I asked Captain Nott-Bower beside me.

"Look around you," said the captain grimly, "The windows are full of women and girls leaning out, there are men and boys watching from the chimneys, let alone the crowds at either end of the street. Artillery fire at this range would do untold damage and the shell splinters or fragments of debris would be lethal. Moscow and Odessa were proof of that. To clear all these buildings of people would take until darkness falls. I really wonder what Winston is thinking of."

I was also about to wonder aloud where Holmes had gone, when the captain scanned the attic floor and said,

"Do you see that tailor's workshop? The sign in the window, on a card?"

"I do."

"It is upside down! It was not so when we took up our position."

"I daresay one of the gunmen went up there to spy on our

positions. He moved the sign away to peep out and replaced it incorrectly without realising."

"Why did he not simply look out of the window beside it or over it?"

"I have no idea."

"Look at it!" said Nott-Bower impatiently. "Do you not see?"

"I see that it is upside down. What can that matter, in the middle of all this?"

He spoke very quietly.

"Do you not know, Doctor, that the Union Jack flag, flown upside down, is the sailor's international distress signal?"

At that moment I knew where my friend had gone. A few hundred pairs of eyes had watched Martin's Buildings that morning and had noticed nothing. But a trivial oddity of this kind was the breath of life to Sherlock Holmes. Just then, there was a murmuring from the crowd. Their eyes were lifted, not to the attic windows but to the roof. White smoke was drifting thinly from the rear chimney of the house opposite where I stood. Just then a bullet smashed the window of a house at the side of the yard gates, not two feet from where we stood. Nott-Bower nudged me and we made our way, with heads down, running across the street to "dead ground" on the far side, out of the gunmen's field of vision.

As we approached the street corner, trying to get round to the rear of Martin's Buildings, the fusillade continued overhead. To my alarm, someone at a ground floor window of the Rising Sun shouted, "There they are! More of them! Let them have it!"

Then I saw that, just ahead of us, a shadow had fallen within the window of the ground-floor room at the street corner. That was what had caused the excitement to run higher. Several bullets shattered that window before a shout countermanded this action for fear that we might be hit. Stories ran through the crowd that two newspapermen had been killed by spent bullets flying off the walls. There were now said to be at least eight Anarchists occupying the houses and some had their women with them. Other spectators claimed to have seen hostages in the buildings. One thing was certain: as I looked back, a second drift of white smoke eddied out round a window on the attic floor, above the gunmen's strongpoint.

There was a fearful expectancy at this and the crowds fell silent. Was the house on fire? If so, had the gunmen set it alight in a last mad act of defiance? It seemed to me more likely that, as they kept up their attack from the floor below the attic, they knew nothing of it. As I drew out into the street a little, there was a brief, bright bloom of flame behind an attic window, and then it was gone. The spectators' excitement was divided now between the duel of pistols against rifles and a subdued glow behind the upper windows.

We took a last view before turning the corner opposite the Rising Sun to get to the alleyway at the rear of Martin's Buildings. There was another puff of flame in the attics, illuminating the interior, and another cry as the crowd recognised the shape of a man. From where I stood, he seemed to be lifting or pulling something, which vanished as the flame died down again. Yet his profile was graven in my mind—or had I seen what I expected to see? If it was Holmes, how had he got in and what was he doing? And how would he get out?

Ahead of Nott-Bower, I worked my way round to the back of the houses. It was a no-man's land of little yards and sheds, providing ample cover. Here and there were police officers in the nondescript plain clothes of city streets, carrying shotguns and sporting rifles, borrowed at short notice from a Whitechapel gunsmith. Any one of them might have been taken for an Anarchist, as was presumably intended, and I wondered that they had not shot one another by now. At last I hailed a uniformed inspector.

"There is a man in that house, a criminal investigator. He is coming out and I believe he is bringing someone with him. Hold your fire. I am a medical man and you may need me."

The inspector appeared to chew this over for a moment before replying.

"There is no one in that house but the men who seized it. Please stand back, sir. Every room was checked last night and the residents removed. No one has come or gone since then."

"There is a man in that house, and his name is—"

"Sherlock Holmes."

It was Captain Nott-Bower just behind me and the change which came over the inspector was wonderful to see.

"For what reason he entered I cannot imagine," Nott-Bower continued, "but Mr. Holmes was illuminated by the fire against an attic window just now. I do not see how we can get him out ourselves, but you will certainly not shoot him if he does so."

"We saw no one enter, sir."

"That does not surprise me in the least," said Nott-Bower caustically.

"The only man to pass this way was the gas company's supervisor, to turn off the supply at the main behind us."

Nott-Bower and I exchanged a glance but said nothing. Just then there was a puff of flame behind a rear window and a crack of timber under the roof. Even here, the exchange of gunfire in the street made the ears sing.

"Holmes was seen in the house at the far end," I added as I followed the inspector and Captain Nott-Bower through the little yards at the back. We reached the end of the row. The door to a back room had been opened and from above us the sound of firing continued. Whatever else had brought Holmes here, it was not a plan for silencing the gunmen. Looking through the open back door into that ground-floor room, I could see that it was filling with the same thin white smoke. It drifted like steam off the padded chairs, as if they might burst into flame without warning.

Then, as calmly as if this had been Baker Street, Holmes came silently down the stairs, leading a girl by the hand. She was slightly built, undernourished, about fourteen or fifteen years old, dishevelled, pale and terrified. My friend's clothes were covered in dust and there were streaks of black about his face.

"This is Anna," he said reassuringly, "she does not speak perfect English but she is no Anarchist. The next time you search a house of this kind, Inspector, you might bear in mind that the upper floor is very likely to be a sweatshop. The girls or children who work for a pittance as seamstresses sometimes hide up there to sleep the night, rather than find their bed under the arches of the bridges or the corners of the markets. They know very well how to conceal themselves from a search."

The inspector ignored him, shouting to his men to fall in with their shotguns and prepare to assault the gunmen's strongpoint by the back door and the stairs. Holmes stared coldly at their sporting weapons.

"You will be slaughtered by their Mausers. They will get off twenty or thirty shots for every one of yours. In any case, you have left it too late. The building is ablaze. The bullets have hit the gas-pipes and set the fumes alight. Even if you are not ambushed on the stairs, you will not reach the room where the men are defending themselves. There are two of them left and they have made their choice of how to die. You had far better grant them that."

As we stood in the yard, the flames were already eating at the edges of the wooden stairs. There was no more talk of storming the building. We soon heard that the crowds in the street had seen one gunman lit by the flames as he stood behind the glass panels of the front door. A burst of rifle-fire drove him back, grievously wounded or dead. A second surge of flame illuminated another of the defenders, face-down on a bed with his face buried in the pillow. It seemed he was already dead.

The firing from the blazing house stopped long before the arrival of the horse artillery. By the time I had accompanied Holmes and his young charge to the front of the building, the shooting had stopped on both sides. A fire engine followed the artillery. It was impossible to imagine that anyone was left alive as the blazing attic, its timbers glowing and masonry crashing, collapsed into the floor below, where the defenders had been.

By now, the guardsmen were firing into the front door and the street-level windows at point-blank range. There was no response. The house was a roaring column of flame as exploding gas fuelled the conflagration. The Scots Guards still knelt with rifles aimed at the doorway lest a fugitive might bolt down the street, but the time for that was long past. When the roof and the floors had fallen in and a volume of flame shot skywards, the besiegers formed themselves up to withdraw. Only the hoses of the firemen played on the remains.

How many of the gunmen died or whether any escaped, before or after the arrival of the police, was anyone's guess. Later on, the remains of the house were searched. Among the burnt debris were the head and arms of one man and the skull of another with a bullet-hole in its back. Several Mauser pistols which had exploded in the heat of the fire lay close by. The remains of a dressmaker's dummy and the bodies of several sewing-machines were all that remained of the Union Jack Tailoring shop. There were parts of metal bedsteads and containers for acetylene or gas, which had the shape of torpedoes and a usefulness as bomb-cases. From these fragments, the world was to construct what explanation it could.

Anna, the protégée of Sherlock Holmes, was handed over with all kindness to the Salvation Army matrons, who had set up their camp beyond the police cordon to minister as they might. They would return her to her mother and sisters in Whitechapel.

"But how could a girl like that know such a thing?" I demanded. "She is Polish? And yet she knows the seaman's distress signal of a Union Jack flown upside down?"

Holmes smiled.

"Her father is Polish and served for many years in the merchant marine. On a humbler level than Mr. Joseph Conrad, but no less usefully, he entertained her with the tales and customs of the sea. This one caught her imagination. It is not a custom that you had encountered?"

I was a little put out by this.

"It was one that I knew perfectly well. But with bullets flying in all directions I was hardly likely to keep watch as to whether someone had turned a tradesman's card in a window upside down."

He nodded indulgently.

"Indeed so. I fear that on such occasions, my dear Watson, you see but you do not observe. The distinction is quite clear and not unimportant."

9

The fire had, as it seemed to me, destroyed many of the answers to the mystery which led to the "Siege of Sidney Street." The most intriguing, if the press were to be believed, was what had become of the sinister and cold-blooded figure of "Peter the Painter." Had he died in the fire, or was he safely back in Paris, or Berlin, or Moscow? He was certainly real enough. He had a history of subversion and assassination in the police dossiers of the world. He also had a future in the revolutionary government of the Soviet Union, though Sherlock Holmes was one of the very few who predicted that. No one could agree as to who commanded him or who obeyed him, let alone in what disguise he might be found. In England, it seemed that he had come and gone, died perhaps, in the few weeks following the Houndsditch murders.

Because I had seen him, I was pestered a little by the press, but I could tell them nothing they did not know already. I thought he was one more paragon of evil who had set out to destroy Sherlock Holmes—and had failed.

So I sat down to compose our narrative of the Anarchist uprising. Holmes was out and it was a fine February afternoon with the rime of the frost still clinging to the grass of the Regent's Park. Being a Saturday, Mrs. Hudson had gone to visit her sister in Dulwich. Even Mary Jane, the maid-of-all-work, had gone walking with her "young man." The house was quiet, the traffic subdued, and I had begun.

> On a morning in early December, three years before the Great War, Mrs. Hedges brought us the unusual story of a yellow canary. . . .

I had written a page or two more when there was a ring at the front door. I cursed to myself, but it is a "rule of business," as Holmes says, to leave no summons unanswered. I put down my pen, descended the stairs, and opened the front door.

"Mr. Hoolmes! Mr. Share-lock Hoolmes!"

I froze with terror—and it was no cliché—or should I say my heart leapt to my throat. There was no mistaking who he was. He had not died in the fires of Sidney Street, whatever the authorities might hope. I thought helplessly that my Army revolver was locked in the desk upstairs and that I was alone in the house. Perhaps if I could make him believe that the landlady or the maid was within earshot he would not dare to murder me. . . .

"You are alone, I think. But whoever you are, you are not Mr. Share-lock Hoolmes. Perhaps when I tell you my name, Piatkoff, you will comprendre."

It was the same coat with Astrakhan collar, the same broad-brimmed hat. But now the voice was quiet and a fine scorn animated his features with his dark neat-cut hair, the aristocratic profile and beaked nose.

Had I known of his visit in advance, I could have prepared myself. For the moment, the shock was so great that the power of speech was beyond me. He stood up a little taller, his head went back a little and he seemed about to utter a laugh of diabolical triumph.

Then, as if in my unconscious mind the entire mystery of the past few weeks was revealed, I exclaimed, "Holmes!"

He laughed, drew breath, and then laughed again. It was not the satanic cackle of Piatkoff but the ebullient chuckle of my friend.

"Holmes, what the devil. . . ."

"My dear Watson—I could not resis. . . ." Laughter stifled him on the doorstep for a moment. "I could not resist one more little impersonation. I could not forgo the sight of your face when. . . . Surely, my dear old fellow, you noticed that when Piatkoff materialised before you on previous occasions, I was always conveniently elsewhere? Truly, truly, you see but you do not observe!"

I was so shaken that I simply stood back and watched him go up the stairs. He shrugged off the Astrakhan-trimmed coat and sent the hat skimming onto the rack. The grease-paint that had subtly flushed his complexion was wiped off. The wads that had heightened those cheeks were pulled from above the gums, he disappeared into his room and disposed of the gum arabic and gutta percha which had made the alteration of his nose possible, and he peeled away the fine set of whiskers.

By the time he returned, I had almost finished the glass of whisky which the occasion demanded. Wiping his hands on one of Mrs. Hudson's clean towels, he remarked, "You must save some of the blame for Brother Mycroft, Watson, for it was his apartment that I used as my dressing-room."

"Your brother knows the truth of this charade?"

"Indeed."

"And Lestrade?"

"The truth is not something that one always tells to a susceptible fellow like Lestrade."

"But to what purpose?"

He sighed and sat down.

"No one in the Anarchist movement here is certain of Piatkoff. Nor of his appearance, for he has so many. Nor of his voice or manner, for it changes in a moment. Nor of his whereabouts. There are so many spies, so many Anarchist movements spying on one another, that he does not advertise when or where he comes and goes. He is like the elusive Scarlet Pimpernel, though far less amiable."

"But he cannot be so secret."

Holmes reached for his pipe.

"Secrecy is all to these people. The names of the few are not known to the many, much less their disguises. They cannot betray, even if they wished to. Piatkoff is still in Paris but most of the Anarchist group in London—and the Metropolitan Police—believe him to be in England, dead or alive."

"But to what end?"

"Mycroft and I devised a plan which we divulged to no other person. It hinged upon making the press, the police, and even you, my dear fellow, believe that Piatkoff was in London and that I in my impersonation was he. We were careful to deal only with those who had never met him. Sidney Street was the arsenal of those who sought European revolution and whose first weapon was assassination."

"Assassination of whom?"

He pulled a face.

"I was told more of assassination than I expected. The list includes the King, the Prime Minister, and Winston Churchill as Home Secretary, who therefore commands the nation's police force. Among many other names, my own appears. I confess I should have been disappointed had it not done so. You, for some reason, are omitted. My performance as Piatkoff in the street below us and the notoriety which the press gave me for that were of great assistance. The search which you and your two policemen undertook through the streets of Stepney was invaluable. I promise you, it was essential that you should all have believed in my masquerade. There are spies everywhere. Imagine trying to get Lestrade to act a part. He would not last five minutes."

"You bought firearms from E. M. Reilly & Co in New Oxford Street and had them delivered to a contact at the Anarchist Club?"

"Indeed, several very efficient rifles of a kind which the trade of assassination thrives upon. You saw them in action at Sidney Street. One of them I managed to rescue during my visit to the burning house. The comrades come by hand-guns quite easily, but they are remarkably short of rifles. I do not believe they possessed one until my gifts to them. Rifles, they believe quite correctly, are 'the weapons of assassination.'"

"But this is madness!" I said.

He shook his head.

"No, Watson, this is cold and absolute sanity. Mycroft and I agreed that I should become their quartermaster. They would look to me for their supplies and they could not do that without telling me of their needs. By knowing of their needs, I should learn their plans and the objects of their campaign of assassination. I should become not their servant but their master."

"And Lestrade?"

"Lestrade still knows nothing of this and never will. As it proves, the charade is over."

I tried to compose myself.

"Let me have this straight. You supplied these men with live ammunition and rifles, which as it turns out were used in an attempt to assassinate the Home Secretary in Sidney Street?"

"They were supplied for that purpose but we had no idea that Sidney Street would be the occasion. Mr. Churchill, of course, was bound to be the target in the circumstances."

"And did he know?"

"He insisted."

I did not want to call my old friend a liar. Yet I could not swallow the story that anyone, Home Secretary or not, would agree to face marksmen's live bullets at lethal range with no protection.

10

The last act of this farce, if I may call it that, was the most extraordinary. Holmes promised to convince me, but I did not see how. Next morning, he said only that we should have visitors that afternoon. Once again, it was one of those occasions when Mrs. Hudson was engaged elsewhere. Just after four o'clock, as the lamps were lit along Baker Street and the shops shone brightly, a cab pulled up and Holmes went down to answer the door.

There were several voices on the stairs. Into the room came Mycroft Holmes with two strangers who looked, to say the least, curious. I recognised one from his carte-de-visite, which he had left one day on finding that Sherlock Holmes was not at home. He was Chung Ling Soo, the Marvellous Chinese Conjuror of the Wood Green Empire Music Hall. With him was his wife, Suee Seen. My first impression was that they were not Chinese at all; indeed, subsequent events revealed that they were William and Olive Robinson.

"In order that you may be convinced of the safety in which the Home Secretary stood," Holmes said to me, "Mr. Chung

Ling Soo and my brother are now going to shoot me. Unless you would prefer to do so."

Mycroft Holmes seemed entirely unperturbed.

"Certainly not," I said.

The pantomime proceeded. Two rifles had been brought, one of them purchased by Holmes from E. M. Reilly, the other presumably supplied by the conjuror. Holmes handed me two bullets, inviting me to scratch some identifying mark on each. With growing unease I did so. He handed them to his brother. Each of the rifles was then loaded and the charge rammed home. There was no question that they were using live ammunition. Chung Ling Soo took one of the guns and Mycroft Holmes the other. I truly believed that I was about to see Mycroft Holmes try to shoot dead his younger brother.

"Stop this!" I said furiously. "Such trickery is dangerous!"

Gunfire had not been unknown in our sitting-room, as Holmes picked out patterns in the plaster with revolver shots from my own weapon. This was far from such amusements. Holmes took up a silver dish, a tribute from one of our clients, and walked to the far end of the room, a range of about twenty feet. He held the dish out at chest height, as if offering it. I sat in my chair and felt sick with anxiety. Mycroft and the conjuror raised their rifles, taking deadly aim at Holmes's heart.

The barks of the guns were almost simultaneous. Flame shot from the barrels followed by a thin cloud of powder and a stink of burnt cordite. Holmes did not even flinch. Instead, there were two sounds, each like a "ping!" as something seemed to fall into the silver dish that he held out to receive it. He walked across and presented to me the two bullets which I had marked with my own initials. It was evident that he had somehow "palmed" these, yet two shots had surely been fired in earnest.

"Our Home Secretary was in no more danger than I," he said

gently. "By his coolness he drew their fire and gave us their positions before they could do us any damage."

"And if they had used the Mausers first?"

"The gunmen could not aim without moving the curtain. The moment a Mauser barrel appeared, he would have been thrown behind a convenient steel screen. One was already in position. Happily, this was not the case."

The secret of the "firing-squad trick," performed twice nightly to great applause by Chung Ling Soo on the stage of the Wood Green Empire, was now revealed to me. It required a small alteration in the mechanism of a rifle. The barrel and its bullet were sealed off from the detonation. The gases and the force of the explosion were directed down the tube running along under the barrel of the rifle, the gun's safety valve and a convenient place otherwise for keeping a cleaning rod. By the time that an assassin suspected such a trick, it would be too late.

As we sat in the aftermath of cordite fumes, I knew at once the answer to the mystery of the soldering-iron fumes at the breakfast-table and Holmes hollow-eyed from lack of sleep. Of course he had spent the night with Brother Mycroft or the Wonderful Chinese Conjuror, preparing three or four Lee-Enfield rifles for delivery to Jubilee Hall.

11

I cannot conclude without adding that some of the actors in the dramas of Houndsditch and Sidney Street were to be heard of again, not least the Home Secretary whose fame was to echo across the world. Chung Ling Soo, Wonderful Chinese Conjuror, fell victim to his own cleverness. Constant removal of his rifle's breech-block at every performance had worn the mechanism dangerously. One night, the bullet in the barrel was accidentally fired. Our benefactor fell dying on the stage of the Wood Green Empire Music Hall before his Saturday night audience on 23 March 1918.

As for Peter the Painter, it was certain that before his arrival in Paris, he had been a medical student in his native Russia and that he returned there from Paris soon after the battle in London. Meantime he had worked as a theatrical scene painter and thereby acquired his nickname. To avoid being conscripted into the army of the Tsar in 1914, he travelled to Germany and was not heard of again publicly until the Communist Revolution of 1917 brought him back to Petrograd.

I have before me a cutting from The Times of 14 April 1920. It was Sherlock Holmes who noticed a letter from Russia and read it out to me at the breakfast table. Its author signed himself only as "S." He revealed that a list of 189 workers had been published in Moscow, men who had been shot on the orders of the Extraordinary Committee for Combating Counter-Revolution. Their crime had been to hold a mass meeting in Petrograd, at the Poutiloff factory, where they denounced the Commissars and demanded "bread and liberty." They accused the Bolshevists of offering them only "prison, the whip, and bullets," denying them even "the small political liberties enjoyed under the Tsarist regime."

As the paper reported, Piatkoff, "the notorious Peter the Painter of Sidney Street fame," had been despatched from Moscow to supervise the wholesale execution of these dissidents. Before being executed, they were informed that their crime had been to sully the name of liberty, which their great leader Lenin had re-defined as meaning the self-discipline of the proletariat.

I could not but shudder at this and at the name of the man who had taken up the trade of executioner. He was not the only ghost to haunt the future. Small wonder that when the Soviet Union created its secret service, the "Cheka," it appointed as chairman the cousin of "The Limping Man," Yoshka Sokoloff, who had died in the battle of Sidney Street. The new chairman, added The Times report, was "one of the cruellest of Cheka officers during the early years of the Terror."

V

The Case of the Zimmermann Telegram

1

For many years after the events which I am about to describe, the papers of Sherlock Holmes relating to them were lodged in the most secure bank vault in the City of London. I held one key to the black metal deed-boxes, and a member of His Majesty's Privy Council held the other. Neither of us could open them alone. Among the contents were letters, telegrams, and folded parchments tied with pink ribbon, like the confidential brief of King's Counsel in a leading criminal trial.

Some of these folded briefs bore a few words written by Holmes himself in black ink on their outer surface. One of them was dated 1917 and had the name "Arthur Zimmermann" written upon it with the instruction "Twenty years." That is the period for which Holmes and I were sworn to secrecy concerning the Great War of 1914–18. Our promise had been given to the First Sea Lord of the Admiralty, at Buckingham Palace, as all Europe careered into the abyss in August 1914. With the passing of time and the consent of His Majesty's Government, the contents of those papers need no longer remain secret.

I had never expected that his records of our war against the German Empire would have survived the domestic bonfires of my friend's final days. Surely he would have burnt this! Surely, surely he would have destroyed that! But I was quite wrong. There they lie, untouched among other letters and memoranda which he made no effort to conceal.

Perhaps he was satisfied that a certain telegraph message which gives its title to the present story would mean nothing to those who chanced to find it. I have it before me now. It is printed on a Western Union telegram form, and it bears the mast-head of that company across the top of its page. It is dated 19 January 1917 and has been wired from Washington to Mexico City, via Galveston, Texas. You may now read it, if you choose. Though it is a little in advance of my narrative, it will illustrate how daunting can be the appearance of a diplomatic cipher from the intelligence service of a great world power. Imagine, if you will, that the lives of millions of people and the fate of the world depend upon your unaided ability to turn the following equation into plain and readable prose within the next two or three hours.

TO GERMAN LEGATION
MEXICO CITY

Charge German Embassy
Washington 19 January 1917
Via Galveston

130 13042 13401 8501 115 3528 416 17214 6491 11310
18147 18222 21560 10247 11518 23677 13605 3494 14936
98092 5905 11311 10392 10271 0302 21290 5161 39695
23571 17504 11269 18278 18101 0317 0228 17694 4473
23264 22200 19452 21589 67893 5569 13918 8958 12137
1333 4725 4458 5905 17166 13851 4458 17149 14471 6706

13850 12224 6929 14991 7382 15857 67893 14218 36477
5870 17533 67893 5870 5454 16102 5217 22801 17138
21001 17388 7446 23638 18222 6719 14331 15021 23845
3156 23552 22096 21604 4797 9497 22464 20855 4377
23610 18140 22260 5905 13347 20420 39689 13732 20667
6929 5275 18507 52262 1340 22049 13339 11265 22295
10439 14814 4178 6992 8784 7632 7357 6926 52262 11267
21100 21272 9346 9559 22464 15874 18502 18500 17857
2188 5376 7381 98092 16127 13486 9350 9220 76038 14219
6144 2831 17920 11347 17142 11264 7667 7762 15099 9110
10482 97556 3569 3670

Bernstorff.

Such is the complete text of this extraordinary document. I will tell you as a clue that no single number corresponds to the same letter of the alphabet on every occasion, though entire words may sometimes be identical. The number "7" may be "a" on one occasion and "q" on another, and "h" on the third. What lies behind this sequence of numbers is an infinitely variable series of ciphers.

Sherlock Holmes was one of the few men on earth who could break the secret of such a transmission within a few hours. His colleagues in Admiralty Intelligence were an unpredictable company of naval officers, classical scholars from the best universities, puzzle-book addicts, eccentrics of many kinds. There were mathematicians, and pioneers of symbolic logic, among them pupils of the late Rev C. L. Dodgson, better known to fame as "Lewis Carroll." Holmes several times remarked that had we been able to enlist the creator of Alice, we should have given German intelligence "cards, spades, and a beating," from the first day of the war to the last.

Holmes himself was supreme—and he knew it. After the Zimmermann adventure was over and the war had ended, I recall him reclining in his fireside chair during one of his more insufferable meditations, shaking out the match with which he had just lit his briar pipe and saying, "All things considered, Watson, and though I found much of the work tiresome, I believe it was just as well that I was at hand when this little matter came to the attention of our government."

He did not intend to be humorous in the least. All the same, I laughed. It was too much like the Duke of Wellington recalling the "close-run thing" of the Battle of Waterloo and adding, "Damn it, I do not know that it would have done if I had not been there."

It would not have done—in either case. Let me now reveal how the career of Sherlock Holmes in the Great War of 1914–18 culminated in that bizarre but momentous battle of the famous telegram.

2

Holmes and I were recruited to this work on the very eve of war. The man responsible was the First Sea Lord at the Admiralty, Sir John Fisher, with whom my friend had worked in breaking Germany's peacetime codes. "Jacky Fisher," as he was popularly known, did nothing so obvious as visiting us in Baker Street. Who was to say whether a passer-by might not be a trained spy, or a German sympathiser in the pay of Tirpitz and his Kriegsmarine?

We knew from our friend Chief Inspector Lestrade, now of the Special Branch at Scotland Yard, that several neutrals in the Baker Street area were under suspicion. They included a Swiss watch-repairer, a Swedish bank courier, even a Spanish restaurateur. Any of these might be the man whose role in the war was to report to Germany on the movements and activities of such men as Sherlock Holmes. Being neutrals, they might inform military intelligence in Berlin, through German embassies in their own countries, without the danger of being hanged or shot in London as traitors.

To foil surveillance of this kind, Sir John Fisher arranged a most unlikely rendezvous with Sherlock Holmes. It was the last Court Ball to be held at Buckingham Palace, before all such good things ended for the duration of the war. The place was well chosen, precisely because it was the type of function which Holmes abominated. So little taste had my friend for what he dismissed as "flummery" that there was an inevitable difficulty as to which ladies we should escort to the occasion. In the end, I was obliged to call upon the services of two astonished spinster cousins from Devonshire.

The Court Ball itself—dancing on the path to Armageddon, as Holmes called it grimly—was no less brilliant for being the last of its kind. It was to have been held a month earlier, before the ultimatums of war were issued. Instead, it had been postponed during a period of court mourning for the assassination in Sarajevo of the Archduke Ferdinand of Austria and his wife Sophie by a Bosnian student on 28 June. Who would have thought that two deaths in a remote and dusty Balkan town would plunge the entire world into such conflict?

Even as a century of peace was dying, the scene at the palace on that gala night was one I shall never forget. The young Prince of Wales, a shy boy who was to succeed his father as Edward VIII in 1936, was his mother's partner and piloted Queen Mary through the Royal Quadrille. King George stood apart, in grave conversation with the ambassador of our Russian ally, Count Benckendorff. The Germans and the Austrians had feigned a diplomatic absence and were packing their bags for the journey home, as the minutes of our ultimatum ticked away.

At the edge of the grand ballroom, Holmes and I found ourselves chatting in a small group round Lord William Cecil, the King's Equerry, who was also an officer of Military Intelligence at the War Office. Holmes had no appetite for small talk of any kind. He soon lapsed into a gloomy and discourteous silence. Even when a reply was necessary, he responded by a monosyllable.

I was only too anxious to be rescued from this embarrassment. I looked across the floor towards the tall and elegant figure of Sir John Fisher, in the formal royal blue uniform and gold piping of Admiral of the Fleet. He caught my eye but gave no sign of recognition. He too was now unsmiling, despite the "laughter lines" round his mouth. Even the brightness in his pale eyes had died away.

Holmes and Jacky Fisher had been firm friends for many years. Fisher was a man after Holmes's heart with his simple policy for naval warfare: "Hit first, hit hard, and keep on hitting." Sherlock Holmes would never hear a word spoken against the admiral, describing Fisher as having "not an inch of pose about him." My friend gave him the motto, "Sworn to no party—of no sect am I. I can't be silent and I will not lie."

Just then, Lord William Cecil ceased to talk ballroom trivialities. As if he had received a signal, he took us each by an elbow, murmuring something about "supper." He led us towards the grand buffet, where a crowd was beginning to gather. However, we were not to reach those supper tables with their sparkling white cloths, their silver and porcelain dishes of salmon and caviar, where royal footmen were waiting to serve us. To one side of this display was a white panelled door with gilt mouldings. Beyond it lay an ante-room. In a moment we had passed through and the door had been locked behind us. The exchanges which followed were to remain under our wartime oath of secrecy.

Sir John Fisher was there to speak for King George. Lord William Cecil held a brief for the General Staff. There was one other man who was a complete stranger to me. Yet if I had never met him again, I should not have forgotten his appearance. He was wearing the uniform of a Royal Navy captain. I recall him as being dapper, alert, with a perfectly domed bald head, a large hooked nose, and a strong cleft chin. Most memorably, he had eyes that were possessed of a dark and penetrating hypnotic power.

As we entered the damask-panelled chamber, Fisher went up to this newcomer and then turned to us.

"Gentlemen, may I present to you Captain Reginald Hall, who is at present commander of the battle-cruiser Queen Mary? You will see and hear a good deal of him before long. He will very shortly be taking up his appointment among us as Admiral Sir Reginald Hall, Director of Admiralty Intelligence."

After that, I needed no further hints to deduce what part Holmes and I were invited to play. When the formal introductions were over, Reginald Hall casually picked up a copy of that evening's Globe newspaper, which had been left on a small occasional table. Its tall black headlines proclaimed the immediate German military threat to Belgium and hopeless Belgian gallantry in meeting an overwhelming attack. As a way of introducing himself, the captain tossed the paper back again and looked at us with his penetrating gaze.

"Well, here's a business, Mr. Holmes and Dr. Watson."

"I daresay, Sir Reginald," said Holmes, rather too coldly as it seemed to me, "but it is not a business of my making nor is it to my taste. I confess that I have killed one or two men in my time—and without regret—but slaughter of this kind is not a dish I can relish."

Fisher intervened at once, before my friend could make matters worse.

"Nor I, Mr. Holmes. However, now that the choice is set before us, we must either win this war or lose it. My sole duty to His Majesty is to ensure that we win."

I could guess what was coming, for I had heard it from many people in the past few weeks. Fisher reminded us that England had fought no great European war for almost a century, since the defeat of Napoleon at Waterloo in 1815. In consequence, we had been caught thoroughly unprepared for this one, as he had repeatedly warned us that we would be. Now there was work for us all, and we must do it with a will. There could be no "civilians." Every man and woman at home had duties to perform, as surely as the first of our front-line regiments who had embarked secretly for France. The particular duties of Sherlock Holmes and myself had yet to be agreed, but that they must be a matter of national importance was constantly implied.

"There can only be one place for you, Mr. Holmes," Fisher said at length, his eyes holding my friend's gaze. "Your gifts belong at the heart of our nation's security. Without such intelligence as you can bring us, we fight blind—and deaf too, for that matter."

"To begin with," said Holmes, more gently than I had feared, "if I were to travel like an office boy each day from Baker Street to Whitehall, I should soon have every spy in London on my back. I take it that when we speak of Whitehall we are talking of the famous Room 40 in the Old Admiralty Building. Room 40 is a secret so well kept that every newspaper boy in the West End streets can tell you a dozen stories about it."

"If there are spies on your tail, the more easily shall they be caught," said Fisher evenly. "We shall get the better of those fellows, believe me. I have given the matter considerable thought."

Holmes seemed only to be half listening. He was looking round the ante-room, as though it were beyond his conception that any sane man should choose to live among such paint and gilt, such damask and satin as this. He responded to Fisher by raising his eyebrows a fraction, indicating a little surprise that a mere admiral of the fleet should presume to think in competition with the sage of Baker Street. Then he sighed.

"Very well. Tell me what you propose."

Jacky Fisher relaxed and began to explain himself.

"Some years ago, you will recall that you first came to my

assistance by recovering the Bruce-Partington submarine plans which had been stolen from Woolwich Arsenal. Indeed, our friend Dr. Watson wrote an account of your adventure on that occasion."

"Not by my wish," said Holmes quickly, but Fisher ignored him.

"At the time," he continued, "I recall that you had made a hobby—or a study—of the choral music of the Middle Ages. Indeed, you were writing an analysis of the Polyphonic Motets of Orlando Lassus, were you not? I was much struck by that."

"Your memory does you credit," said Holmes dryly. Sir John brushed this aside.

"I will make a suggestion. Our adversaries in Berlin would give a good deal to know of your activities in the course of this war. I intend to appease their curiosity by feeding them something to chew on. Now, then. Your reluctance to go to war is humane and sensible. I will not ask you to compromise your views. Indeed, I suggest that you should compose a letter to the editor of the Times or the Morning Post or both, expressing your disapproval of this coming entanglement with Germany and your hopes for an early resolution of the conflict. . . ."

"Not merely a disapproval of this war but of all such unnecessary wars," Holmes retorted.

Captain Hall blinked, but Fisher took this in his stride.

"The fact that the letter is genuine in its sentiments is entirely as I would wish. Having let your feelings be known, you should then openly pledge to dedicate yourself to the study of Orlando Lassus. Of course, the Germans may doubt the sincerity of your objections to the war, but they cannot be sure. A suitable library should be chosen for your work. It must not be open to the public. If there is free access, your movements could be spied upon even while you were at your desk. That would never do. You will be seen coming and going to the institution, but that also is as we would wish it."

"And behind this charade of Achilles sulking in his tent?" Holmes inquired.

"I propose," said Sir John Fisher, the eyes twinkling at last, "or rather His Majesty proposes, that you should become Director of Admiralty Signals Intelligence at Room 40. We divide our surveillance into Human Intelligence and Signals Intelligence. We offer you Signals. You see that your fame goes before you!"

Holmes began to mellow a little under Fisher's charm. As we talked of the proposed arrangement that evening in the ante-room, the dancers whirled in a twisting of silk and a glitter of diamonds, a few feet away beyond the locked door.

The very existence of Room 40 was supposed to be known only to the trusted few. Despite Holmes's scornful aside, that was still the case. At the rear of the Old Admiralty Building, this room and its offices looked out beyond the expanse of Horse Guards Parade and St. James's Park towards the heavy Renaissance pile of the Foreign Office. It was the centre from which the best brains of Naval Intelligence struggled with the coded signals and secret telegraph messages that filled the night sky between Berlin and Ankara, Vienna and New York, Valparaiso and Tokyo.

In addition, Fisher confided to us that the German deep-sea cables carried both naval and diplomatic ciphers, as well as conventional telegrams. They ran from Bremen on the bed of the North Sea, westwards down the English Channel, then across the Bay of Biscay to Vigo in northern Spain. From here they extended across the Atlantic to New York, and alternatively to Buenos Aires, touching first at Tenerife in the Canary Islands.

These sea-bed cables were not destined to survive the outbreak of war by more than a few hours. The Cable & Wireless company's cable-laying ship *Telconia* was lying at Dover, already commandeered by the Admiralty and with a Royal Navy crew aboard. A few hours before the British ultimatum to Berlin expired, she would put to sea in darkness, carrying sealed orders. Her course had been set for the neutral Dutch coast to strike at the weakest point, where the cables must run in shallow waters. There the vessel would ride at anchor in the darkness and the mist, where the territorial waters of Holland meet those of Germany, awaiting the midnight signal from the Admiralty to all shipping that war had been declared.

As soon as the signal was received, Telconia was to trawl with her grappling gear for the five transatlantic cables in their iron sheathing. They would be hauled to the surface at the invisible sea-frontier. Royal Navy cable engineers were to sever them through their iron casings and let the broken ends fall back into the depths. Neutral Holland might continue to signal to the world. Our enemies in Germany would be obliged to communicate openly by wireless from the powerful transmitter at Nauen near Berlin or through neutral countries, most probably Sweden. Every one of the coded messages sent by such means could be intercepted by a new chain of Admiralty signal stations established round our coasts.

Having explained this, Fisher came to the supreme consideration of security and secrecy. "Your presence at the Admiralty, Mr. Holmes, is to be kept from public knowledge. Our opponents almost certainly know that you have broken their code in the past. We must try to persuade them that you have not been given the chance to do it again."

Captain Hall interposed, rather diffidently, as became a newcomer to the debate.

"Our first measure has been an attempt to convince our adversaries of the existence of a vast and efficient network of British spies on the Continent. Indeed, two Royal Navy officers, Lieutenant Brandon and Lieutenant Trench, have served prison sentences in Germany. It seems Tirpitz prefers to believe that his cipher-tables may have been given away by indiscretion, or even betrayed, but not deciphered. We have a small number of spies in Europe, to be sure, but nothing like the total that the Wilhelmstrasse believes. A few of our most skilled and important agents play the part of traitors to us. We know that German intelligence believes such disloyalty to be the most valuable source of their information."

Holmes turned away and stood silent for a moment. Sir John Fisher interrupted his thoughts with growing impatience.

"You say that you disapprove of this war, Mr. Holmes. You do not disapprove of it more heartily than I do—or more deeply than the King himself. So long as it continues, the best of our young men face death in the trenches or on the high seas. The sooner it is over, the better. With your abilities we may win bloodless victories. If there is war, there must be battles, of course. But many more battles that would have cost tens of thousands of young lives may never need to be fought. How much better to triumph in this way than through the hecatombs of the slaughtered young."

Holmes turned to him, calmly and with his decision made.

"Very well. I am His Majesty's subject and shall obey. May the end be as quick and as bloodless as you propose."

In the white ante-room with its gold-laced furniture it, was impossible to miss a collective breath of relief.

Our negotiations with Fisher and Hall were not before time. In the course of that evening, a score of officers in their medalled mess jackets and formal dress took an unceremonious leave of the Court Ball. Despatch riders had brought orders to the Palace that two of our most famous regiments must return to camp. There was to be no delay, not even to enable reservists to reach them. Their battalions were to mobilise at present strength. At Liverpool Street station, they were to entrain for King's Lynn to meet a possible German raiding party on the East

Coast. The enemy might be expected as early as the next day's summer dawn.

Such news brought with it a sense of complete unreality, as if we were taking part in a new play at the Haymarket or the Lyceum. All too soon, the same news was to be the talk of the hour.

3

Even as we discussed Fisher's plans for Sherlock Holmes, I was doubtful that the enemy would be deceived for long. It was all very well for Sir John Fisher to boast how easily he could make fools of the Germans. The truth was that enemy spies might be anywhere in London, in guises of every kind. A citizen of a neutral country, let alone our own, might have private German sympathies. Holmes and I must assume, each time we left Baker Street, that either of us was being followed by a man or woman whose presence we had failed to detect.

We came to recognise one or two of those who quite plainly kept watch on us, though it would have been difficult to prove what law they were breaking. In any case, Holmes insisted that we must "let them be." Far better to have such hangers-on where we could see them, than behind prison bars. We might not recognise the enemies who took their places, until it was too late.

There was a stout young man with a high flush and breathless movements. He would frequently appear in cap and gaiters where Cornwall Terrace joins Baker Street, like a stable-groom setting out for the park, just as Holmes stepped into his hansom cab. But this young look-out went no further. He crossed the road and turned away in the opposite direction, towards Marylebone. We could accuse him of nothing—and yet we were sure. His turning away was the signal for another watchdog. As the cab moved forward, this second man would very often appear round the corner from Park Street. He rode a bicycle, convenient for keeping a cab in view, and appeared much the older of the pair. His dark hair and pointed beard had the suggestion of being rimed by white frost. All the same, the nimbleness of his movements on the bicycle pedals hinted strongly to me that he was a younger man disguised. But we could hardly have him shot for that.

With one exception, these watchers were never interfered with. Our only mishap, early on, was the arrest of a ginger-haired giant with an entirely Germanic face. This was done by my intervention, largely to placate our nervous landlady, Mrs. Hudson. Holmes was not in the house at the time. The man proved to be a plain-clothes sergeant of the Criminal Investigation Division, stationed at Paddington Green police station specifically for our protection. Needless to say, this well-intentioned error on my part delighted my friend.

His letter denouncing the futility of war, from Holmes to the Morning Post, had duly appeared. It was written with sufficient feeling to carry conviction to the unprejudiced reader. I feared we should receive a deluge of hostile post from wartime patriots, but such was not the case. We were at an early stage of the conflict, and tempers were not as hot as they subsequently became.

Every morning Holmes went by cab to the St. James's Library, off Pall Mall, to resume his work on the counterpoint of Orlando Lassus. The St. James's was a private library, founded by the great John Stuart Mill in the 1840s and restricted to members only. Membership was granted after personal recommendation and election, so that it was easy to check the names of those who made use of it. Holmes the musicologist appeared to work there until late in the afternoon, when he was driven back to Baker Street.

We were informed by Naval Intelligence that those who spied upon the library during the day probably did so from the rooms of an otherwise respectable European Club on the far side of the square. Its windows overlooked the library building. Yet even if these hidden onlookers in St. James's continued to keep watch, they saw no evidence of Holmes among the readers leaving or returning between his arrival in the morning and his departure for home at the end of the afternoon. They must content themselves with a young carpenter, who had been at work erecting shelves in the reading room, swinging his long bag and whistling as he went on his way to another job. Perhaps a bluff middle-aged fellow in a country suit arrived from Sussex or Surrey for an hour's browsing among the shelves. An elderly scholar with pince-nez and an old-fashioned stove-pipe hat might appear from the Oxford train or the ecclesiastical figure of an avuncular rural dean would set out for his return to a West Country parish.

Those who have followed the adventures of Sherlock Holmes may at once guess the identity of the whistling carpenter, the bluff countryman, the shrivelled old scholar, or the rural dean. Happily, it was a fact unknown to German intelligence that in 1879, as an anonymous understudy and at short notice, Holmes had played Horatio to Sir Henry Irving's Hamlet at the Lyceum. It was his one and only appearance on the London stage. Almost at once he was engaged to sail on an eight-month tour of the United States with the Sasanoff Shakespearean Company. It was not merely that he adopted the costume of the role he played; he assumed the expression, the manner, and the very soul of that part.

Yet I believe my friend considered that he reached the height of impersonation when the cab stopped in the Piccadilly square, the familiar figure strode up the library steps, the driver whipped up the horse and clattered round the corner into Pall Mall. As so often, the spies saw what they expected to see. Yet it was a trustworthy amateur, perhaps resting from the stage, who went up the steps to the library door, while the consulting detective covered by a shabby coat and hat drove the hansom smartly round the corner. Fifteen minutes later, he brought the horse and cab to rest in the securely guarded precincts of Old Admiralty Yard.

If anything more was needed to lay German suspicions to rest, Holmes published in the following spring two impeccable reviews of the polyphony of Orlando Lassus. His learned references to texts and manuscripts were in themselves several pages long. Orders for the journal were placed with Lindemann in neutral Geneva. The destination of two copies proved to be the Bureau of Military Intelligence in Berlin. It was from this moment that a noticeable falling off began in the numbers of those who tracked the hero of Baker Street on his daily journeys to Piccadilly and, presumably, among those who watched forlornly from the windows of the European Club.

4

If my friend expressed his reservations in the first months of the war, when the hopeful belief was that it would be over by Christmas, you may imagine his feelings as the Western Front settled into mud and slaughter. On a pleasant June evening, after almost two years of the conflict, we were sitting either side of our window, discussing the losses of British battle-cruisers in the engagement off Jutland a fortnight earlier, and the loss of Lord Kitchener, Minister of War, in the sinking of the cruiser HMS Devonshire the previous week. Holmes seemed to be at his lowest ebb.

"I fear that we and Germany may end as two corpses, manacled together," he said gloomily. After a pause, he stared down into the quiet street and added, "Even were we to defeat the powers of central Europe utterly, the result could only be to destabilise that area completely for fifty years to come."

"That is something beyond the power of Room 40 to remedy," I said philosophically.

He stood up and went to the cigarette-box on the mantelpiece. It was a few days before midsummer and the setting sun glowed like molten gold on the far wall of our sitting-room.

He lit his cigarette, shook out the match, and said, "I cannot make Hall understand that the only way to control German intelligence is to let them read our ciphers."

As he returned to the window, I wondered if I had heard him correctly. Possibly I had missed a tone of irony in his words. He stood in the golden light, tall and gaunt, emaciated by months of constant work. I was struck by the sudden impatience of his grimace, a growing sense of his consuming energy, an onset of that passionate reasoning power, which I had learnt to recognise with some disquiet.

"You want the Germans to penetrate our codes and ciphers?"

"Of course!" he said emphatically. "We cannot control their thoughts simply by reading their cables. The time has come to let Germany win a battle of the ciphers. It will not do for Hall's handful of spies to feed them stories of our intentions. That trick is done with. Tirpitz is not a Teutonic clown but the equal of Hall or Fisher. He has been stung too often and will now believe only what he reads for himself."

"Then what is the answer? Surely not to give away our secrets?"

He shook his head impatiently.

"We must give him the means of reading our codes and ciphers. We must make him feel that he is winning, rather than losing. There has been too much triumph on our side and the braying that goes with it. He must read our wireless messages and signals with the assistance of our own code-books. He must read our confessions of being baffled by his new ciphers."

"He will not believe any of that!"

To my surprise, he smiled.

"Suppose that we should present him with our Secret Emergency War Code, containing a complete set of our cipher-tables for the next six months."

"He will not believe anything that we give to him!"

"I think he will, if we allow him to steal the emergency code-book. You and I could arrange that on our own. I hardly think we need trouble Admiral Hall. Let this be our own enterprise. I believe we could be successful in passing such information to Berlin."

In that moment my heart seemed to stop.

"I believe we could be shot by our own side!" I said desperately. "Or assassinated by the Germans!"

"My dear Watson, they will be only too happy to believe in the value of a code-book, provided that it is served up to them in the right way. In every neutral country their spies are now ready to pay for whatever information our so-called double-agents betray to them. This is far better. All we need in this case is an apparently indiscreet leakage of our naval and military intelligence, including codes and cipher-tables. I grant you, we shall also need an impersonating agent of our own who must appear simple enough and gullible enough to carry conviction."

"And what sort of man is that?" I asked scornfully.

"You are," he said.

Holmes declined to discuss the matter further just then, and I was left to my own thoughts. I confess that I had never imagined myself as a secret agent. Now that the suggestion was made, I was surprised to find that I was not entirely averse to the challenge. So far, I had played my part conscientiously in the Watchkeeper's Office of Room 40. I had collected copies of intercepted telegrams as they fell from the pneumatic tubes and filed them as "Admiralty," "Military," "Diplomatic," or "Political."

That work was so humdrum that I would scarcely have been human if I had not felt that I was cut out for more exciting things. Without telling Holmes, I had offered my skills to the War Office the previous year as a military surgeon, on the basis of my experience in Afghanistan. To my chagrin, I was turned down as being at least twenty years too old! At least, if I became a make-believe agent, I should find myself on active service. I recalled the famous saying of Dr. Samuel Johnson that a man always thinks meanly of himself for not having been a soldier. In Holmes's wistful adventure, I might answer the call to arms.

Sir John Fisher summoned me several days later. He assured me that our enemies were ravenous for whatever information might come their way, provided their appetites were suitably stimulated. I knew that he had just been talking to Sherlock Holmes

"How will you know if they believe what is given them?" I asked.

He chuckled.

"If they believe it, they will come back for more. That is to say, they will continue to pay for it. Oh, yes, Doctor. Our most successful and most valued agents in neutral Europe are those who have posed as traitors with secrets to sell. The money that comes to them from the German Abwehr, as their military intelligence is called, goes into our special fund at Room 40. We shall share it out among deserving causes when we celebrate victory at the end of the war."

"Then you are offering them a traitor?" I had not liked the sound of this.

"I think not, on this occasion. We may have played that card too often."

"Then whom?"

"We need a. . . ." His eyes wandered a little as he avoided the words "fool" or "buffoon." Then he smiled. "An innocent is what we want. One who appears naive enough to have information stolen from him."

Within two more days, Holmes had put to Fisher a plan for selling to German Intelligence a bound volume of a counterfeit Secret Emergency War Code. Its contents had been devised by my friend, as a permanent means of introducing false information to the Wilhelmstrasse, including variations in codes and ciphers, for as long as the war might last. The way would be cleared by one of our best double-agents in Holland, working under the cover of being an importer of Sumatra tobacco, but in German pay since before the war began.

This agent was fastidious. He did not claim access to British intelligence. He was merely an international businessman and an admirer of Germany who had an old school-friend in the Foreign Office, William Greville. From this garrulous source, he was now able to alert his German clients to the forthcoming revision of our Secret Emergency War Code. Copies would be restricted to a handful of officers authorised to receive it. On previous occasions, the agents of the Wilhelmstrasse had no hope of laying hands upon it.

The tobacco importer did nothing so foolish as to offer the code himself. That would have alerted German suspicions at once. He merely passed on a piece of information that his easy-going friend at the Foreign Office had let slip. As the threat of war spread, the distribution list of the code would include for the first time the British Consul in neutral Rotterdam. Greville, a Foreign Office courier who had acted in the past as a King's Messenger, was to deliver it at the beginning of August. The story had only come out between trusted friends because this affable diplomat had let slip that he was greatly looking forward to a weekend of peacetime luxury in the neutral Dutch city. So much for William Greville, the long-serving Foreign Office courier, an old Army man, genial but not formidably sharp-witted.

So I was to travel as "William Greville." Before I assumed that role, our own people had watched me at home for several weeks and found no visible interest in me on the part of German agents. With the addition of horn-rimmed glasses, the temporary absence of my whiskers, a darkening of the hair, and an inch or so added to my height by the aid of built-up heels, I became the emissary and an assistant secretary to a junior Foreign Office minister. Or so my diplomatic passport described me.

Before I left the Pool of London on a Dutch ship, the nature of my mission was allowed to leak out by means of several loud and indiscreet conversations in hotels and bars frequented by neutrals with German sympathies. I was not convinced that this would be sufficient bait, but my guardians thought otherwise and, after all, they knew best. The proof of the pudding would be in the eating. It was in this frame of mind that I sailed for Holland on the first Friday evening in August.

In Rotterdam, rooms had been booked for me at a hotel near the docks, where the hall-porter was known to our naval intelligence as being in German pay. By the time I came ashore, I could be assured that my presence in the city was not unnoticed. The time of my arrival was of the essence. It was the Saturday afternoon of an August bank holiday weekend, observed in England but nowhere else. The British Consulate behaved as though it were in England. In other words, it had shut on Saturday morning and would remain closed until Tuesday.

I acted the part of a frustrated emissary, spending my time reading newspapers in the hotel foyer, drinking whisky and twiddling my thumbs. After an hour or two, the hall-porter fell into conversation with me, as hall-porters are apt to do in such places when business is quiet. I complained of a tedious wait, caused by offices that did not open on the first Monday in August. After that, there could be little doubt who I was or where my business lay. In any case, the porter had only to glance at my passport, which now lay behind the hotel desk. Whether or not he knew that the British consul was due to receive a copy of the Secret Emergency War Code, I could not say. I was quite sure by now that his masters had been warned.

Nothing more was said until the following evening—Sunday—when the obliging porter suggested that it was a pity I could not have a little "fun" while delayed in Rotterdam. I complained again, this time that I was a perfect stranger in the city and had no idea of where fun was to be found. He tendered the name and address of a house, also near the port, where a warm welcome and a good deal of amusement could be depended upon by the lonely stranger. I began to brighten up at this information. I went up to my room and changed. While there, I opened the locked briefcase with its code-book and papers, in order to take out some cash. In my apparent eagerness to experience the delights on offer, I omitted to lock the case when I put it back, clumsily hidden under a pile of clothes in the wardrobe drawer.

I now followed the plan prepared for me. It was simple in the extreme. I made sure that I was not followed immediately I left the hotel. Then I ordered a cab from the rank and loudly gave the address of the "house" recommended to me. Once round the corner and out of sight, I ordered the driver to drop me as I had decided to have my dinner first. He shrugged and drove off. Making sure again that no one had followed me, I diverged from the hall porter's route. On my way to the hotel the previous day, I had noticed a pleasant enough quayside brasserie and now took a table outside it. This looked directly back across a stretch of water, giving me a view of my own window.

The window of that room was the third along from the right on the second floor, and I had naturally left it in darkness. I waited for more than an hour, drinking my schnapps slowly on the quayside. Another twenty minutes passed and then, to my relief and excitement, the light went on in my hotel window.

This was no visit by a maid, turning down the bed. The light remained on for over an hour, quite long enough for someone to photograph every page in the Secret Emergency War Code, as well as to search my effects and confirm my assumed identity as

William Greville. Before they began the search, the intruders had allowed me time to get to the house where amusement might be found and to immerse myself in it. No doubt the hall porter was on guard at the desk, watching for any unexpected return, but they had every reason to believe that there was ample time in hand, more than enough to copy the bound cipher volume.

I waited for a little while after the light had gone off. Then I made my way to a restaurant near the famous statue of Erasmus and spent another hour or so eating my dinner. As for my return to the hotel, I have seen and heard enough drunkards during my career to put on a pantomime of being a little the worse for wear. I welcomed help from the kindly hall-porter in climbing the stairs and getting into bed. He was very insistent in seeing that I got there.

I tipped him generously and, as soon as he had gone, went to look for the attaché-case. It was once again under the pile of clothes but not quite as I had left it. Moreover, someone in closing it had caused it to lock automatically. Such was the end of my three days of active service in the pay of British Military Intelligence. I cannot pretend that I found it exciting; it was more than anything tedious and a matter of waiting around for something to happen. However, Holmes seemed well pleased with the result and Sir John Fisher appeared positively affable towards me.

5

For more than six months after this, Admiral Hall and his colleagues were able to transmit messages from our own chain of wireless stations in a code which the Germans could decipher, thanks to the present I had made them, but which meant nothing to our own side. All the same, this advantage was only to be exploited with great care.

Counterfeit cipher messages must correspond in most details to subsequent events. It was the few significant variations which would plant false information in the intelligence bureau of the Wilhelmstrasse. On one occasion, at least, Admiral Beatty altered by two days the date on which he was to take the Home Fleet to sea on gunnery exercises, in order that this should verify the counterfeit version of the war code ciphers. It was a small price to pay for giving apparent authenticity to a masterpiece of deception.

On the basis of false information fed to Berlin through the counterfeit cipher tables, my friend engineered what became known sardonically in Room 40 as "The Sherlock Holmes Invasion of Belgium." This was at a time when detachments of our troops were being withdrawn from the Western Front to reinforce the expeditionary force to Salonika. As Holmes remarked, it seemed desirable that the Germans should be induced to withdraw units of their own troops in return.

In messages based on the new ciphers, the intelligence bureau of the Wilhelmstrasse was allowed to read an ingenious fiction of closely guarded movements by our small naval craft on the eastern coast of England. Flat-bottomed boats of the kind used for landing troops on a sandy coast were being marshalled there. A further message contained an instruction to stop at short notice all cross-channel shipping between England and neutral Holland. The order would remain in force for a fortnight, so that merchant shipping should not compromise the movement of an invasion fleet on course for the coast of Belgium.

These enciphered orders, based upon the counterfeit code and its appendix, then revealed details of an imminent invasion of that coast, in the rear of the German army in France. It was gratifying that the enemy's High Command diverted some 20,000 men to the defence of the Belgian sands and dunes along the North Sea. Little by little, the Admiralty's orders to an imaginary invasion fleet were received in Berlin. The vessels would sail in three groups, from Harwich, from Dover, and from the mouth of the Thames. The command for the temporary prohibition of sea traffic to Holland was authorised, though not yet issued.

As a final persuasion of the truth of this story, a special edition of the Daily Mail was printed. This was done in consultation with Admiral Hall and the paper's editor. It consisted of only twenty-four copies for sale in Holland, where it was routinely bought by German agents. The paper contained a front-page paragraph reporting "Great Military Preparations on the East Coast" and "Flat Bottomed Boats." Within hours, this was followed by a further edition of the Mail with the whole story blacked out, as if the censor had intervened.

In order that the plan did not seem too easily revealed, it was allowed to appear that the author of the feature had got the wrong end of the stick, as Holmes put it, and that he believed the East Coast was being prepared against an attack by the Germans. Officers of the German High Command knew that they did not intend to invade Eastern England. Therefore they were bound to assume that the journalist had got the rumour wrong and that it must be the British who were going to attack Belgium. In the confusion, they had felt compelled to switch an entire division or so to the defence of the empty sands round Ostend.

Both sides were now changing ciphers with greater frequency, every day on the stroke of midnight. It was a race which Holmes was prepared to run. Before the end of the year, he penetrated the most complex of all, the German diplomatic code. This was, in truth, a gift from the Kaiser's vice-consul in Persia. The unfortunate diplomat had fled in his pyjamas, abandoning his luggage, after witnessing a failed German attack on the Abadan oil pipeline. This paved the way for our final victory in "the war of ghosts and shadows."

6

By the autumn of 1916, the neutral nations included Holland, Latin America, and, most significantly, the United States. Many in the Admiralty and the War Office spoke wistfully of a new order of things. To put it plainly, they meant the entry of the United States into the war on the Allied side.

Homes "drudged" by day, as he called it, and read by night. Increasingly his thoughts seemed to be elsewhere. One evening, he was occupied by a history of the Russo–Japanese War of 1904, when Britain had backed Japan against Russian expansion in the Pacific. In the outcome, a primitive Asiatic nation had defeated a great European power.

I noticed later what Holmes had written in the margin.

"Japan will remain our ally in the present war until she has acquired Germany's possessions in China and the Pacific. If ever the war should go against us, it will be in her interest to turn her eyes upon the possessions of Britain and the United States in the Far East."

It was a cynical but not impossible conclusion.

A day or two later, he was absorbed by John Reed's account of the 1910 Mexican revolution, Insurgent Mexico. What had we to do with that? Mexico's recent history seemed to me no more than a chronicle of one tyrannical revolutionary succeeding another, by courtesy of Pancho Villa and his bandits. Next evening, while he was engaged at his work-table, I saw that he had jotted a note in the margin of this book as well. "United States military strength 40,000. Three-quarters of these with General Pershing in Mexico or on the frontier."

Anyone who read the newspapers knew how President Wilson had sent the U.S. Marines ashore at Vera Cruz. The USS Prairie had also intercepted the German cargo ship Ypringa. On board were 200 machine-guns and several tons of ammunition for Pancho Villa and Carranza's troops, with thirty or forty German officers to train them. What had all that to do with Armageddon on the Western Front? I tried facetiousness.

"Let us hope, Holmes, that we shall be spared the sight of Pancho Villa and his bandits galloping down Baker Street with dripping swords!"

He said nothing, but got up and went to the bureau. Unlocking a drawer, he took out a sheet of paper. I recognised it as the decryption of a diplomatic telegram. From the date, Holmes must have deciphered it within the last twenty-four hours. My eyes caught three sentences.

> Despite the presence of General Pershing and the United States army upon their mutual frontier, the power to decide the Mexican question has passed from President Wilson to President Carranza, from General Pershing to Pancho Villa.

It was a contentious view but hardly a secret. I read what followed.

> Whatever measures President Wilson may threaten in reply to our orders for unrestricted submarine warfare, his

> inclinations and those of the Congress are for peace. His scope for military action scarcely exists.

This was far more alarming. What were "our" orders? Who were "we"? There could only be one answer, and it lay in the Wilhelmstrasse.

> It is clearer and clearer that the American government has drawn back from breaking off relations with Germany because its military forces are not sufficient to face a war with Mexico.

A war between the United States and Mexico was surely a lunatic vision of the German High Command. But there was another line, edged with a chilling truth.

> Without Tampico's oil-wells, the British fleet cannot leave Scapa Flow.

"A fevered brain in the Kriegsmarine!" I said contemptuously.

"No, Watson. The brain is at this moment several thousand miles from Berlin."

"Where does the cipher come from?"

"Our old friend number 13042," he said quietly. "The German diplomatic code. It was employed yesterday by Count Bernstorff as Ambassador in Washington to communicate with Arthur Zimmermann at the Foreign Office in Berlin. It is Bernstorff's weekly appreciation of what he calls 'The War Situation.' The code and the cipher-tables are still those which came into our possession thanks to the German vice-consul at Abadan." He put his pipe down and shrugged. "The message is only the latest of its kind."

"But why should the Americans want to fight Mexico?"

Holmes's eyebrows contracted, as if I had wilfully misunderstood him.

"They do not. It is Germany who wants America to fight Mexico. The Western Front is at a stalemate, but Zimmermann, Bethmann-Hollweg, and the Kaiser believe that Germany can starve England into negotiation by unrestricted submarine warfare. Yet Germany knows she must not provoke America to fight her. If America is involved in Mexico, as three-quarters of her regular army already is, she can fight no war in Europe before Germany's U-boat campaign succeeds. Without a war in Mexico, American troops might land in France in a few months."

"The whole thing is absurd."

Holmes shrugged.

"I can only tell you that the ciphers from Bernstorff, which we have intercepted in the past few weeks, tell us that Mexico and Japan are already in negotiation with Berlin over the fruits of victory. Indeed, the Japanese battle-cruiser Asuma with troops on board is known to have anchored in the Gulf of California. I do not think that can be a lie told by an ambassador to his foreign minister."

"But the German army cannot reach Mexico!"

He shook his head.

"In one sense, it is already there. Bernstorff boasts that the patriotic Union of German Citizens has twenty-nine branches in Mexico, supported by seventy-five branches of the veterans' Iron Cross Society. He claims 50,000 willing recruits in the Americas, and our own Foreign Office confirms it. The present 104 branches in Mexico include some 200 German officers who have entered the country recently as skilled workers but are ready to fight and are already training others. For that matter, there are also half a million Germans of military age in the United States."

"They can hardly fight the rest of its population!"

"If only one in a thousand is prepared to sabotage ships, trains, and refineries, there will be 500 active agents. A score of time-bombs has gone off in the past few months on ships sailing from the eastern seaboard to Britain and France. Together with Mexico, it is enough to hold America back while we and the Germans fight it out."

That night, I lay awake and remembered a mad story I had heard a few years earlier. It was during gossip at my club, the Naval and Military. An officer of the Coldstreams, whom I knew only slightly, entertained us after dinner in the smoking-room with an account of how Japan, in an alliance with Mexico, might land troops on the very coast where the battle-cruiser Asuma was now said to have anchored. In a single spearhead to regain Mexico's "lost provinces," the two countries would fall upon the peaceful and unsuspecting south-west of the United States. They would strike through Texas into Louisiana, invade the Mississippi Valley and cut the nation in two before its inhabitants could rally. If Holmes was right, this force, when reinforced by trained German troops, would easily outnumber Pershing's 40,000 peacetime army. I was still awake when the winter morning dawned.

7

What became known as the Zimmermann crisis followed almost at once. A neutral Danish observer, the captain of a coaster returning home from the port of Kiel, passed information to our naval attaché in Copenhagen. The talk among officers of the German High Seas Fleet was of U-boat production already reaching the level necessary to sustain unrestricted warfare by mid-January 1917, six weeks away. An unknown number of the new submarines had sailed from Wilhelmshaven with stores, fuel, and torpedoes for three months.

"Which can only mean operations off the American coastline from Florida to Maine," said Holmes quietly. "No commander-in-chief would send his vessels to the Bay of Biscay or the Western Approaches for such a length of time and with no available port. It may take them three or four weeks to cross the Atlantic. They will be in the American coastal shipping lanes by early January, counting on a base in Mexico."

There had been German threats to United States shipping before this. When the British liner Lusitania was sunk with the loss of many American lives, it had been all that President

Wilson could do to hold the country back. America's own ships, like the Gulflight and the Sussex, had fallen victim to U-boats, but still a fragile neutrality persisted. So far, each crisis had passed after a protest by Washington.

Woodrow Wilson continued to urge the combatants in the war to find a peace without victory, a peace without conquest, for the benefit of mankind. In this, Holmes was his supporter, though for more practical reasons. He argued that in a general war, a million young Americans might die, for the sake of paltry gains on the Western Front, compared with a few dozen or a few hundred in the submarine war. It was a high price to pay for national pride.

As the latest U-boats sailed from Wilhelmshaven, the German diplomatic ciphers revealed that Arthur Zimmermann at the Foreign Office in Berlin had been assured by the Kriegsmarine that Britain could be starved into negotiation in six or twelve months by the new fleet. Those in Whitehall who believed that American arms could yet change the course of war began to lose heart. It was surely too late.

During that Christmas season of 1916 and into the New Year, Sherlock Holmes was a stranger in Baker Street. If he slept in his own bed, he was gone before breakfast and absent until after midnight. Often he slept on a camp bed at the Old Admiralty Building, in a shabby panelled office allotted to him by Signals Intelligence. When grander accommodation was offered, he declined it. He worked alone in his "cubby hole" and there was little sign of him elsewhere in the building. The departure of the U-boats on their voyage kept our wireless interception busy day and night with ciphers to be decoded.

The New Year brought us the freezing January of 1917. I had taken three days leave to go alone to the Exmoor cousins at Wiveliscombe. I returned to Baker Street very early one morning, before the office workers were at their desks. An overnight sleeper had brought me on the train from Taunton to Paddington. There was no sign of Holmes in our rooms. It appeared as if he had not been in the house since my departure. I summoned Mrs. Hudson.

"Why, Dr. Watson, sir, I thought he must have gone down to Devon with you, after all. There's been no sign of him here since you left."

I called a cab off the rank and set off at once for Whitehall. If Holmes had been away for three days and two intervening nights, it must be at Room 40. When I arrived, only those who had been on duty since the day before were still there and the new watch had not yet taken over. I went to the Watchkeeper's Office. Here the printed intercepts arrived through pneumatic tubes. A row of clocks told the time across the world from London to New York to Tokyo and back to Berlin. Closed-circuit telephone lines ran to the Director of Naval Intelligence, the War Office, Special Branch at Scotland Yard, and the Prime Minister in Downing Street. The waste-paper baskets were usually full of pages, crumpled and discarded during the long night, all of which would be emptied into the Horse Guards incinerator by Royal Marine sergeants.

As a rule, several of the night watch would sit at their desks until 10 A.M. In the morning light, their faces were pale from exhaustion and drawn from lack of sleep, eyes staring unnaturally bright from the dark shadows of their sockets. Even then, if necessary, they would wrestle for several hours more with some new naval or diplomatic cipher which had been changed at midnight in Berlin or Vienna.

This morning, Holmes was in the Watchkeeper's Office alone. He sat in a wooden chair, the desk before him clear, head back, arms folded, and eyes closed. Yet he was not asleep. His eyelids lifted as I came in.

"Where are the others?" I asked.

"They have gone," he said wearily. "There was no purpose in staying. They had no work to do."

"And the ciphers?"

"They have vanished." He stood up. "The diplomatic ciphers between Berlin and Washington, that it is say everything that matters in the present state of affairs, have disappeared from the ether. So far as we are concerned, they are neither being sent nor received. There have been no intercepts for the past two days."

I stared out of the window, across the mist of St. James's Park where two Jersey cows were grazing on the frosted grass that stretched between us and Buckingham Palace. I tried to make sense of what he had just said.

"Surely the signals are being sent. Now, of all times, when Wilson and Zimmermann are trying to avoid war. Zimmermann must be in contact with Bernstorff and their Washington embassy."

Holmes sighed.

"Not through his own signals. Negotiations between the two countries are at a delicate stage. The last messages that we received merely confirmed that Chancellor Bethmann-Hollweg had agreed to consider President Wilson's fourteen-point proposal for a general peace on all fronts. I have a private assurance of that, from Edward Bell at the American Embassy. Bell tells me in confidence that President Wilson authorised the use of America's own diplomatic telegraph for transmission of German peace proposals in code."

"And what of the U-boat fleet heading for the American coastline?"

"So far as we are concerned, that has vanished off the map. So far as the Americans know, it never existed. For a time, it was communicating through Sayville, Long Island, disguised in the codes of commercial or steamship company telegrams. That has ceased."

"How will Berlin's signals carry to Washington?"

"During the present negotiations, Zimmermann has requested that his own telegrams to Robert Lansing at the State Department shall be transmitted from Berlin with those of the American Embassy, in the American diplomatic code. The route is through neutral cables from Berlin to Stockholm, then to Buenos Aires and so to Washington. Wilson's Ambassador in Berlin, James Gerard, has agreed."

"To transmit German diplomatic intelligence? Preposterous!"

"Perhaps. However, Gerard and Secretary Lansing have accepted this, apparently on Wilson's instructions. Still worse, they have accepted Zimmermann's insistence that his telegrams to Bernstorff must be transmitted by the Americans in the usual German diplomatic code—undeciphered—so that they remain confidential to Bernstorff. These telegrams are forwarded, unexamined, from the State Department to the German Embassy. Lansing and Wilson have no idea of the contents. Negotiations between the two countries are too delicate to permit the risk of interception in London or elsewhere."

"It is unthinkable!"

"So is war," said Holmes gloomily. "To Wilson, war is an abomination. If he can end it, why not allow Zimmermann this small concession? Zimmermann must send diplomatic telegrams to his ambassador in Washington anyway. Wilson does not want the British or the French eavesdropping at this point."

"Why can we not eavesdrop through our own efforts?"

"Because we should have to break the American diplomatic code, before we can get at Zimmermann's telegrams. Imagine a friendly power discovering that we had deliberately broken its code and were reading its confidential messages. In any case, Balfour at the Foreign Office has categorically forbidden it—at eight o'clock last night. We can only sit here and see if the ciphers in the German Diplomatic Code—13042—resume."

"Well, here's a pretty pickle!" I said helplessly.

"Not quite. Stockholm is a link in the route. I have been trying my hand at the recent Swedish ciphers in our archives—so far without much reward. They have never merited attention before. I have established, however, that the new Swedish envoy in Mexico City has German sympathies. In one case, he has so far forgotten himself as to send in plain text an appreciation of the situation in Mexico. Unforgivably careless."

Holmes drew a transcript from his pocket and read out what he had copied.

"Dated 1 September 1916. President Carranza, who is now openly a friend to Germany, is willing to provide support if necessary, and if possible, for German submarines in Mexican waters."

The chill that ran through my blood was no figure of speech.

"For the U-boats from Wilhelmshaven!"

"It had clearly been arranged before they sailed." Holmes continued to read the Swedish envoy's report.

"The Imperial German government proposes to employ the most efficient means to annihilate Britain as its principal enemy. Since it intends to carry its operations across the Atlantic with the object of destroying its enemy's merchant fleet, it will need shore bases to fuel and supply the submarines. In return, Germany will treat Mexico like the free and independent nation which it is."

Holmes paused.

"There is a good deal more, but that is the gist of it."

I looked round the dim, gloomily boarded watchroom.

"And the Americans know nothing of this?"

"No one else knows as yet. Arthur Balfour at the Foreign Office fears that if we reveal the contents of the Swedish telegram now, senior figures in America will treat it as a British hoax, designed to draw them into the war. In any case, it is no more than the opinion of one diplomat. No more than a foreign correspondent in Mexico City might write in his newspaper."

8

There were innumerable fragments in this mystery. We needed one more which must be, to put it crudely, the centrepiece of the puzzle. For the time being, it seemed as far away as ever. Neither Holmes nor I were great believers in sudden strokes of luck providing an answer to an insoluble problem. Nor was it so here. What came our way was not the answer to our problem, but an Englishman who could unveil the clues, Mr. Varney of Mexico City.

Holmes had never met his protégé face to face. Mr. Varney was a printer who had been in trouble a year or two before. Unknown to him, several of his workers had made blocks, which they then used for printing off counterfeit small-denomination Mexican currency. When Mr. Varney discovered this crime, he hurried to report it. To his dismay, he was arrested as though he were the culprit, brought before a revolutionary tribunal, and sentenced to be shot.

His sister, Miss Varney of Muswell Hill, hurried to Baker Street and recited a tearful story to Sherlock Holmes, while her brother in his cell awaited a summons from the firing-squad. Holmes at once secured the intervention of the Foreign Office in London, and the Mexican Ambassador was summoned. In Mexico City, the British Minister confronted President Carranza himself. Between them, Mr. Balfour and his Minister persuaded the Mexican authorities that Mr. Varney was unlikely to be the originator of a plot to forge notes that were worth only a few English pennies. Within two days, he was released.

Mr. Varney had vowed to do anything for Holmes in return. Several months ago, he had redeemed this pledge by infiltrating the office of Posts and Telegraphs in Mexico City. Under revolutionary law, coded telegrams were forbidden for fear that they might be used to start yet another revolution. However, the government minister responsible frequently permitted commercial codes to escape scrutiny, in exchange for a small bribe. Mr. Varney, in his turn, had been able to bribe a lesser functionary. This man would alert him to the texts of incoming Western Union telegrams from Count Bernstorff in Washington to Minister Eckhardt at the German Mission in Mexico City.

"It is simple enough," said Holmes, next morning at the breakfast table. "The United States Embassy in Berlin may forward German telegrams to the State Department in Washington—and so to the German Embassy. However, the State Department will not forward them to the German Minister in Mexico City. In any case, there is nothing beyond Galveston except the services of Western Union. Mr. Varney is able to confirm that such telegrams are passing to Herr Eckhardt. They are in code, but any coded texts in the archives of Western Union in Mexico City will henceforward be available to us. Perhaps we shall no longer be working blindfold after all."

Within days, there came into our hands at Baker Street, late one afternoon, a wire from Mr. Varney. It had been forwarded by courtesy of Captain Guy Gaunt, the British Naval Attaché in Washington, who was also Naval Intelligence officer at the embassy. This wire accompanied the secret message which is known to history as the "Zimmermann Telegram"—and which the reader will find quoted as a coded text at the opening of this memoir. What follows is the best sense that Sherlock Holmes and I could make of it that evening.

We sat at either side of the work-table while Holmes made two copies of the coded message and passed one to me. I hardly knew how to start upon it, but the keen energy of my friend's brain began to illuminate the darkness of the cipher like forked lightning.

"Let us dispose of the first two groups of numbers, Watson. At the start, 130 is simply the number of the telegram and tells us nothing. The next, 13042, is the current prefix for communications in the German diplomatic code and tells us a good deal. Then you will see 13401, which identifies its source as the German Foreign Office, not the embassy in Washington. The source, if not the message, is genuine. The next item, 8501, confirms that this began its journey as a 'Most Secret' telegram from Berlin to Count Bernstorff, who has now forwarded it to Mexico City. Between them, such clues narrow our area of search a little."

"We have intercepted no messages between Berlin and Washington in the past fortnight," I said cautiously. "May this not be a hoax of some kind by the German intelligence service?"

He frowned and ran his pencil across the rows of numbers.

"I think not," he said presently. "By its number, this is a recent telegram which Zimmermann has passed to Bernstorff under the cover of the United States diplomatic code. Had Bernstorff not forwarded it to Mexico City, we should never have seen it. I believe that disposes of any hoax. Now then, there are recurring words in this cipher and I fancy they will show us the way."

His pencil was busy for a moment. Then he looked up.

"The framework of the telegram is in a cipher system we have encountered before; therefore, what follows must be related to it. The message, I concede, appears to be encrypted according to a new code; that is the challenge; but the system which sustains it should be the same."

He pushed his paper across to me.

"See here. In the preliminary instructions, we have 17214, which has previously been used for ganz geheim—strictly secret. Well that is no surprise—it is an old friend to me. And then, here, 6491 11310 18147. That is also familiar from previous use. Selbst zu entziffern—decipher this yourself. From there on, the code has been varied and everything is a little opaque."

I worked my way through it, trying to pick out any groups of letters whose position or repetition might help us to "get a lever" under the rest. Holmes took another approach.

"We know that Eckhardt in Mexico City must be able to decode it. It has been sent as a matter of urgency and therefore probably in a code that can be read by anyone who knew the previous one. Eckhardt is not allowed to refer the matter to his underlings, he can ask for no assistance, therefore it must be a familiar system to him."

He bowed his head over the paper, the harsh white gaslight throwing the shadow of his aquiline profile on the wall. Presently he chuckled. His pencil was ticking the most frequently used words. He selected one of them.

"Here, here, and here, Watson. The group of numbers most frequently used is 69853. From its position, as compared with earlier messages which we have decrypted, it appears to be a noun, almost certainly a proper name. In an urgent and secret diplomatic message to the German Minister in Mexico City, what is that word likely to be?"

"I would say most probably 'Mexico.'"

"And here it is used with the cipher 5870, which also occurs just before it and immediately after it. The same 5870 occurs again two words further on. May I be kicked from here to Charing Cross if that is not a comma! What else can it be with such frequency? Now, such a series of commas would suggest a list, would it not? A list of three items in this case, the second of which is in two words. The second of those two words is 'Mexico.' So we have a compound noun, the second half of which is 'Mexico.' To me that strongly suggests 'New Mexico.' Let us see."

It was a characteristic leap of intuition. Beforehand, the answer might have appeared an outside possibility. As presented by Holmes, it now seemed the only answer that made sense.

"In all probability it is a list of American states," I said quickly.

"Excellent, Watson. New Mexico, with an item before and an item after. The one in front of it appears as five letters. Try 'Texas.' The one that follows it has four syllables. What state associated with Texas and New Mexico has four syllables?"

"Arizona?" I replied hopefully.

"And what unites Texas, New Mexico, Arizona? All three were at one time part of Mexico and were lost to the United States by conquest. What plan has Herr Zimmermann for those states now?"

"To return them to Mexico? Impossible!"

"Not at all impossible, provided that there is a sufficient bargain upon the table. Another name 52262 recurs closely. You will recall that all nations in the last diplomatic cipher to be broken by us were reduced to five digits and I fancy this is one of them. Allow me the luxury of supposing that it stands for 'Japan.' You will recall that the battle-cruiser Asuma lately paid a prolonged courtesy call to Mexico, as the papers tell us. That news was contained in one of Bernstorff's previous 'appreciations' of the war situation. The ship was in Turtle Bay so long that she ran aground and had to be attended by other units of the Japanese fleet."

"What about the United States?" I inquired cautiously. "Surely a more likely country to be mentioned than Japan in the context of Mexico?"

"Not quite in the proximity which we find here. If my instinct is right, this telegram is about the part to be played by others in respect of the United States. In that case, 'United States' may have a lower frequency than the protagonists. You will find 39695, here, and here, and here, occurring almost incidentally. That I deduce is more likely to be the United States. I shall be surprised if I am not right."

We worked long into that cold January night, deaf to the sounds of the street below, indifferent to the supper which Mrs. Hudson brought on a tray and which remained untasted.

"Yes, yes!" said Holmes impatiently to her kindly reproach. Presently the sitting-room air was clouded with the smoke of his pipe and the food still remained almost untouched.

I was little help, I fear. Yet I could not have torn myself away as I watched him working at the blocks of numbers on the telegram form. He had the previous cipher of the German diplomatic telegrams to hand and now established to his own satisfaction the five-number groups which represented the nations, like pieces on a chess-board.

As the hours passed, Zimmermann's text began to appear in groups or clumps of letters and signs, like islands in a sea of numbers. Just after midnight, Holmes hit another vein of inspiration. Nouns were divided into groups of four or five letters. Other words varied a little to identify each occurrence. He made out that 6926, 6929, and 6992 were varying forms of "and," determined by which letter began the next word. This in turn gave him the first letters of "Japan," "understanding," and "suggestion." With fewer than half the words deciphered, the purpose of the telegram was plain. He recognised 5903 as "krieg," or "war." A repetition of 98092 from an earlier telegram gave him "U-boat." This left him with an incomplete phrase, "ersten 13605 un-14963 U-boot krieg."

"What is the date, Watson?"

I was quite unprepared for this and had to think for a moment.

"The twenty-third of January. That is to say, the small hours of the twenty-fourth."

"Admirable! Then the crucial date in the telegram must be 'ersten Februar'—the first of February! The first of the next month in the immediate future. One does not use telegrams for dates that are far off, there is no urgency and the decision may not yet have been taken. Therefore we have, 'The first of February un-14963 U-boat war.' There is already a U-boat war being fought but what is to come is in some way different. What can that be but 'The first of February un-restricted U-boat war'? It is an instruction to Bernstorff in Washington and an order to Eckhardt in Mexico City, to the effect that Germany will sink on sight, in a week's time, neutral shipping entering European waters."

"Wilson cannot hold back from war, if that is the case!"

"I fear he may. The decision lies with Tirpitz and his master. If the Germans use the threat sparingly, Wilson will hesitate to commit his country to all-out war. Who would not? The loss of a few ships is nothing compared to a million men slaughtered on the battlefield and the nation's prosperity in ruins. In any case, the likely outcome is that neutral vessels will keep well away from our shores, our own merchant fleet will be destroyed by Germany's torpedoes, and our goose will be cooked. That is the plan in Berlin. They want to preserve peace with America, if they can. If not, they hope to trap her in a war on her own continent."

By three o'clock in the morning, his pessimism seemed confirmed. We now had a translation of the text of the earlier passage: "Zimmermann to Bernstorff. Strictly Secret. Decipher this yourself. We intend to begin unrestricted U-boat warfare from 1 February. We will attempt to keep the United States BLANK. If this should not be BLANK, we offer Mexico. . . ."

"The first BLANK is 'neutral,'" I said; "the second is 'possible.'"

The rest of that night was spent in teasing out from the sets of numbers just what it was that Mexico might be offered in exchange for a German alliance. We made out "united in war, united in peace." Then we returned to "Texas, New Mexico, Arizona" and the single word "zuruck"—"back." Preposterous though it might seem, President Carranza was being offered the return of Mexico's lost territories in return for loyalty to the Kaiser.

This reading was confirmed when Holmes deciphered the two occurrences of 22464 as "President," referring to President Carranza of Mexico, who was to be both a German ally and mediator in the alliance. He must induce 52262—Japan—to join the pact. England, which now appeared for the first time, would be "compelled" to make peace in a few months by a massive U-boat assault now being prepared. This would be sustained by supplies and fuel from Mexican ports. So long as the United States had only its small peacetime army, it could be invaded along the Mississippi Valley by a Mexican army with the support of German "legionaries" and Japanese troops, conveniently cutting off those territories which were now to be returned to President Carranza. It was a complete confirmation of the tall story I had heard in the Army and Navy Club several years before!

I burst out laughing at the apparent absurdity of the suggestion. Holmes remained solemn.

"You cannot take it seriously," I said, "the notion of the Japanese occupying the Mississippi Valley!"

"What I take seriously, Watson, is that America is strong at sea but weaker on land, as England has been. Such have been both our historic priorities. I take seriously the prospect of a small American peacetime army fighting valiantly, suffering reverses at first, but eventually being victorious. Pending that eventuality, which may be months or years away, I also take seriously the probable triumph of the U-boat campaign, while the Tampico oil-wells supply German submarine bases in Mexico. I take seriously the choking of our supply lines by U-boat fleets, stalemate on the Western Front, the Royal Navy starved of fuel-oil, immobilised, and a peace treaty leaving Germany with all her European conquests."

"What a peace!" I said, as if to myself.

"Belgium would be her puppet state, giving her a seaboard opposite our own shores. France would lose all that she lost in the war of 1871 and more besides. Morocco would be a German colony, opposite Gibraltar. Remember the German gunboat Panther's seizure of Agadir in the crisis of 1911."

It was in a sober mood that we abandoned the half-finished puzzle and went to our rooms as the first sounds of the milk-carts and the bread-vans disturbed the early winter morning of the street. In a few hours more, we should have enough of the German text before us to compose a report for Sir Reginald Hall.

The contents of the Zimmermann Telegram were released to the world in instalments. At first it seemed that we need not have bothered to decode the message, for Count Bernstorff called at the State Department on the afternoon of 31 January and gave notice to Secretary Lansing that Germany would commence unrestricted sinking on the following day. Bernstorff was handed his passport and ordered to leave for home. Yet Wilson was still the man of peace. "I refuse to believe that it is the intention of the German authorities to do what they have warned us they will feel at liberty to do. Only actual overt acts on their part can make me believe it even now."

There were to be overt acts in plenty, but Holmes had not

been wasting his time. In the privacy of his room at the Foreign Office, Arthur Balfour presented a copy of the infamous telegram to the American Ambassador, Dr. Page. Woodrow Wilson, who had striven so long for peace and had hoped that even the U-boat campaign might not mean general war, was aghast at Zimmermann's audacity. In the cause of peace, the President had put at the disposal of Zimmermann the diplomatic cipher channel of the United States, so that America's peace proposals and Germany's responses might be confidentially exchanged. The Foreign Office in Berlin had even been allowed to use the channel for coded telegrams to its own embassy in Washington. How this facility had been abused as a means of preparing for war was now plain to see.

Too late, Arthur Zimmermann telegraphed urgently and in plain text to Eckhardt in Mexico City, "Please burn all compromising instructions."

Woodrow Wilson became as implacable for war as he had been adamant for peace. Yet for weeks afterwards, the Zimmermann Telegram was still described in the United States Senate as being "probably a forgery of the British Secret Service." Sherlock Holmes was not much given to outbursts of passion. On this occasion, having read of the allegation, he went so far as to crumple the Morning Post and hurl it from the breakfast-table into the grate.

He need not have worried. The American Secret Service had already established that the telegram indeed had been sent by Western Union from Bernstorff in Washington to Eckhardt in Mexico City. Worse still, it revealed that Zimmermann had so far violated the decencies of diplomacy as to propose an attack on the very nation which offered peace and the means of friendly negotiation.

Woodrow Wilson's resolve broke the nerve of those who had been conspiring against him. Zimmermann admitted to the world the bad faith of which he had been guilty in sending the famous—or infamous—message to Count Bernstorff. Three American ships were sunk without warning on 18 March, and President Wilson declared war on 6 April. President Carranza quickly denied any intention of offering Germany submarine bases or a military alliance to attack Texas and New Mexico. Japan, it seemed, had no such intention, and Zimmermann was denounced for maligning the Imperial Court by imputing these designs to it.

So badly had events turned out for Zimmermann that he was soon to be dismissed from office. Germany's U-boats found that their base and fuel supply at Tampico had proved a will o' the wisp. The Royal Navy's oil reserves were secure. In alliance with the United States naval squadrons, it soon had the U-boat wolf-packs by the throat. The outcome of the war was no longer in doubt, only the date of victory.

9

Sherlock Holmes remained in government harness until the end of hostilities. Yet he was increasingly able to return to his private practice as a consulting detective. The first case of this kind is one that I remember with particular pleasure.

We received a visit from Sir Henry Jones, Laird of Tighnabruaich, whose son was Captain Obidiah Jones, a young Scots officer reported missing, feared dead, in a battle against the Turks. Sir Henry heard no more until he received a postcard from Turkey, written in a hand he did not recognise. It was entirely blank except for the address: "Sir Henry Jones, 184 Kings Road, Tighnabruaich, Scotland."

As if to celebrate the gentler ways of peace, Holmes had instructed Mrs. Hudson that a glass of mid-morning Madeira and slices of seed-cake must be provided for our first civilian client. It woke memories of the pre-war world, a far cry from the intellectual austerity of Room 40.

Sir Henry had brought his curious post-card to us in some distress, not knowing what had become of his son. Since there was no message on it, he feared the worst. The curiosity of the address was that his village of Tighnabruaich is a remote collection of a few houses. It is so small that those houses need no numbers, and there is certainly no "Kings Road" to be found there.

Holmes studied the postcard for a long moment and then looked up.

"I believe you may have every confidence, Sir Henry, that your son is alive and well. He may soon return to his regiment, for he and his company have escaped the enemy pursuit, though they were cut off from their comrades. He is leading his company back, under cover, to their headquarters. Their provisions are spartan, but he and his men are so far safe. Indeed, he has been able to smuggle out this message to you."

There was no mistaking the old man's delight, but he looked at us in the most startled manner, as if afraid to believe what he had been told.

"How on earth, Mr. Holmes, can you tell such a thing from that card—which seems to me to bear no message whatever, merely an incorrect address?"

Holmes drew himself upright.

"There you are in error, Sir Henry. You will appreciate that the equipment of the criminal investigator must contain a working knowledge of the world's great texts, not least those of Classical Languages and Holy Writ. They are frequently employed in forming military codes. It was General Sir Harry Smith—was it not?—who, having seized the province of Sind during the Indian wars, communicated this by a message in one word. 'Peccavi.' To those with no knowledge of the Latin tongue, it must be meaningless. Yet every English schoolboy would know that it is translated as 'I have sinned.' You see? The Horse Guards understood at once that Sind was in our power."

"I daresay," said Sir Henry impatiently, "but what has that to do with my son?"

Holmes picked up the postcard again.

"This address. There is no Kings Road in your village and no house numbered 184. I suggest to you that 'Kings 184' can only be a reference to the Old Testament—the First Book of Kings. If that is correct, the number 184 can only stand for Chapter 18, verse 4."

"How extraordinary!"

Holmes bowed his head a little in acknowledgement and then continued.

"You will, I am sure, recall how that verse runs. 'Obidiah took a hundred prophets and hid them in a cave, and fed them with bread and water.' A hundred is a regimental company, a little under strength as his might well be. Obidiah can only be your Obidiah. And now let us drink a health to this brave young man—and wish him well."

In this matter, I must record, Sherlock Holmes was later proved correct. We heard from his proud father that Captain Obidiah Jones had been awarded the Military Cross for gallantry and was now a youthful Major Obidiah Jones.

On that morning, however, after Sir Henry had thanked us several times and left us to seek further particulars of the story at the War Office, Holmes stretched out in his chair and stared at the gentle dancing of flames in the grate.

"I believe, Watson, that Sir Henry is the first client whom we have seen in these chambers for a very long time."

"I believe he is."

"Then I think we may say that the war is over at last. From now on, this office is open as usual for business. I take a good deal more pleasure in seeing my clients face to face, in this homely manner, than in being the servant of the government. Be so good as to pass me this morning's copy of the Morning Post."

He took another sip of his morning Madeira and a crumb of seed-cake, and, opening the pages of the newspaper, began to read the reports of yesterday's proceedings in the Central Criminal Court. In this manner, peace returned to Baker Street.

Donald Thomas is the author of fifteen novels, including four collections of new Sherlock Holmes stories, and seven biographies, notably Cardigan: The Hero of Balaclava and Cochrane: Britannia's Sea-Wolf. He received the Eric Gregory Award from T. S. Eliot for his poems Points of Contact. His writing on crime includes The Victorian Underworld, followed by an account of World War II's criminals and black marketeers in An Underworld at War, and Villains' Paradise: Britain's Post-War Underworld. He has also contributed to the BBC several series of broadcast documentaries on historical crimes and trials.

JAICO PUBLISHING HOUSE

Elevate Your Life. Transform Your World.

ESTABLISHED IN 1946, Jaico Publishing House is home to world-transforming authors such as Sri Sri Paramahansa Yogananda, Osho, the Dalai Lama, Sri Sri Ravi Shankar, Sadhguru, Robin Sharma, Deepak Chopra, Jack Canfield, Eknath Easwaran, Devdutt Pattanaik, Khushwant Singh, John Maxwell, Brian Tracy, and Stephen Hawking.

Our late founder Mr. Jaman Shah first established Jaico as a book distribution company. Sensing that independence was around the corner, he aptly named his company Jaico ('Jai' means victory in Hindi). In order to service the significant demand for affordable books in a developing nation, Mr. Shah initiated Jaico's own publications. Jaico was India's first publisher of paperback books in the English language.

While self-help, religion and philosophy, mind/body/spirit, and business titles form the cornerstone of our non-fiction list, we publish an exciting range of travel, current affairs, biography, and popular science books as well. Our renewed focus on popular fiction is evident in our new titles by a host of fresh young talent from India and abroad. Jaico's recently established translations division translates selected English content into nine regional languages.

Jaico distributes its own titles. With its headquarters in Mumbai, Jaico has branches in Ahmedabad, Bangalore, Chennai, Delhi, Hyderabad, and Kolkata.

SINCE 1946